Chronicles of Ytria

Chronicles of
Ytria

Matthew Buscemi

Published by Matthew Buscemi, 2021
Seattle, Washington USA

ISBN 978-1-62802-029-8

Typeset by Matthew Buscemi in Dutch Medieval Pro with Paciencia display.

to Jon Luke
in the hope that we'll be boxing again someday soon

Table of Contents

Ytria
Vorei
Makrin
Thano
Sart
Chys
Ksohk
Seira
Epeyen
Sfi
Intok
Endok
Ikim
Gallos
Potro
Oterik
Frax
Semm
Wellesper
Aemis
Dossen
Iofuin
Calens
Poan
Ediad
Qelem
Koilada
Delz
Pannouk
Bota
Daicis
Velyg
Reiar
Eikres
Yvenia
Fobbyn
Jela
Noso
Reodis
N
E
S
W

We Were Here First

Bruce pulled open the door to the public house with a mighty gasp. He glanced about the dimly lit room, clasping his right bicep with his left hand. Some eyes turned toward him, but not many. Good.

He scanned the interior of the pub, quickly assessing the counter on the right and the oaken tables scattered throughout the room. He let his gaze stop only briefly on the buxom barmaid. In other circumstances he might have evaluated how he might best court her, but so many other matters pressed on his mind this evening that his carnal impulses would have to wait. In the back of the large space, he spotted a group of tables half-secluded by a partial wall and window panes—a cloister of sorts. Its tables lay empty.

Bruce hobbled quickly toward it. He hoped his leg was not bleeding too badly. He'd been to public houses in Reiar that would turn away the wounded at the first sign of running blood, even those who bore a royal crest upon their breastplate. A few more eyes strayed his way as he shuffled across the wooden floorboards, but no one moved to stop him. He half-hoped the barmaid would, but she paid him no mind.

He found the table at the farthest back corner of the pub in a small area of three tables, partitioned off from the main chamber by an additional wall. He threw down his two packs, and slowly lowered himself into the chair. His leg and arm ached, and pain seared within them anew. He took deep breaths as he slowly unwrapped the bandage on his arm, threw it into the pack for dirty things and retrieved a clean one from the pack for clean things. The dirty pack had begun to bulge and his supplies in the clean pack had reached critically low levels. And he still had miles left to travel through Reiar.

His arm seemed fine; he could still move his fingers. That arrow had just glanced his shoulder. His leg, however, was worse. He winced through the pain as he changed its bandage. Eventually, with both wounds staunched, he pulled up a second chair, put up his bad leg and leaned back in his seat. He scanned the pub again briefly—still no sign that anyone cared about his presence—so he closed his eyes and tilted his chair back into the wall.

"Milord?" a voice before him.

His eyes shot open. "Yes?"

A young man stood before him, clearly the youngest of the staff. "What can we do for you this evening, milord? Do you require assistance? A drink? Lodging?"

Annoyance that they'd sent this stupid squire instead of the hot barmaid surged within him anew. "Any news of the road to Yvenia this evening?"

"I have heard nothing out of the ordinary, milord."

"Good. You may go." Bruce closed his eyes and leaned back again.

He would restock in Yvenia. This town, whatever its name was, would not offer him sufficient protection from his pursuers. There were, however, people in Yvenia who owed him a favor or two. If he could just get there he could finally get some sleep.

"Hi!"

The voice sounded female, and Bruce imagined that the buxom barmaid had decided to join him, but when he opened his eyes, he started at the sight of a young man, who stood across the table from him. He had done up his hair, and his clothing bore flamboyant frills. Clearly a poofter. Revulsion surged through Bruce, and the poofter's smile faded.

Three women came in behind him, one middle-aged and the other two the same age as the poofter. The poofter, to Bruce's horror, threw his things down on Bruce's table. Right across from him. Just threw them down! In front of a man bearing the leather armor and royal sigil of Jeia! The two younger and reasonably attractive women joined him at Bruce's table, opening up bags and producing scrolls, parchment, and quills. The older woman seated herself gracefully at an adjacent table.

The women had done up their clothes, too. They wore bulky but very extravagant dresses, but there was something not quite right about the styles, something artificial, something feigned—and that's when it dawned on him—they were performers.

"What is going on?" Bruce asked the group.

"I am Madam Origoire of the Northwest Reiar Theatre Company." No 'milord'. No recognition of his title. Nothing.

"I've had quite an evening," Bruce snarled.

The group of them nodded, and their smiles drooped, but continued pulling out their parchments and quills and setting them on Bruce's table.

Bruce huffed. "Now look here!"

The theatre troupe's movements slowed, and they eyed him warily but made no move to leave their seats.

"I've had a very difficult journey, and I just need a couple hours silence, if that's alright."

"Our troupe has reserved this space," Madam Origoire said. "Every Amnday from midnight 'til dawn."

Bruce furrowed his brow. "Reserved? In a public house?"

"Yes," Madam Origoire responded matter-of-factly.

"How are you feeling? Better?" The poofter asked Madam Origoire.

"Yes!" she replied jovially. "Actually much since last week."

"Splendid," the poofter replied with a disgustingly effeminate wave of his hand. He turned to his colleague at the table beside him. "Those are beautiful quills! Did you get them from Master Trellain's?"

"I did. I noticed them yesterday and just had to pick some up."

"I'll have to get some for myself next week."

Bruce's frustration boiled over. "Do you mind?"

The troupe's expressions soured into frowns once more.

Bruce huffed. "Do you usually... converse at these meetings?"

The poofter snickered, but then silenced himself as Bruce's

glare turned toward him.

"Yes, *milord,*" the poofter said. "Our performances do require some amount of conversation to work out."

Bruce pushed himself up out of his chair and hobbled toward the bar while the troupe snickered behind him. He came to the counter, and clasped the cold metallic edge with both hands.

"Excuse me!" he called to the buxom barmaid, the one who should be servicing him in more ways than one.

She caught his eye, finished pouring a draught, then picked up a rag, cleaned a part of the counter, and finally wended toward him. "Yes, milord?" Her tone was hostile and forced. He'd have to go easy.

"There seems to be some kind of theatre troupe in the back room there—"

"That would be the Northwest Reiar Theatre Troupe, milord."

"Yes. I had set myself up there, but they just barged in and threw down their things—"

"They are very amenable to others using the tables with them, milord."

"Yes, but they are quite... grotesque, if you catch my drift." The barmaid's frown deepened. He'd heard this about Reiar. They were famous for their tolerance of queerdom. "Anyway, it is difficult for me to rest my eyes with them there..." Bruce rolled his hand in the air, hoping the barmaid would catch his drift.

"With them doing what, milord?"

"You know. Talking."

"This is a public house, milord."

"That it is."

"People may talk in a public house, milord, at any table

they choose."

"But do they get to use that space exclusively?"

"No, milord. But as I said, they have been very amenable to others using the space with them."

"So, you can't kick them out?"

"I'm afraid not, milord." The barmaid hurried away.

Bruce sighed and begrudgingly hobbled away, back towards the poofter and the crone and the young women who liked the company of poofters better than real men like him. Such an off-kilter country, Reiar. He couldn't wait to get to Yvenia. Best brothels on the whole damn continent. He'd get some nice play there. Presuming his leg healed properly by then.

He threw himself back into his chair, put up his leg, and eyed Madam Origoire. The poofter was saying something to her, but Bruce talked over him. "I talked to the owner of the establishment and she said that you don't get exclusive use of this room or any of the tables."

Madam Origoire turned her gaze slowly toward him. "And neither, milord, do you."

"Yes, but you were wrong." With that, Bruce leaned back and closed his eyes. At least the tones in which the troupe talked were more sedate thereafter. Bruce lost himself in his thoughts. He wondered what the king would have to say about Bruce's report on what had happened to him in Calens. With Reiar in between them and his home country of Jeia, it was unlikely that the two nations would come to blows. But still. If diplomatic relations broke down completely...

A low rumble from somewhere above, at the very periphery of Bruce's perceptions, grew louder, demanded his attention, crescendoing into a roar. Bruce's eyes shot open. The whole public house had grown deathly silent as tables and chairs and beer steins all rattled, patrons and employees both staring up at the ceiling. The noise suddenly ceased, and while most of the staff and patrons remained stunned, a few rushed up out of their seats and out the door.

The troupe stayed put, but Bruce pulled himself up and hobbled to the door. Never had he heard such a cacophony as blared through the sky above him.

He exited and turned, discerning a crowd in the dark night, distinguishable by the light of a few torches held aloft. But that light was nothing compared to the bright white glowing thing that was descending into the forest behind the public house.

"What the devil?" Bruce muttered. People ran about and around him, some carrying weapons, most carrying torches.

The large group down the road began toward the thing in the woods, which had now descended below the tree line, though its bright white light still lit up the sky and made the green of the leaves and underbrush visible despite the night.

Bruce followed, albeit more slowly on his injured leg. He pushed ever forward, stopping to climb over logs and pull himself out of brambles.

He found the group from the village stopped at the edge of a grove, which was brilliantly lit up, as bright as though it were day. The light emanated from an enormous metallic bubble that sat on the ground atop little metallic feet. Fear convected off the herd of villagers in waves, all standing morbidly still. They stared at a trio of strange men, who puttered about near the metal contraption, each wearing the most bizarre clothing and tapping at little rectangular hunks of metal in their hands.

"Hey there!" Bruce shouted.

A small gasp went up from the crowd of villagers. The eyes of the three men turned toward him.

Bruce hobbled into the clearing. "Yes, you! On the authority of the Kingdom of Jeia I demand to know why you have invaded this land, Jeia's friend and ally, the Kingdom of Reiar."

The three men shared bemused glances, then their attention returned to Bruce.

Bruce drew closer to them. "Well?"

"We represent a higher authority," one of the men said.

"Which land do you call home then, that you can craft metallic steeds as bright as the sun that fly through the air?"

The men went back to poking at their metal rectangles.

"Excuse me. You are addressing a knight of the Kingdom of Jeia!"

One of the men shot him a look. "You are excused."

Fear shot through Bruce. What could such people as these do if he angered them? Was their weapons technology on par with their modes of transportation?

"Good sirs," Bruce tried again. "Look at these fine people here. You have most certainly upset them. As a representative of a nearby kingdom, I can use my authority to ease their worry if I can only understand your intentions better—"

"That won't be necessary," one of them men said while his compatriots continued tapping. "They will lose the capacity for abstract reasoning within the next ten minutes, as will you."

"I don't understand—"

"And in under an hour, you will understand even less. We have released a number of genetic modification drones into the environment. Most of you will all be very different creatures within the hour."

Bruce gulped. "What kind of creatures?"

"You have pigs, don't you? Something like that."

Fear shot through Bruce anew, then rage. "Don't do that to us! Please. I beg you. We're not... you can't just..."

"But we can," the man said. "Our ship is badly damaged and in need of repairs. If this planet were protected, that would be one thing, but the Galactic Consortium's designation for your world is Delta-Four. Unprotected and unmanaged. We can make whatever modifications to the environment we please."

"Gal-tic Consortium? What country are they? Where is their stronghold?"

That got the two other men chuckling, as well as Bruce's interlocutor.

"Farther away than your feeble mind can imagine," the man said.

Bruce reached for his knife, pulled it out and slammed it into his interlocutor's neck. Instead of slicing through his target, Bruce's hand was forced away. He lost his balance and fell into the grass, but caught a glimpse of the man's whole body shimmering.

The crowd at the edge of the forest shouted and dispersed into the trees.

"Even if you were to kill us, it wouldn't stop the drones. You and every person within about a hundred kilometers will change."

"Why?" Bruce gasped.

"As I explained, our ship is damaged," the man said. "Our crew is hungry, and also rather tense, if you catch my drift. They need some appropriate companions for relaxation and recreation. Oh, don't look at me like that. Not all of you will be turned into pigs. Some of you will just get fitter and leaner, better... endowed. But even in such cases, the mind has to go."

"Savages!" Bruce shouted.

They laughed at him. All three of them laughed.

"This is our land!"

Their laughter intensified.

"We were here first!" Bruce tried.

The man shrugged. "We were here second."

Bruce scrambled to a stance and ran. Perhaps he could outrun this change. Perhaps he could stay himself.

He ran to the public house and threw open the door. The whole room was now eerily desolate. He grabbed up his two packs, then hobbled out and down the road as fast as he could away from the horrible light still shining up out of the woods. He kept on furiously thinking as he ran into the night, without a torch, down a road only dimly lit by the moon. He felt as though, if he kept on thinking, he could keep thoughts in his head, that they wouldn't flitter away from him, like the strange men had said they would. He had lost his knife, he realized. No defense from brigands, but that was of negligible concern now—he directed all his effort into escaping those strange men in that terrible grove and thinking, desperately thinking.

Perhaps it had been a dream. Perhaps any moment he would awaken, sitting tilted back in his chair in the public house. He would give anything for the company of Madam Origoire, the poofter, and those two women right now. And he'd stop calling men like the young performer poofters, he decided. He might even go to a few shows in Jeia the next time he had the opportunity.

A pain flared through his back and he fell to the dark ground. The two packs fell off his back and rolled away. He gasped and gasped. The pain in his leg and arm grew more intense, then he realized it was in both legs and both arms. His whole body spasmed, and he yelled. The sound of his voice changed.

Thought drifted away. He stomped his hooves and sniffed with his snout. An irresistible desire for eating truffles and rolling in mud overwhelmed his thoughts. He meandered off the dirt path, and into the underbrush of the forest, looking for both.

Ergo Sum

What a stupid question.

"It's just a name," Nax said.

His professor folded his arms and gave him that wide, confident smile, which annoyed Nax all the more. "Does the name remind you of anything?"

Nax released a sigh, not even bothering to try to hide his irritation from his classmates. "No. Should it?"

"The writer has named the character 'Koga Nessis,' which is an allusion to the character of Kreega Gnessis, the narrator of Rikar's novels."

Nax rolled his eyes and mumbled.

The professor's countenance gained an air of malevolence. "I'm sorry. Would you like to say that again?"

"You made that up."

"Made what up?"

"The connection between the two characters. It's not actually there."

"Then, how do you explain the similarity of the names?"

"It's just a coincidence. Tennith pulled a name for the character out of the air and used that. While we're on the topic, it seems Tennith pulled a great many things out of the air. His story has a lot of details, but no drive, no purpose. It's boring."

Gasps went up from the class. Nax's friend Soch jerked his wide-eyed countenance to Nax and shook his head vigorously back and forth.

The professor's face took on a new air, not so much angry as confident. He even broke a kind of grim smile. "I see. Well, Nax, if you'd be so kind, please tell the class what we should be reading."

"Easy. Puruk Quisik."

The professor's smile grew wider. "The Equentian writer."

"Yes."

"And why him?"

"His novels contain all the important themes for humanity, and he relates them using interesting, compelling plots."

"I see. Does anyone else have an opinion on the Equentian writer?"

None of the other students dared speak. Soch's face was half-covered by his hand.

"How many of Quisik's novels have been translated into High Glissian?" the professor asked.

"Just two," Nax admitted.

"And how many has he written?"

"Eleven."

"And why do you suppose that is?"

Nax's simmering anger boiled over. "Maybe it's because Glissian scholars have bad taste."

Soch stared at Nax, his jaw slack.

The professor cast his gaze over the room, smiling. He seemed, Nax thought, to be saying to the rest of the class, "See, everyone? This is what happens to you when you read debased writers."

The professor finally turned his sight back to Nax, his countenance perfectly equanimical. "One last question. We've been talking this whole time about all the relationships between the details in Tennith's novel and those in other novels, or to historical events. Are Quisik's novels connected to history and literature in the same way? Would you be willing to consider that Quisik's novels haven't been translated because they aren't, in fact, very good?"

Nax stood. "These connections we keep talking about aren't real!"

The professor refused to be goaded. "But I have noticed them. They are part of *my* interpretation. Are you saying that my understanding of this novel isn't real?"

"Yes! Just read a book without going and searching for *connections* for once! Maybe you'll end up enjoying it."

Now the professor seemed merely sad. "I do enjoy reading books. Quite a bit."

Nax huffed. "May I leave?"

The professor nodded, his face making him seem not so much angry as distraught. Nax couldn't find a shred of remorse within himself. Let the professor be sad, reading his novels to understand all the connections between every other novel he'd ever read. A life wasted building connections when the whole point of reading was to lose oneself in the narrative, the flow of the plot.

Nax grabbed up his things and stormed out of the classroom. The professor had already moved on to his next question about Tennith's novel and the discussion had resumed before Nax was even out the door. Once he was, the professor's voice faded. Nax marched down the hall and glided down Eske Hall's central stairwell, his footsteps resounded off the large, domed ceiling overhead.

He had just reached the door when he heard his name called from behind. He turned to see Soch careening down the stairwell. "Nax! Where are you going?"

"Wellesper," Nax said. "I've heard the monks at Wellesper Abbey know Nipic. Maybe they can teach me."

"What about your family? You said they paid the university a lot of money—?"

Nax shook his head. "I'm fed up, Soch. I can't take it anymore. All these people who think they know things that don't exist, who have opinions about writers they've never read. I'll translate Quisik's novels myself!"

Soch gulped. "You're not leaving the city now, are you? You'll never make it to Wellesper before nightfall. And have you thought about food and supplies?"

His friend had a point. "I suppose you're right. But my mind's made up, Soch. I'm doing this. And you're not to write a word about this to my family."

"But they'll be so worried. Your father—"

"Not a word!"

Soch bit his lip. "Fine."

"Thank you." Nax marched off toward his dormitory. He had a journey to prepare for.

Nax skipped the rest of his classes that day and instead prepared a travel bag. He put his two Quisik novels in first, then went down to the kitchen where he procured some thick rolls and a pair of apples. He returned to his room and stashed those in his bag, then added some select notebooks and pencils from his school supplies.

"Go to university," his father had insisted. "Learn more about real writers. Then tell me who you want to emulate."

Every last literature scholar he'd met here had been a moron. Literature wasn't about finding all the stupid details that referenced other stupid details from all the moron writers going back centuries. Reading was about losing yourself in a narrative. Nax still remembered how he'd accidentally discovered a battered copy of Quisik's first novel in the back room of a bookstore he and his father had been visiting in Calens. Its pages had browned, and the price on the tag was a scant two azmi, but having read the first few pages, Nax was already hooked and knew he would love the rest. His father had bought it, thinking nothing of it at the time. But once Nax started clamoring to have other translated Quisik novels, his father's curiosity had been piqued. His father had gone searching and had found one other book for him, but had also begun encouraging Nax to expand his interest in literature. For a time, Nax tried to comply, but he found everything written by Glissian writers droll. And then, one day when he was fifteen, Nax had been talking to a bookseller in Jeia, who had casually informed him that Quisik had in fact written nine more novels, but the monk who had translated the first two had grown disinterested and moved on to other projects, not bothering to translate the others.

Nax had become incensed. How dare that monk! How dare the world deny him *nine more* novels by the greatest writer known to mankind!

There was nothing more for him at the Semm University, Nax decided. The next day, he would go to Wellesper Abbey, and he would join the monks on the condition that they teach him the Nipic language. All other possibilities had fallen away. His father could even show up at Wellesper, for all he cared. Nax would read Quisik's other novels if it was the last thing he did.

Nax woke before dawn and left the university before the first bell had rung. It was early spring, and the last frost had passed, but it was still quite chilly. Nax had worn an extra layer and taken his warmest coat with him. The pack was not too heavy, and at first, the cold wasn't so bad, even though he could see his breath in the air before him.

The Kingdom of Semm was composed mostly of wooded hills and valleys, interrupted only by small farms and the occasional village. It stretched outward for many miles before dropping down into the valley containing the Kingdom of Wellesper. The road between the two cities was well-traveled and stone markers appeared at the roadside at regular intervals, showing his progress toward his destination.

The first mile or so outside the walls of Semm, Nax wished he'd perhaps worn a few more layers, intermittently rubbing his hands together and stuffing them in his pockets. He quickened his pace, too, as much as he was able. However, as the morning wore on, the sun rose higher and the air grew warmer. A flock of madricas, Spring birds, alighted on a nearby tree, singing, and Nax's heart warmed at the sight of them. A good omen, he decided.

About the time the sun reached its zenith, Nax noticed that his stomach was rumbling. He'd also managed to empty his small canteen. Frowning at that, he walked a mile more, listening carefully to the sounds of the forest. For a time, he heard nothing but the sounds of birds and the occasional scampering of a rabbit or squirrel, but finally, near a marker indicating the fourth mile from Wellesper, Nax heard the sounds of running water.

For just a moment he considered perhaps continuing on to city, as he was so close, but the scratching feeling of his parched throat won out. He dashed off the road toward the sound, pushing through tree branches and underbrush, the sound of the water growing steadily louder. At last, he emerged into a field of tall grasses surrounded by trees on all sides except one, upon which lay a small stream of water, not very deep, with a bed of visible stones of all colors. Tiny fish darted to and fro, and the whole scene would have been quite tranquil were it not for the bizarre metallic structure sticking up out of the grasses. It was the shape of an egg and perhaps as tall as the tallest building Nax had ever seen, a full three stories, perhaps taller. The metal was perfectly smooth and glistened in the sun. It was perhaps as wide in diameter as Eske Hall had been long. It filled more than half of the grove. A metal staircase led from the grasses up to the edge of the egg, where its shell contained the faint outline of a door-like portal, but as far as Nax could tell, the 'door' was just a solid slab of metal. There didn't appear to be anything like a handle or a knob.

Nax stood and stared at it, canteen in hand, his hunger and thirst forgotten.

He had just decided to turn away from the grove and go back to the road, when the door-shaped metallic slab in the egg's shell wobbled and then dissolved, melting into the air like evaporating water. A man strode out of the newly-formed hole, stood upon the top step of the stairs, and looked down at Nax. He had a shock of brown—almost black—hair, was light-skinned, and looked like a normal enough human, though perhaps maybe a Northerner, except that his clothes were unlike anything Nax had ever seen. They looked so smooth and perfectly sewn. In fact, Nax couldn't see any seams. And the material wasn't like any cloth Nax had ever seen. It glimmered in the sunlight like wax.

"Hello there," the man called down.

Nax gulped. "Hello."

"What is your name?"

"Nax. What's yours?"

"Anith."

"What is this... metallic structure, Anith?"

Anith smirked. "My home."

"What happened to its door just now?"

Anith smiled, a smile Nax thought a bit too forced. "I opened it, is all."

"I should be going..."

"You help travelers in need here, in the Glissian kingdoms, do you not?"

Nax blinked a few times. "Yes. It's very important to help travelers in need. What land are you from?"

"It's called Impett."

"I've never heard of that kingdom."

"It's very far to the north."

That made sense. He did look like a Northerner.

"Where are you from?" Anith asked.

"My family lives in Eikres, but I'm a student a Semm University. Well, I suppose I *was*. I'm on my way to Wellesper to join the abbey."

"Why is that?"

"I'm going to learn Nipic from the monks so that I can translate Nipic books into Glissian."

Anith smiled. "Have you ever tried your hand at translation before?"

"No. But I don't care. I'm going to learn. I'll do whatever it takes."

Anith nodded. "Very dedicated. Is there a particular Nipic book you are interested in translating?"

"Yes, well, nine of them, actually. By a writer named Puruk Quisik."

"And why those nine books?"

"He's written eleven books. Two have been translated into Glissian, but not the others. Those two are the best books I have ever read. What are you doing in a glade off the Semm-Wellesper highway, Anith?"

"I am a researcher," Anith said. Then, noticing Nax's look of confusion, added, "a scientist."

"Ah," Nax said. "Astronomy? Physics?"

"Biology. In a sense. I study how people understand each other when they speak."

"Huh," Nax said. "I've never heard of a science like that. But we have many biologists at the university. There's a big symposium tomorrow about the most recent studies on the four humors."

Anith smiled wider. "I'm sure there is. Nax, I'm afraid I'm in a bit of a bind, and I need the help of someone in Semm."

"What's the matter?"

"My scientific studies require that I talk to people, but I'm a foreigner and afraid of going into the city. I can make myself clothes like yours. That part is easy. But until I understand how to behave in your land, I can't study what I need to. If people think I'm not Glissian, they'll talk to me differently, and I won't learn what I need to learn."

Nax looked up at the sun. It was probably about one. Maybe even two. If he didn't hurry onward now, he wouldn't arrive at Wellesper before dusk. "I'm really sorry, Anith, but it would be dangerous for me to be on the road at night. I should get back to the highway."

Nax started to move back toward the forest, but Anith called out. "What if I could get you copies of all eleven of Puruk Quisik's books in Glissian?"

Nax turned and took a few steps toward the metal egg. He looked up at Anith, trying to gauge the man. He seemed completely genuine. "How? They haven't been translated."

"I think they have been. And I think I can make copies for you. Here, in my home."

Nax didn't believe in dark magic, or wizards, or any of that other nonsense. His father said people still told tall tales, like the stories about the Unholy Night in Reiar ten years ago. There were no such things as people becoming animals, his father had said. And the other part of that tale, about the people with engorged organs and blank minds, that was mere puerile fantasy. They believed these things because people were generally superstitious, gullible, and had sinful minds, but his father had taught him to think hard about such stories, to understand the world with reason, with rationality. Anith's claim seemed absurd.

"You have a printing press in your home?" Nax asked.

Anith nodded. "After a fashion. Come on in and see for yourself."

Nax bit his lip. He should get on to Wellesper. But—all eleven books, translated already, waiting for him to read them. He needed to know, and so he crept slowly toward Anith's home, walked up the metal stairs, and followed Anith through the hole into the metal eggshell.

They walked down a long hallway of metallic floor, walls, and ceiling. Light somehow burst from the ceiling at intervals although no flame could be seen and no heat radiated down onto him. Besides that, the hallway was rather plain, but at its terminus, Nax came into a circular room, which he could only describe as a kind of chamber of wonders. Multicolored lights danced about the walls, like a portrait made of light and constantly changing its shape. Like the hallway, light without fire emanated from the ceiling, illuminating the space. At the center of the room lay a circular table and a pair of chairs, each seemingly fixed to the floor and made of materials Nax couldn't describe.

"I had no idea the northern kingdoms possessed such marvels!" Nax gazed about the room.

Anith smiled and sat down at one of the chairs, encouraging Nax to do the same. He tapped at the table, and a sea of squares rippled out across the table's surface, each with a letter of the Glissian alphabet inside it.

"Tap the buttons," Anith said, "and spell out Puruk Quisik's name, please."

Nax stabbed at the table, the name forming on the table's surface as he did so. When he'd finished, the table lit up in front of Anith. He set his palms down on it and began rapping his fingers methodically against its surface. He seemed to notice Nax staring at him. "This will take just a few minutes. Tell me, why this author?"

"When I was thirteen, I discovered one of the two translated books. It was hidden away in the back of a bookshop, and my father bought it for me. I loved it. I loved the way that the text pulled me in. I've never been so engrossed in a story. I wanted to read more stories like it. But Glissian stories aren't like that. No one here in these kingdoms can write."

Anith raised an eyebrow but continued rapping his fingers against the table. "Don't you think that's a bit harsh?"

Nax shook his head. "All anyone here cares about is *references*. The professors care about how all the little details in one book are like those in another, and then they make up ideas about what all those details supposedly *mean* but that's all just something they invented. It's not real, not like the plot. We don't care about plot like they do in Equentia. Our books are just big tapestries of interlocking details that don't ultimately matter."

That stopped Anith typing. He swiveled in his chair—the chairs *swiveled*?—and looked at Nax. "I find that quite interesting. You want to read without references? Any at all?"

"That's right. They don't matter. It's the plot that's important."

Anith seemed to be going over something in his mind. "Very interesting." He then swiveled back to the table, put his hands back, and rapped his fingers against the table once more. After another furious bout of typing, he gave a triumphant nod, withdrew his hands, and sat back in his seat. Nax tilted his head, which Anith noted, then pointed at the table.

Nax turned and spotted a gray goo seeping out of the table's surface. Instead of pooling, it rose upwards, forming itself into a bulbous tower a few feet high, gaining color and surface detail until it had become a stack of eleven books. What other wonders was Anith capable of?

Nax turned to Anith. "Those are all—?"

"All eleven of Puruk Quisik's books."

"May I...?"

Anith nodded, and Nax jumped to his feet. He picked the top one off the stack. The title on the spine read, *The Visitor at the Temple of Hosp*, in his own language. Nax couldn't hold back his tears. He opened up the book. He moved from the title page, through the table of contents to the main text. He began reading, losing himself in the prose.

"Why don't you sit down?" Anith said.

Nax ambled to his chair and found himself sitting down once more, remaining fully captivated by the text throughout.

"Sorry," Anith said. "Just one more thing. You said you want to read without any correlations. No connections between this text and any others. Is that right?"

"Uh, yes. That's how I read." Nax paid no further attention to Anith. He lost himself in Quisik's story.

Soch watched from his dormitory room window as Nax strode confidently across the quad, through the university gates, and away into the City of Semm. He did not like how dismissive Nax had been of his father the day before, and Nax had been so determined. It had made Soch feel as though he shouldn't bother trying to stop Nax, but the thought of his best friend throwing himself fearlessly into this particular abyss nagged at him now.

He couldn't help but feel that Nax was setting himself up for disappointment. It wasn't that Soch found Quisik's books particularly bad, it's just that they weren't particularly good, either. Perhaps the translator had stopped for a reason. Perhaps their literature professor was right. What was more likely, that all the scholars in the Glissian kingdoms were wrong, and that Nax, a partially-educated twenty-year-old was the only person able to perceive Quisik's true depths, or that Nax had glommed on to the writer as an adolescent and was refusing to give it up despite all evidence that he should?

Nax had done a lot for Soch. He had shouted down Soch's tormentors during their first month at the university and had then gotten Soch involved in the training and the monthly tournaments that had helped build his confidence and taught him to stand up for himself. They'd started studying together, and Soch had to admit that Nax's mathematical and scientific aptitude was higher than his. Soch's marks had certainly benefited from those study sessions. Soch cringed to think what his university life would be like without his best friend.

It took him until halfway through his first class, a lecture on chemical reactions he found he couldn't concentrate on, to decide he would go after Nax and try to talk some sense into him. He got up in the middle of the lecture, walked out of the hall, went to his room, dressed in his warmest clothes, packed a bag, and headed out of the university grounds, through the City of Semm, past the gates, and out into the wooded road to Wellesper.

He walked briskly but kept a healthy pace. With the start Nax had gotten, Soch would never be able to catch up with him, but he figured that didn't matter. Nax would not waste any time in Wellesper. He would go directly to the abbey and inquire about joining. Even if the monks wanted to turn him away, which seemed unlikely, they would not do so immediately. Soch should certainly be able to find Nax there.

The road was busy that day, and Soch passed by soldiers, farmers, and numerous merchants. The road began weaving downward as the sun dropped in the sky, and just as dusk arrived, he found himself at the Wellesper city gates. He showed the crest of his family's house, and the soldiers let him pass. He wound his way through the city and came to the abbey grounds, themselves enclosed in a second ring of walls.

Once inside, he sought out the nearest monk, who happened to be tending the garden near the gates. Soch introduced himself and described Nax. The monk shook his head and explained he'd seen no one fitting that description. Soch continued around the abbey ground, inquiring in the apothecary, the smithy, the infirmary, the refectory—no one had seen a young man fitting Nax's description.

Soch came back to the center of the abbey grounds, the sun a mere red streak of twilight against the sky, and the light of candles now glistening in the windows of many of the abbey buildings.

"Excuse me," came a voice from behind him.

Soch turned. "Yes?"

"Are you Soch?"

"Yes."

"I am Abbot Renek. I understand you are looking for a friend. And you're of House Belgwor. Is that correct?"

Soch nodded.

"It is late, and I would be remiss if I let you spend the night in the city. We will find a room in the dormitory for you here. But perhaps first you'll join us for dinner?"

"Thank you," Soch said, appreciative, but miserable.

It must have shown on his face. The abbot tilted his head slightly. "You're worried about your friend?"

Soch nodded.

"Come to dinner. You can tell me how you came to be looking for him here. Perhaps we can help."

—

Nax rubbed his eyes. His mind felt like jelly. He set down *The Visitor at Temple Hosp* on the table.

"How was it?" Anith asked.

Nax blinked a few times. He wasn't sure.

"Nax? How was the book?"

"It was..." His mind was a blank. "I'm tired. What time is it?"

How long had he been reading? The artificial light coming from the ceiling was the same as when he'd entered. But it had been so long. Hadn't the sun set?

"There's a bed against the wall if you'd like to get some rest. And I can provide food if you're hungry."

"I should really—" Nax had had a thought in his head, but he found it had slipped away from him, and he couldn't quite grasp it. "There was... I mean..."

"Are you hungry?" Anith asked again.

"No." Nax shook his head.

"Tired?"

Nax nodded.

"Come over here."

Anith guided him to a bed, where Nax lay down and closed his eyes.

The Abbot sat Soch down at a long, wooden table in the center of the refectory, one amongst many rows of such tables. Most of the monks had already assembled. The abbot brought two plates of bread, cheese, and soup, set them both down, one before Soch and another at his place. All the other monks had procured plates as well, but no one ate. The abbot moved to the front of the hall, took his place before all the tables, and began chanting a prayer spoken in

Old Glissian, which Soch couldn't understand a word of. He wouldn't learn Old Glissian until his next year at the university. If they didn't expel him for his disappearance.

The Abbot continued chanting, and occasionally, the assembled monks would chant a response. This continued for some time, but eventually, the prayer finished, and the Abbot returned to his seat across from Soch. The other monks had begun eating, and the Abbot took up his bread and motioned for Soch to do the same. The moment Soch tasted it, he realized he was famished, and hunger overwhelmed concern.

"Tell me about what brought this friend of yours on a journey to us," the abbot said, and Soch proceeded to tell the whole tale, about Nax's argument with the literature professor, his insistence that the novels of Puruk Quisik were held in lower esteem than they deserved, and his ardent passion to translate the entirety of Quisik's work into Glissian.

The Abbot grinned. "Have you read either of the two translated Quisik novels?"

"Sort of. I read the first few chapters of his first novel."

The Abbot gave a wry grin. "I read that one fully. It wasn't very good. You say your friend, he got good marks?"

"Oh, yes," Soch said. "He does pretty well at all the subjects. He's better than me at mathematics and physics, and he does pretty well in literature, too. When he's not argumentative, anyway."

The Abbot nodded sadly. "I am very glad that you and I met first. A young person showing up demanding to become a Nipic scholar... I would probably have agreed to take him on without knowing Quisik to be his single-minded goal. If Nax had given his life over to this translation project, I suspect it would take him a decade or so to realize his error. On the other side of that journey would lie a mountain of regret. Best to dissuade him from this now."

"But where is he?"

"That is a good question. Get some rest tonight. Let yourself sleep. In the morning, I will help you find him."

"But... your duties...?"

"Don't worry about that."

"Thank you, Father Renek."

The Abbot waved it off and proceeded to ask about how the University of Semm was doing these days.

After dinner, the Abbot assigned an elderly monk to find a room for Soch in the dormitory. The one they gave him was on the second floor, its window facing East. He would wake with the sun, it seemed. Soch thanked the elderly monk, who left him and closed the door. Soch did not bother to light the candles. He merely got onto his cot and lay, his head heavy and filled with worry for where Nax might be and what might have happened to him.

Nax awoke from slumber into a kind of fog. There wasn't any literal fog inside of Anith's home, but rather, before him lay a field of forms and colors, which he had trouble putting any names to. He knew that it was supposed to have been Anith's home, but everything was somehow hazy and indistinct, even though there was nothing wrong with his vision.

A blob of mauve, grey, and blue moved toward him and noise erupted in his ears. "Zzzzt zzt zzzt book zzzt? Zzzt zzt read zzzzzt zzt zt zzzzzzt?" He instinctively knew the sounds to be words, which should have been understandable, but he found himself unable to distinguish them from mere noise.

Nax found himself gliding through the sea of shapes in Anith's home, guided by the arm, and as he did so, he found himself struggling to reconstruct his past. He was a student... where again? His family was... which house? What was their crest? How old was he? Where had he been going?

A memory slammed into him just then—he had been in Calens with his father and they had seen a preacher from one of the heretical orders shouting in the city square. Nax's father had hurried him away from the scene, but before they had, Nax had caught a line about demons from the abyss sent to torture humans on Ytria and drag them down into hellfire. He wanted to cry. Is that what had happened to him? Had he been ensnared by a demon? He wasn't supposed to believe in such things. He wasn't to tell the monks or the priests that those were superstitions because that could get him in trouble, but now, he wondered, had his father been wrong? He turned to Anith to ask the question, but the idea fell apart as he tried to construct it into words. He spoke something at Anith, who's colorful blobs formed momentarily into a face wearing a calm, cool, smile. A blob of mauve and blue pushed a book toward him.

Nax took hold of it and looked at its spine: *Seenit's Land*. He could read the words. He opened up the novel and found its writing comprehensible. While he read, his mind seemed clear of the fog. Anith spoke something, but Nax ignored it. He continued reading, which kept his fear, for the time, at bay. It seemed the only thing he could now do.

As expected, Soch woke with the sun, which pierced his window and bathed the room in its luminous rays. He looked out of the window and saw that the monks were already busy, moving from the refectory and scattering about the abbey complex, some to the library, others to the chapel, others the infirmary and the gardens.

Soch gathered up his things and hurried outside, making toward the chapel, but the voice of the Abbot called out to him from behind, and he turned. The Abbot strode toward him, himself with a satchel thrown over his shoulder.

Soch quirked his head. "Abbot?"

"I am going to help you search for Nax today."

"Father Renek, I really—"

"I insist."

Soch blinked a few times. "But where shall we begin? If he didn't come here, I can't imagine where he might have gone. He could be anywhere."

"There is a place we shall check along the Wellesper-Semm roadside. I believe he might have been waylaid there."

"Why there?"

"Call it divine inspiration."

Soch decided it was best not to argue with an Abbot. If there was anyone in the world he should trust, it was the head of a monastic sect. The Abbot led Soch out of Wellesper Abbey, through the city, out the gates, and back down the road as the sun rose and warmed the earth.

At about the halfway point of *Seenit's Land*, Nax grew weary of reading. He had the vaguest of impressions that he had read this novel before. Not exactly this novel, but a novel like it, a novel that was similar in shape, in narrative texture, in characters, and in plot. However, none of those details came readily to his mind. In fact, Nax struggled to articulate to himself anything about *Seenit's Land*, although the text had made perfect sense as he'd been reading it.

He looked up from the book and found his environment had degraded further. He could no longer make any sense of the shapes and colors about him. He could no longer distinguish any pieces that could be called 'a wall' or 'a table' or 'a chair.' He had a vague sense of what those things should be, but not enough to help him bring order to his perceptions.

Nax was terribly, terribly frightened. His head flailed about, and he made noise with his mouth, trying to make the sounds have meaning, but words failed him. He felt a pressure on his arms just then, and another pressure on his head. His arms became fixed in place, and his legs too. He struggled, but he couldn't move. Within his gaze, the blotches of colors formed into a page, and the page contained words, and he realized he was looking at *Seenit's Land* again.

He read the words, and his fear dissipated. He stopped struggling, and he read. A tear rolled down his cheek, but the sensation of it was oddly distant. What was 'a tear' exactly? What did it look like? What did it taste like, if it happened to touch the lips and the tongue?

Nax didn't concern himself with such horrifying questions. He read the words in the open book that lay before his field of vision.

As they walked, the Abbot asked about Soch's family and about how he and Nax had become friends. Soch explained about the rough time he had had during the prior year, his and Nax's first year at the university, and about how Nax had not only stood up for him but also taught him the athletic pursuits that had given him the confidence to stand up to his tormentors himself. Not only that, but they had done most of their studying together, too. Nax helped Soch with an assignment in a roughly four-to-one ratio with instances of Soch helping Nax. Their friendship, Soch had to admit, had felt a little imbalanced, with Soch always struggling to catch up to Nax's level.

However, there had been moments when Nax would allow his temper to carry him away. Before the incident with their literature professor, Soch had been able to pull Nax aside, where he could calm him down. In such instances, Soch had been able to talk him out of following through on his rashest impulses. Two days prior though, Nax had been so angry with the professor that he'd blown up publicly instead. Soch had not been able to talk Nax down that time.

"Here we are," the Abbot said all of a sudden, pointing to the side of the road.

Soch quirked his head. It looked like merely trees to him. The fourth mile marker lay just behind them, and he heard the sound of moving water somewhere in the distance, but that was all.

"What is 'here?'" Soch asked.

"My hunch," the Abbot said, and he moved toward the trees at the edge of the road.

Soch followed him into the underbrush. They pushed aside branches, weaved around brambles, and stepped through tall grasses until eventually the trees fell away, a stream came into view, and a grove spread out before them, one with an enormous metal egg sitting in its center.

The Abbot smiled. "That's what I thought." He turned and looked at Soch. "I promise you I am here to *help* your friend Nax. Please do not be frightened."

Soch was frightened. He was ready to bolt from the scene. What unholy, monstrous thing was the Abbot involved in?

The Abbot removed his satchel a pulled out a metallic device about the size of a bread roll. He tapped at it and his whole body shimmered. The wide chest and shoulders shrunk inward, his hair grew longer, and the whole shape of his face changed. The shimmering subsided.

"My real name is Aequa." A woman stood before him wearing the abbot's robes, her voice completely different now, a woman's voice. Soch stood rigid, unmoving, and unblinking.

"Your friend is in trouble," Aequa said. "In this structure. I know its owner. I can help Nax, but you have to trust me. He will likely need your help, so please do not run away."

"Is that magic?" Soch demanded, nodding to the metallic rectangle in her hand.

"No magic," Aequa said. "Just science you can't imagine yet. Now, while I'd love to answer the dozens of other questions I'm sure are on your mind, Anith may, at any moment, decide that we're more interesting than your friend. If he notices us and decides to take off in his ship with Nax, your friend will likely be lost for good."

"Ship? What ship?"

Aequa gestured toward the metallic egg, then began marching toward its stairs.

Soch hurried after her. "That's a ship? It's on the ground."

"Right now. It's capable of sailing between stars."

Soch blinked a few times. He recalled an author who had written a novel about kingdoms on the sun and moon and ships that could sail past the clouds. He'd never read the novel, but his tutor had described it to him. "Have you been between the stars?"

"Yes." Aequa marched up the metal stairs. She tapped at her metallic rectangle, and a part of the metallic egg wall wobbled, then dissolved into the air. Aequa stepped inside. Soch took a few deep breaths and plunged in after her.

They walked down the strangest hallway Soch had ever seen. Everything was made of metal, and light erupted from the ceiling at intervals, although there was no visible flame. The hallway opened up into a circular room with moving pictures of light dancing about the walls. At a circular table in the room's center sat Nax, his arms and legs seemingly fixed in position on a chair, although there were no visible restraints. A book hung, suspended in the air just above his hands. With the slightest gesture, Nax turned a page. His eyes possessed a vacant, faraway look that Soch had never seen in his friend before. Over him stood a man. He was tall with fair skin and deep brown hair. Soch didn't like the look in his eyes.

"Oh, really, now." Anith scoffed. "I am *so* close to a breakthrough."

Aequa marched forward. "Undo what you've done."

Anith folded his arms. "He gave consent."

Aequa marched up to him, fuming. "He did not give consent, Anith! Your victims never give consent. And how can a boy in medieval society *possibly* give consent?"

Soch crept slowly toward Nax, whose eyes were still scanning the words of the book in his lap.

"He's the one who came up with the whole thing!" Anith insisted. "He said he wanted to read these books without knowledge of anything else sullying his experience."

Aequa's face fell. "Oh, Anith. You didn't..."

Anith became animated. "Think of what I have learned in the last day! We will be able to treat so many neurological conditions with this research!"

Soch reached Nax and began tugging at his arms, but they were fixed in place. He whispered in his friend's ear, but his eyes turned crazed and agitated, before falling once again onto the lines of text.

Aequa's face hardened. She pulled out her metallic rectangle and stabbed at it. Half of the pictures of light on the walls in the circular room flickered and died. The ceiling lights dimmed. Nax, presumably unable to read the words as well, strained against his bonds and began to cry out. Soch tried to calm him.

"Undo what you've done," Aequa said. "Now."

Anith released an annoyed sigh, moved to the table, leaned over, and rapped his fingers against it. A few moments later he turned back to Aequa. "There. It's done."

"And the restraints?" Aequa demanded.

Nax was crying out louder now.

"It's me! Soch!" Soch took the book from Nax, and Nax seemed to calm, but in his eyes was only the faintest spark of recognition.

Anith released a second impertinent sigh and tapped at his table again. All at once, Nax jolted upward out of his seat, and the Quisik book fell to the floor. Nax ran to the table and pushed the stack of the ten other books onto the floor, then dropped to his knees, beating the nearest book with his hand. After a few punches, he tore it open and began ripping at the pages. Soch ran to him and pulled his arms back, and Nax struggled against him, howling wordlessly, like an animal.

"That's brain damage, Anith." Aequa spoke somewhere behind them.

Anith drenched his retort in sarcasm. "This world's not protected, Aequa."

"That mistake is being corrected."

"Well, I don't want to see any charges coming my way. This planet is *delta-four*. Those are official Consortium records. I'm within my rights."

"Get off this planet. And if I ever see so much as the first byte of your hyperlane registry code on my scans again, I'm calling Enforcement. Is that clear?"

"Crystal."

Soch had managed to get Nax's arms pinned, but he sat now, amongst the battered and torn books, merely sobbing.

Aequa appeared at their side. "Come on."

Soch pulled Nax to a stance, and the two of them followed Aequa through the hallway, out of the ship, and down the staircase. Soch only then had the thought that he might have looked back at the strange man named Anith, but Anith was now sealed away in his ship. He hadn't understood most of the last part of Aequa's conversation with him, just that Anith had skirted some kind of law, and now Nax was injured.

Just as they reached the tree line, there was a rumbling behind them. The whole ground shook. They turned and looked at Anith's egg. All at once, it launched off the ground and shot into the sky, disappearing beyond the clouds. The rumbling subsided. Soch looked at Nax and found it difficult to tell if his friend had understood what he'd just seen. In Nax's eyes lay the intelligence Soch knew, but dampened, somehow restrained such as his arms and legs had been.

When Soch looked over to Aequa, he discovered that she had become Abbot Renek again.

"Abbot?" Soch asked.

"Yes?" The Abbot possessed a masculine voice once more.

"How do I help Nax? Is he ever going to be the same again?"

The Abbot's eyes exuded sadness. "None of us is ever the same as we were after some time has passed, no matter what has happened to us. Anith altered some chemicals in Nax's brain. He prevented certain parts of it from growing and he blocked other parts that had already grown. His influence is now gone. Nax's brain could continue developing normally toward its same potential. There could be lasting damage. It's impossible to be certain. The best thing for him would be to try to read and study as much as he can, to get him to learn the way he did before. That is his best hope."

They came back out onto the Wellesper-Semm road.

"I'll help him," Soch said.

"He's lucky to have a friend like you."

"It's the least I can do."

They headed down the road toward Semm, Soch still supporting Nax, his arm slung over Soch's shoulder and his eyes darting around, confused, certainly, but not agitated, either.

"Are there more people like Anith?" Soch asked.

"Unfortunately, yes," the Abbot said. "That's why I'm here."

"And... Did I understand correctly... There's some kind of mistake in some law somewhere, and that's how Anith was able to come here?"

"Yes," the Abbot said sadly.

"I know that laws here take a very long time to change. Is that really so hard for people with ships that can move between the stars?"

The Abbot smiled just then. "A great many things that we never imagined became possible, all while some things we hoped would change remained fixed. One of the latter was systems of human bureaucracy. The principles by which those operate appear to be universal constants."

That was the last question Soch asked about the Abbot's secret life amongst the people of the stars. For the rest of the journey back to Semm, they talked about how best to help Nax.

—

With the Abbot's help, Nax and Soch were able to avoid any disciplinary measures from their professors. Nax's condition was explained as the result of head trauma he'd incurred when attacked by a highwayman. They said they had been closer to Wellesper than Semm, and thus had taken Nax to spend the night at the abbey, where they'd tended to his wounds in the infirmary.

Nax remained silent the whole time. Soch noticed that, during the interviews between the department heads, himself, Nax, and the Abbot, Nax's eyes had stopped darting about, and he seemed calmer and more focused, but he did not speak.

Soch requested they room together so that he could keep an eye on Nax, and the request was granted. On the next day, Soch brought breakfast up to their room, and they ate, Nax still saying nothing, and Soch had begun to narrate to him, merely relating what he thought would be interesting, but expecting no particular reply.

Late in the day, Soch went to gather up their things. He went to Nax's room first and, while there, had to explain the situation to Nax's former roommate, who sent his regards. Soch brought Nax's things into their new room, set them down, then went to get his own. When he returned to their room with his things, he noticed two books had been placed in the hall outside the door—Nax's two Quisik novels. Soch dropped off his own things in their room, then took the two Quisik books and donated them to the university library.

The next morning, Soch had gotten up early and was sitting at his desk, quill in hand, thinking through the outline for a paper he was writing for one of his classes.

Nax pulled himself to sit upright in his bed, stretched, and then said, "I'm hungry."

Soch jolted up out of his chair and looked at Nax, blinking a few times. "I'll... go get us some food. How are you feeling?"

"Just hungry."

Soch got them breakfast.

Nax spoke more as the days wore on, Soch getting the distinct sense that it was not so much that Nax couldn't speak, for when he did, he seemed as keen as ever. It seemed to him that Nax was more afraid of tripping over his words than anything else. He occasionally did so. More and more over the following days, Nax would let himself get momentarily lost in conversation with Soch, and then there would come a moment when Nax would garble a word, or trip over a phrase, or lose his train of thought, and the moment would silence him, his face twisting up in revulsion.

Soch instinctively changed the topic, ignoring the momentarily lapse. It didn't work so well at first. The first few times, Nax grew so distraught that he shut himself up completely and refused to talk further. But after a few weeks had passed, Soch found he could easily encourage Nax into discussion once more.

One of the most concerning things for Soch during the first month was that Nax seemed to have lost all of his memories of everything he had read and studied before the incident. Soch wondered how many years he would have to sit by while Nax made his way through basic mathematics, principles of physics, chemistry, and biology all over again. However, after Soch had procured for him grammars and textbooks for much younger students, Nax proceeded to relearn those topics with remarkable speed. He claimed all the knowledge was new to him, but he hurtled through it nonetheless.

He read many books, too. He devoured the books on Soch's reading lists and then asked for more from the library. At this point, he was still not going to classes or talking to anyone but Soch, but over the next months, Soch would slowly integrate Nax into university social life again, first through the athletic training sessions (which didn't require him to talk at all, only to follow the coach's instructions), then a few months later, Soch would discover Nax had been checking out books from the library himself, which must have required some amount of verbal communication with the librarians.

At the start of their third year, Nax began attending lectures again. The professors avoided calling on him, still, out of respect, which seemed fine by both Nax and Soch. There was no literature class during the first term of the year, but during the second they found themselves assigned to the same professor that Nax had stormed out on the year prior. Soch had a pleasant conversation with the professor before the start of the first class, and the professor seemed not to be holding any ill will. If anything, he seemed concerned about whether the class would help or hinder Nax's continued recovery. Soch and the professor discussed this during a private session, and they ultimately decided to go forward with it. Nax was still reading voraciously, and his verbal skills were improving every day. He stumbled over his sentences much less often and he'd begun to articulate complex ideas to Soch once more, very similar to their conversations during their first year.

They talked about the books they read for their literature class much in the course's first few weeks, but always within the confines of their dormitory room. Nax remained silent in class, and the professor never called upon him.

One warm spring day, about a year after Nax's incident, they sat in the professor's literature class, the professor leading a discussion about a novel by Tennith, this one titled *All My Saints*.

"Why," the professor asked the class, "do you think Tennith chose a smithy as the setting for this scene?"

"Because he's talking about religion," Nax said. All eyes shot toward him. Nax continued undeterred. "And metalsmithing is the job our Lord and Savior had in his youth."

"Yes..." the professor sputtered.

"And all the details of the town are allegories to the savior, too—the three hills, the merchant being next to the temple, and the figures sitting at people's doorsteps are reminiscent of idols. And so on. There are references to the ancient philosophers, too."

The professor blinked a few times. "And... what do you think of these connections?"

Nax smiled. "They're beautiful."

Soch smiled, too.

Habitat

Ephi gazed out behind the boat, watching the Fobbyn coastline recede into the distance. There was still no sign on the horizon of Reodis Island. The first mate had told her that it would not appear until the following morning, and yet she couldn't help but feel untethered and adrift without the sight of it. Not that anyone on board the ship would commiserate with her predicament.

She spotted her twelve-year-old son climbing up onto the guard rail and leaning over, looking down at the crash of waves spilling over the sides of the great ship as it cut through the ocean.

"Perri!" she called down the deck in her usual tone of admonishment.

Perri stepped down off the guard rail. "Sorry, mom."

She walked over to him. "You have to be more careful on board a ship. What did you see?"

Perri's face lit up. "I thought I saw a fish. A big one. Maybe a dolphin? They skirt along the edges of ships, right?"

"Sometimes."

"When dad's better, do you think he'll take me fishing again?"

Ephi instinctively drew her son close. "I'm sure he will. Come on. Let's go see how he's doing. Go grab one of the flasks of water from that crate there."

Perri ran to the crates that held the provisions for the ship's six passengers—Ephi, Perri, Ephi's husband Genno, and three others she hadn't yet more than glanced at. The captain and first mate had clearly wanted the passengers to tend to divvying up the rations themselves. He had told the group of passengers where to find their provisions, where their cabins were, to direct any questions to the first mate, and then dismissed them. Ephi was not about to go out of her way to ensure any particular method of distribution method so long as Genno and Perri got enough to eat and drink. Especially Genno. Ever since he had returned from Equentia, he had downed more and more water every day, which pained Ephi all the more to watch, as it meant he had to relieve himself more, and whenever he would return from such an outing, he would be sweating and red in the face. The effects seemed to be getting worse, not better.

Perri met her with the leather flask of water, and mother and son retreated below the deck to the small room with three wooden slats for beds set into the walls and sacks of their meager possessions in the corner. Genno lay on his side on the middle bed slat, curled up in the fetal position.

"Genno?" Ephi asked

"Yes?" His voice was as raspy as ever.

"Are you thirsty?"

"Yes."

Perri rushed forward and handed his father the flask. He gulped it down, and handed it back, his hand shaking.

The disease was well known in Equentia. The Equentians called it nefr, and it came from drinking tainted water. Genno had marched under King's Fobbyn's decree alongside an army of thirteen other Glissian kingdoms into the Equentian lands where their Lord and Savior had been borne, and to this day heathen hordes made it their home. The Glissian kingdoms had been unsuccessful in holding any territory against them, and Genno had returned home in this condition, his symptoms growing worse every day. The Glissian doctors did their best, but clearly they were clueless. The disease didn't seem to pass easily from person to person. It did not spread like a plague, as far as anyone could tell. The doctors had suggested perhaps a cool climate with a strong ocean breeze would help, and so this trip had been decided upon.

Ephi, through having to run the bakery while Genno was away, had quickly picked up reading, writing, and enough of numbers to keep the books. She had written a letter to the governor of Reodis Island, and he had agreed to put them up in a small farming estate of his, in the hope that the island climate would do Genno some good, and on the condition that Ephi renovate the dilapidated house's kitchen and put it to good use.

Ephi sat down beside her husband.

She wrapped her hands around one of his, and he brought

his other hand out from under himself to clasp them both. "You mean the world to me," he said. "I want to get well for both of you."

"You will," Ephi said.

Genno turned to look at Perri. "What did you see up there?"

"I think I saw a dolphin!"

Genno managed a smile. "I'm sure you did." His smile faded and he turned to Ephi. "I need to go."

Ephi nodded and stood. She held her hand out for Genno. He tried to stand on his own, but eventually took Ephi's, and she helped him pull himself off the bed. He ambled toward the door, then paused, clutching the door frame, then ambled away toward the ladder to the deck.

Each time he went, she worried about his state and how he would make it back, but she didn't dare suggest that she go with him. Even in his current state, that was a dignity she dared not violate.

Ephi saw the island when she went to get food and water from the deck early the next morning. It had rained overnight, leaving the deck damp, but the sky was now clear, and the island glistened, a halo of light forming around it as the sun came up behind it.

She hurried the food and water back to her family. Perri was still asleep, but Genno was awake. He declined the bread but took a flask of water.

"I saw Reodis," Ephi told him, keeping her voice low so as not to wake Perri.

"How far away did it seem?"

"Close. Probably only a few hours now."

"You said the governor is giving us a bakery?"

"He called it a farmhouse. He said that particular farm has been derelict."

"He doesn't expect Perri to plow the fields, does he? I could teach him if I were better..."

"The governor didn't mention anything about that. He just wanted me to fix up the farm's kitchen. Perri can help me with that."

"I'm worried he'll want more."

"I told him you were a decorated soldier who had served his King honorably, and you have. Your health is what's most important, not impressing the governor."

Perri stirred, silencing their conversation. Shortly, he stretched, rolled over, and pulled himself up off his bed.

"Mom?"

"Yes, dear?"

"Good morning." Perri yawned widely. "Should I go up and get the food?"

She was so proud of him. If she could teach him how to keep his curiosity in check, he'd grow up to be both strong and kind, like Genno. "I got some already. She reached behind herself, picked up the other flask, and a paper-wrapped bread roll, and handed them out to her son, who shuffled toward them and took them from her outstretched hand with a smile.

"Thanks, mom," Perri said before stuffing the roll in his mouth. After he'd chewed and swallowed the first bite, he asked, "Is it still raining?"

Ephi shook her head.

Perri's eyes widened. "The island?"

"I saw it. You can go see it, too, once you're done with your breakfast."

Perri grinned and took another enormous bite of his roll,

chewing as quickly as he could.

"Chew properly, Perri, or you'll upset your stomach."

He gulped down the bread. "Yes, mom."

Ephi gave Genno a pensive look.

"Go show him the island," Genno said. "I'll be fine."

Ephi squeezed his hand.

When Perri was finished, she took him up to the deck. As she left, she smiled at Genno, but his face, she noticed, even in the weak light of their cabin, was looking paler than ever.

Three hours later, a deckhand stopped by their room to tell them that the ship would soon dock at Reodis Harbor. Perri packed up their belongings, and Ephi took one large bag, slung it over her back, and helped Genno to stand. Perri took all the rest.

The look on Genno's face pained her. To see his wife and twelve-year-old son carrying all of their belongings, and him carrying nothing, must have cut him deeply.

"We're good, aren't we Perri? Nothing too heavy."

"Nope," Perri said. "This is nothing."

Genno gave them a weak smile and led them slowly out of the cabin, and up onto the deck. The ship was docking just as they stepped onto the deck. A gust of salty ocean wind blasted them, sending Ephi's hair flying. The family squinted in the sun. Land lay before them, a beach stretching off for miles into the distance on either side. A road wound from the port uphill and came to a ring of walls some half a mile up the gently rising hill that lay before the harbor. Forests dotted the island, in a few spots off the road, Ephi caught glimpses of fenced-off pastures with roving cows and sheep.

Once the ship had docked, the three of them disembarked.

As her feet touched the dock, Ephi felt a rush of joy at having something beneath her feet that wasn't swaying. Genno seemed to feel the same way, though under the bright sun he still looked much too pale for her liking. Perri gazed about the island scenery, his eyes wide with anticipation.

"Genno and Ephi Pystin?" called a voice to their right.

They turned and found an older man approaching them. He was well dressed, wearing a black overcoat and a brimmed hat. "I'm governor Diacherie. Welcome to Reodis."

He and Genno shook hands. "Thank you for your generosity, governor. We'll do everything we can to bring the farm back into working order."

The governor raised a hand. "You, Mr. Pystin, are a national hero in need of convalescence. I insist you focus on getting well, and then we can discuss what is to become of the farm."

Ephi watched Genno closely when the governor had referred to him as a hero. It was a sensitive subject for him.—

"They told us it was for God, Ephi, but it wasn't. Do you know who they asked us to fight? The 'invading forces' turned out to be barely kids. They were wearing rags and wielding spears made of badly chiseled tree limbs. And I... God save my soul... I had to cut them down because those were the orders. Our God became human and died so that we could venerate him by slicing up children barely older than Perri? I'm not a hero. You may call me a good baker, or even a good husband, if you think I deserve that, but never a hero. Never."

—Genno's facial muscles tightened somewhat, but that was all. He was not about to argue with the governor. Ephi was so happy she had married a sensible man. The smithy next to their bakery in Fobbyn had a temper, and his wife would often come and tell Ephi about who had rubbed her husband the wrong way, who was no longer a customer, who was refusing to speak to them now. Ephi had once caught the sight of bruises near her wrists, and the smithy's wife had quickly adjusted her sleeves to cover up her injuries. There had always been such sadness in her eyes. Ephi was thankful to be free of such concerns. Both for her sake and for Perri's.

"We'll take my coach to the farm." The governor said.

Perri's eyes practically beamed with delight. Genno and Ephi shared a look.

"Sir," Genno said. "We've been on board the ship for two days. We'd hate to dirty the inside of your carriage. If we might walk alongside, I'm sure—"

"Nonsense," the governor said. "This way please." And he continued walking down the dock. Ephi and her family followed.

Ephi remained concerned at them indulging in such luxury, but she was also secretly glad that Genno would not have to walk all the way to the farm in his condition. At the road outside the dock, they found the governor's carriage waiting. Two men took the sacks of the Pystins' belongings from Ephi and Perri, then opened the doors to the carriage. The governor climbed inside, and Genno went next, then Ephi and Perri. Perri gazed about wide-eyed. Ephi leaned over and whispered to her son. "Don't swing your feet like that, and don't touch anything."

Before long the carriage got underway. They followed the road toward the city only briefly. After passing over one hill, a road broke off of the main path, heading parallel to the town's walls. The island seemed mostly rolling hills and forest, dotted intermittently with pastures and fields of wheat and barley, although about half of them seemed vacant and disused. One vacant farmhouse, she noticed, had a partially caved-in roof. However, the farms that were occupied with animals and people did at least appear in good condition.

The governor was polite, asking first about Genno's experiences on crusade, then later about his condition and what the doctors at home had said.

"Yes," the governor admitted, "the sea breeze on the island is quite lovely. I hope it helps your convalescence along."

Within twenty minutes, the coach turned down a path leading through a break in a short cobblestone wall. Overgrown farmland appeared on both sides of the coach, and overtop of the grasses, Ephi spotted a small, brick farmhouse. It was in decent enough shape. The roof seemed sturdy enough, and it possessed a tall, brick chimney. It had seen some use, judging from the soot stains at the top. The door looked aged and slightly battered, and the interior, which she glimpsed through the windows, was dusty and covered in cobwebs, but, all in all, it seemed usable. Ephi thanked God for their good luck. Her concern had been the governor foisting upon them a home that would make Genno's illness worse rather than better. This, however, she could work with.

"This will make a proper home for us," Genno said. "It's very generous of you, Governor Diacherie. Thank you."

The doors were opened, and the four of them exited in the same order they had entered. The men driving the coach brought the bags of the Pystins' things around and set them by the front door of the farmhouse.

"Well—" The governor smiled and seemed to be on the verge of saying something next, but everyone paused to listen to a low, rumbling sound that was growing steadily louder. Momentarily, the ground began to quake, and the coach rattled. Ephi grabbed up Perri's hand, and everyone's heads turned upward as an enormous, metallic—something, Ephi couldn't find words to describe it—glided overhead toward the town, descending as it went. By the time it passed over the nearest hillock, it was close to the ground. The rumbling diminished, then was gone.

Genno broke the silence. "Governor, what was that?"

"I do not know. I apologize, but I must get back to the town. The well behind the house should contain fresh water, at least, the men who came here two days ago reported it drinkable. I will be back as soon as I can." The governor motioned to his two assistants, all the warmth of his demeanor having vanished completely, and he was off and away down the road, the horses bursting into a full gallop once they had passed the cobblestone wall.

Perri's face was still twisted up. "What *was* that thing?"

"I don't know, son," Genno said. "But I'm sure the governor will tell us all about it when he gets back. Now go inside and you help your mom with the cleaning. I'll check the well."

Ephi cast her husband a look.

"I'll be fine," he said. "I need to take care of business, anyway."

Ephi nodded her consent, worrying ever more about his condition. She hoped that the doctors were correct, and the island air would indeed help.

Ephi got right to work cleaning up the kitchen. She opened all the windows, then unpacked her cloth towels and began cleaning. She sent Perri to the well to fetch some water, reminding him to be mindful of his father. The well turned out to contain water, and the water lacked any odor, seemingly drinkable. Still, after what had happened to Genno, she decided to take no chances and boil their drinking water regardless. She prepared a cauldron, poured half the water in, then began to scrub down the entire kitchen after sending Perri out to chop wood. When she'd exhausted her supply of towels, she decided to see if she could find a stream to wash out the dirty rags in. Genno, by this time, had retired to the house's bedroom, where he lay atop a dusty mattress, having pulled open all the windows. Ephi spotted him resting as she left. She found the stream just at the edge of their property.

Ephi worked throughout the morning, and the family gathered in the kitchen at noon to eat the remaining apples and bread rolls they had brought with them from the ship. After lunch, Genno went for a walk around the property, while Perri continued chopping wood and Ephi began cleaning out all the jars, bowls, plates, and utensils in the kitchen, carrying them in a wicker basket to the stream in small batches and washing them there. When Perri had prepared a sufficiently large pile of wood, she sent him with the wicker basket searching for berries, nuts, and fruit for their dinner.

Genno returned, remarking solemnly that Perri had done a good job with the wood. He looked paler than ever though, and was that a cold sweat that Ephi noticed on his brow? He was beginning to look gaunt, too. He had only had half an apple for lunch and given the rest to Perri. Then he had insisted on guzzling a full jug of water.

Throughout the afternoon and evening, Ephi glanced more and more often through the kitchen window and down the path, looking for some sign of the governor. He did not return. Perri, however, returned, his basket full of fruit, nuts, berries, and even some mushrooms. He, of course, knew better than to eat any of them. Genno was their resident mushroom expert, and he sorted the good ones from the bad ones before they started dinner.

"What do you think that thing in the sky was?" Perri asked over dinner.

"No idea," Genno said.

"Iste told me a story once." This was the greengrocer's son, whose store was just down the street from their bakery in Fobbyn. "He said that there was something called the Unholy Night in Reiar twelve years ago, and that a whole bunch of people disappeared, and that the ones who were left were turned into monsters. Is that what's going to happen here?"

"You shouldn't believe everything Iste tells you," Ephi said. Though, to be honest, she had wondered the same thing herself. She'd heard the stories. However, nothing monstrous had happened. Still, it was concerning that Governor Diacherie had not returned as he had said he would.

Perri changed the topic, asking if there were fish in the stream and if there were a way to make fishing poles, and this got Genno and him planning how they would do so. This made Ephi smile.

However, later in the evening, when they lay down to sleep, she noticed Genno sweating again. Just as she was drifting off to sleep, Genno jolted her awake by creeping out of bed and going off outside, probably to relieve himself, and she then found herself awake for much longer with worry, even after he returned to bed. He lay shuddering for many minutes after that, before finally settling in and falling asleep.

Her husband's condition, she decided, had not improved,

but they had only been on Reodis one day. These things took time, and she reminded herself that she would need to keep a positive outlook for both Genno and Perri's sake. She managed to fall asleep after that, and, as always happened when she went to bed late, she didn't rise with the sun in the morning.

She arose to Perri shaking her shoulder.

"Mom..."

There was an urgency to his voice that snapped her out of unconsciousness. Her eyes shot open, fully alert. She pulled herself upright. "What's wrong, Perri?"

"You should come see this, mom."

She got out of the bed, where Genno still lay asleep, his chest rising and falling. She followed Perri out of the bedroom and into the kitchen, where the door stood open. In the field of grass, there now stood three metallic obelisks, each about ten feet tall. They glowed red, the glow oscillating in intensity, bright and then dull and then bright again. At the base of the three obelisks, for about ten feet in all the directions, the grass had disappeared, and the earth had grown dry and cracked as though it had been scorched, but outside that radius, the grass appeared unaffected. The area of the effect reached right up to the edge of the road and the entrance to their house.

"Wake your father up," Ephi said. Perri ran off behind her.

Ephi stared at the glowing metallic structures, her mind poring over the stories of Reiar's Unholy Night.

Ephi and Genno told Perri to stay in the bedroom and talked quietly between the two of them about what they should do. They needed to go into the town and report on what had happened to their farm. They also needed to find out why

Governor Diacherie had not returned. Genno should not stay, they decided, just as Ephi and Perri should not go alone. The idea of leaving Perri alone in the house near the obelisks was clearly out of the question. In the end, they decided that the entire family should walk into town together.

All three at a quick and silent breakfast, then packed up some food, and headed away from the farm and down the road leading to town. At first, nothing seemed particularly amiss, but then they began to notice things. Another field held a trio of obelisks, although these glowed blue instead of red, and the ground surrounding them was damp and sunken in around them. Bubbles slowly engorged themselves upon the surface of the pool of water—was it water?—before finally popping. On another farmstead, a cluster of trees had lost all their leaves, and the branches had become covered in some kind of webbed netting, reminiscent of spiderwebs, but much thicker and metallic. The family hurried on down the road, growing more anxious all the time.

The wall of the city came into view, and the road skirted it. The city, at least, appeared free of obelisks and webbing, but when they came around to the gate, they found it unguarded. Ephi and her family trod inside, discovering eerily deserted streets.

"Where is everyone?" Perri's voice wavered.

"Stay close, son," Genno said, his voice low and harsh. He was sweating profusely from the walk.

Ephi caught a glimpse of eyes in a window before a curtain covered them up.

"The people are here," Ephi said. "They've locked themselves indoors."

"Look at that!" Perri pointed.

Down the road, at the center of the town, lay a circular

plaza. The metallic thing they had seen in the sky the day prior sat there. Beneath its belly lay a pile of stone rubble. It looked as though a statue had been pulverized when the thing had landed. It was essentially bird-shaped but bulbous, smooth, and metallic. Its wings were stiff and contained little fins, making it look more like a hybrid between a fish and a bird. It sat on the ground atop metallic feet, which Ephi had seen as it had soared through the air.

"What is it?" Perri asked.

"I don't know," Genno said.

"What should we do?"

Genno and Ephi looked at one another. "I suppose we could get closer," Genno said, and Ephi nodded.

They crept forward down the street toward the plaza. More eyes in windows watched them as they went. Eventually, they came to the edge of the plaza, where they stopped and stared at the thing.

"It's unholy, isn't it?" Perri said.

"We don't know—" Ephi started to say, but she was interrupted by a visage. A man appeared, seeming to coagulate out of thin air, his body translucent, like a ghost, and he wore the strangest clothes. He appeared in front of the metallic thing, some thirty feet away, but made eye contact directly with them and he waved.

Ephi grabbed Perri's hand and pulled him close.

"Hello!" the man called out.

The family did not respond.

He took a few steps closer to them. "You are unregistered. Please state your names."

Ephi and Genno looked at one another, and Genno, seeming to use all his energy moved to place himself between Ephi and the strange man.

The man took a few more steps toward them. "You appear frightened. Please do not be frightened. So many have run away and not listened, and it is important that my message be heard."

"What message?" Genno called out.

The man walked closer, closing the distance. When he was ten meters away, Genno held up a hand. "That's far enough."

The man stopped.

"What is your name?" Ephi asked.

"I do not have a name. My serial number is HCD-127-b2c97e. I am a Biotopp Corporation habitat construction drone. For the purposes of communication, you may address me as Hacad."

"Why have you come here, Hacad?" Genno asked.

"I was damaged en route to my next construction site, and I require terrestrial materials in order to affect repairs. This was the closest planet in my databanks with the designation delta-four. Did you not know that this planet was unmanaged when you set down here?"

Ephi could feel Perri trembling, and she wanted to scoop him up and fly away with him. How she wished that were possible.

"What do you mean 'unmanaged?'" Genno asked.

"The Galactic Consortium has designated this planet delta-four, meaning anyone may make any modifications to the environment and organisms as they please. My repairs require me to collect a significant amount of carbon, silicate, and other minerals. The means by which I do so may be dangerous for human organisms. I recommend you leave the general vicinity for the next twelve planetary rotation cycles."

"Leave?" Ephi said. "This is an island. How do you propose we leave?"

Hacad's face remained flat. "You could board your ships and relocate to a different landmass. But, as I mentioned, this planet is unmanaged. It would be advisable for you to go to another planet entirely."

"There are red obelisks on our farm," Genno said. "Is that your doing?"

"Yes. As I mentioned, I am collecting carbon and silicate. Would any of you like me to construct a habitat? I would be happy to generate one for you once I am repaired. I estimate that I will have two rotations before I will need to leave, and I can construct anything for which I possess schematics."

"There is a town here," Ephi said. "Three hundred people live on this island. We have no ships that can take us all away to the mainland. My family and I only just arrived ourselves. Can you repair yourself somewhere else?"

Hacad's face again remained emotionless. "I'm afraid that aborting the process would do irreparable damage to my systems."

"What about the red obelisks? Are they dangerous?"

"Carbon-based organisms such as human beings should stay at least fifty meters from the collectors, as they emit a significant amount of radiation."

"How long is a meter?"

"I am nearly two meters tall."

Well, that settled it. Ephi was keeping her family well away from that entire farmhouse. And after all the work she had done to put the kitchen in order the previous day.

"Where is the safest place on the island right now?" Genno asked.

"Here in the immediate vicinity of my ship," Hacad said.

"My collection operations must happen at some distance from it. Will you talk to the others and convince them to leave this planet? They yelled at me when I tried to explain to them before."

Ephi shook her head. "We can't leave our planet."

"This is highly problematic," Hacad said. "Delta-four is a classification for uninhabited planets without sentient life, yet this planet has a variety of fauna, flora, and human settlements. I have filed a report to the Galactic Consortium. Hopefully, they will rectify the matter."

"So... we should stay in the town, then?" Genno asked. "For twelve days?"

"That is advisable, yes."

"Okay, Hacad. We'll be going now."

"Please send Governor Diacherie back to me if you find him," Hacad said.

"We'll tell him," Ephi said. "Goodbye."

"Goodbye," Hacad said, then promptly vanished, fading away to nothing.

Ephi and her family left the square and sought out the governor's house, a large estate situated at the top of the tallest hill in the town. Halfway up it, Genno had to stop and rest. Ephi retrieved a flask of water, and he drank. Ephi and Perri waited while he went to relieve himself in a wooded area off the road, and it took him so long that Ephi nearly went in after him. He eventually did return, sweating profusely and looking paler than ever.

"Maybe we should wait a bit," Ephi suggested.

"No," Genno insisted. "I'm fine. Let's keep going."

They reached the governor's house some time later but learned from his staff that he was in town at some kind of impromptu meeting of the island elders. They explained about the farm, the red obelisks, and Hacad's warning that staying near them was dangerous. A member of the staff wrote them a letter to show to the owner of the island's inn, explaining Genno's condition and insisting that the Pystin family be housed there under the circumstances. Genno and Ephi both thanked them, and they retreated down the hill, tracing out the path to the inn from their vantage point.

The sun had reached its zenith by the time they arrived. They found Governor Diacherie stranding atop an upside-down barrel outside of the inn, a crowd of at least thirty citizens gathered around him. Ephi and her family remained at the periphery of the group and watched.

"Who's he to tell us to leave our own island?" a man in the crowd said. "I say we give him the same we gave those pirates two years ago! We get our weapons and ask him *nicely* to leave."

"Pirates are other human beings," the governor said. "We do not yet even know if we can hurt Hacad. We should fear what he would do if threatened. Three farmers and four militiamen have already died trying to clear his pillars and webs. He is clearly some kind of demon sent to torment us. We all need to stay quiet and hidden from him until the ships I have sent for arrive. No one is to threaten him. Would you threaten the Lord of the Underworld if he were to rise out of the ground? A member of his menagerie has fallen from the sky instead. We *must* flee. Reodis belongs to him now."

"Slabs of metal have destroyed half my crops!" Another man said. "I won't have enough food to make it through the winter."

"We will gather what supplies we need when we get to the mainland, but I need everyone to stay indoors and stay away from Hacad until the ships can arrive."

The impromptu meeting continued in this vein for ten or fifteen minutes more, before the group finally scattered, many faces still looking irate, frightened, or both. Ephi and her family approached the governor, and his face lit up when he spotted them. "Genno! I'm so sorry for not returning. As you can see, we've had our hands full. I'm glad to see you got here safe and sound. As people trickle in, they are bringing tales of all sorts of demonic manifestations across the island. It appears to be unsafe anywhere except inside the town walls. I can only hope that the path to the dock is still safe when the ships arrive the day after tomorrow."

"So, we're evacuating then?" Genno asked. Ephi noticed just then that he was sweating beads, and his chest was heaving up and down.

The governor seemed to notice this, too. "Yes... Genno, let's perhaps get you inside the inn to lie down."

Genno did not argue. He simply nodded. Ephi handed the governor the note from his staff, and the governor took it inside and talked to the person at the inn's front desk. They took Genno to a room down a hallway on the inn's first floor, Ephi supporting him. His knees quaked as he walked, and he dripped sweat onto her blouse.

She lay him down on the bed, and he closed his eyes. His breathing, she noticed was erratic.

"Ephi," the governor called to her from the door.

"Stay with your father," Ephi told her son. She moved to just outside the door and the governor closed it.

"I've also sent for the doctor," the governor said. "But you said he has nefr?"

Ephi nodded.

"Two men who went on crusade came back to us with this

disease. They are with God now. We will do everything we can for your husband, of course, but I wanted you to be prepared—"

"Thank you." Ephi was both appreciative of everything the governor had done and mildly irritated at his current behavior. "I will tend to my husband."

"I just wanted you to be prepared, is all. I apologize that the present crisis prevented us from attending to him sooner."

He was supposed to be at home convalescing, not traipsing all over the island. But then, that wasn't the governor's fault.

The governor gave her a smile that she was sure was intended to be reassuring. "If there is anything I can do—"

"I will let you know," Ephi said.

"Take care," the governor said. "The next two days will be hard for all of us, I expect."

He turned and left the inn.

Ephi went back into her family's room. Perri had set their things in the corner. The room contained three plain beds, a table, three chairs, and a window. It seemed to her a much more comfortable version of their room on the ship. Her dream of starting a new life on the island with Genno gradually getting better and spending more time with Perri had evaporated before it had even begun.

And yet, she found herself strangely fascinated by Hacad, rather than angry with him. Part of her felt she should be. The thing was, she didn't think he was a demon at all. He was far too polite, too eager to ingratiate himself. It made her feel sorry for him. Perhaps he really was from another planet. There certainly wasn't any other way to explain his manner of arrival, or his obelisks, or the webs they'd seen in the trees. Ephi wondered if perhaps there wasn't a way to reason with him, but the governor had ordered everyone to stay away from him.

Ephi gauged the things she would need—a jug of water, a washbowl, clothes, and more. Once she'd made the list, she sent Perri off to get everything. There was nothing left for them to do but to tend to Genno.

Perri dutifully returned with everything they needed, and Ephi tended to Genno. Sometime after lunch, the doctor arrived. He was an older man and probably made an excellent country doctor. He was likely an expert at tending to the myriad of farm injuries and other common ailments, but no one in Glissia had had any experience with nefr until the soldiers had brought it back from Equentia. The doctor prescribed rest, plenty of fluids, and for Ephi to tend to him with wet cloths.

Genno's condition deteriorated as the evening wore on, and Ephi found herself thinking more and more about something Hacad had said—"I am happy to construct anything you desire." Of course, it seemed too good to be true, but what had she left to lose? She knew what awaited her if she and Perri returned to Fobbyn without Genno. She had run the bakery dutifully for two and a half years while Genno had been away, and that was quite enough of that. Only with Genno in the picture would she have time to teach Perri how to read and how to do numbers. Who knew what he would be capable of if he learned those skills at his current age rather than in his twenties as Genno had or in her thirties, as she had.

While she and Perri ate their dinner, Ephi decided that she had made up her mind. She instructed Perri on how to run the towels with cold water over Genno's forehead and then said that she was leaving to run an errand and that she'd be right back. She made him promise twice not to leave for any reason at all until she returned, and that his father needed him.

Perri bunched up his lips and looked at the floor for a moment, then finally looked up and promised that he would. She thanked him, commending him on how well he was handling this situation, then, taking a look at both of them, she closed the door to their room and walked out of the inn.

The sun had grown low in the sky. It had just dipped behind the western gate, the one leading back to the port behind her. Long shadows shrouded the empty street, and eyes watched her from windows. She hurried on toward the plaza ever faster. She prayed as hard as she could that the governor was not lurking behind any of those doors.

At last, she reached the plaza and the strange craft atop the demolished statue.

"Hacad?" Ephi called out.

"Hello!" a voice said from behind her.

Ephi screamed, turned, and jumped. She put a hand to her breath. "Hacad... you scared me."

"I am sorry. The human beings of this island do not respond to me as most do. I admit, my behavioral adaptation algorithms are struggling to learn how to interact with this community. Humans would call such a situation 'distressing.'"

Ephi had no idea what Hacad was trying to convey, so she decided to get straight to the point. "Hacad, earlier today, you asked me if there was anything you could construct for us. I have a request."

"As I have accidentally invaded your homes, it is the least I could do. What kind of habitat would you like?"

"Not a habitat. A medicine. To treat nefr. Can you make it?"

"I do not know of a human disease called nefr."

"It is contracted by drinking the water in a land called Equentia, over a thousand miles north and east of here. Genno has it. My husband. He was with me earlier."

"I see. Just a moment."

Ephi waited many moments. "Hacad?"

"Very interesting," Hacad said. "Yes. I believe I have found nefr. Tell me, is your husband the only person on the island with this disease?"

"Yes. The governor said that the two men from the island who had it died."

"That is understandable. The disease is the result of a virus that attacks the liver and kidneys. It disrupts their normal functioning. Eventually, the body cannot process the toxins within it. Death would be due to blood poisoning."

"Can you cure it?" Ephi demanded.

"This is my first time seeing nefr, but the virus is genetically similar to a number of other viruses in my databanks, ones for which I possess anti-viral treatments. I could modify one of those. However, I cannot be certain it would be effective."

"Genno is very unwell and getting worse. I will try it if there's any chance at all it will cure him. If you could make me that, I would be most grateful."

Hacad held out his translucent hand, palm up. Waving strands of thread appeared atop his palm, twisting and turning in the air. They spun together, forming a cube half an inch square. Hacad stretched his arm out toward her. Ephi reached out and snatched up the cube. It was much lighter than she expected, barely even the weight of a feather.

"How does it work?" Ephi asked.

"Simply dissolve it in water and have Genno drink it. He will have a negative reaction at first, but then, if it works, he will recover quite rapidly."

"And if it doesn't work?"

"His condition will continue to worsen."

"Thank you, Hacad. If there is anything I can do—"

"Have you seen the governor?"

"I have."

"Did you relay my message?"

"Unfortunately, he wasn't very receptive..."

"I don't understand. I am not adapting quickly enough to this community. If you could convince him to come talk to me, I would be most grateful."

"What do you want to talk to him about?"

"There are many places I could choose to extract the minerals I need. I have chosen spots at random, but clearly, many of those are occupied by people. I cannot leave this island until I am complete, but there are many ways for me to get what I need here. Some of the extractors I have placed near homes could be moved, but not all of them. If he were to negotiate, I could perhaps move some of them, but I would need to know which matter more, and which less."

"I see..." Not a demon at all, Ephi decided. He was a strange being, certainly, but not a demon. "I will see if I can convince him to come talk to you."

"Thank you..."

"My name's Ephi."

"Thank you, Ephi."

"Thank you, Hacad. For the medicine."

"I am happy to be able to do something for the people here."

"It means a lot to me. Goodbye."

"Goodbye."

Ephi hurried back to the inn, clutching the cube in her pocket. The sun had set and candle lights were starting to appear from behind curtained windows. She got the distinct impression of eyes watching her, and this only made her hurry faster onward.

She burst into the inn panting, and took deep breaths at the door, noticing looks from both the staff at the counter and the few customers talking at the bar. She ignored them and took off down the hallway to her room. She opened the door and burst in upon the scene of Genno shivering and turning frantically from one side to the other, while Perri desperately tried to run the cloth over his forehead.

Perri looked at the door with the most forlorn expression on his face.

"Perri..." She rushed to the both of them. She felt Genno's forehead and discovered he had developed a fever. "Fetch me one of the flasks of water and glass from the table."

He did as she asked. She took the glass and dropped Hacad's cube inside of it.

"What's that?" Perri asked as he handed over the water pouch.

"Medicine. Hacad gave it to me."

"Wow! I sure never thought he was a demon."

"Me either." Ephi poured the water into the glass, and the cube dissolved as the water touched it.

"Genno!" Ephi said, but he continued to fidget and twist around in bed. "Genno, I need you to sit up."

He seemed to register her words only barely. With Perri's help, they got him into a sitting position, and Ephi helped him drink the water in the glass. Ephi took the empty glass and set it on the table, then returned to Genno's side. He sat at the edge of the bed, staring at the far wall.

"Genno?" Ephi asked. "How do you feel?"

"Oooouu!" Genno howled and threw himself back down on the bed clutching his abdomen with his arms.

"Dad!" Perri wrapped his arms around his father and his eyes watered.

Ephi put her hands on his shoulders. "Hacad said he would seem to get worse before he got better."

Genno continued to moan.

The door to their room crashed open. The following moments were a blur. Men rushed in, perhaps five or six of them, all crammed into the tiny space. Two grabbed up Ephi, one by each arm, and hauled her out of the room, Perri screaming at them incoherently and Genno moaning. At the front counter, they came to meet Governor Diacherie, his face stolid.

He turned up his nose at her. "Witch," he rasped.

It was only then that Ephi realized that the governor had a sword sheathed at his side, and the men around him all held either swords or crossbows themselves. Ephi struggled against them, but their grip was firm.

The men hauled her outside and down the street, the governor leading them toward the plaza. Ephi continued to struggle with all her might, but she failed to break free from her captors. They came to the edge of the plaza, where more men had erected bales of hay around a tall pole set in the center of the street.

Ephi heard Hacad's voice and stopped struggling so that she could hear what he was saying. "Do you realize that this material is rich in carbon? If you burn it, that carbon will be lost as gaseous carbon dioxide."

"Hacad!" Ephi howled.

"Ephi?" Hacad moved out from behind the hay bales. He seemed utterly unperturbed by the events transpiring around him. "Welcome back, Ephi. Was the medicine effective?"

"They're going to burn *me*, Hacad!"

The men were already moving her toward the hay bales.

Hacad bunched up his face and turned to the governor. "Governor Diacherie, what problem is solved by burning—?"

"Be gone!" The governor roared the words. "Foul demon! Get ye back to the underworld from whence ye came. Your demon succubus will be joining you there shortly."

The men were now tying Ephi to the pyre. She struggled as hard as she could, but to no avail.

"Governor, I have told you, I am not a demon, but an artificial intelligence, a computer program designed to construct—"

The governor began chanting hymns over top of Hacad.

Hacad turned and looked at Ephi, then he looked back at the governor, then he looked at the men who had fixed her to the stake at the top of the pyre and were now climbing down from the hay bales. Ephi tried to read his expression but found it inscrutable as ever. All that power, the ability to concoct exotic medicines, to make metallic obelisks and webs that drained the minerals from the earth, and here he was, incapable of simply relating to people.

One of the men approached her holding a torch, and she struggled harder against her restraints.

All at once, the form of Hacad exploded upward, his clothing fell away and his skin grew bright red. Horns erupted from his head and his eyes took on a yellow glow. Fire sparked and erupted from his fingertips. He towered over them all, a full twenty feet high, as high as the buildings encircling the plaza.

Demon Hacad threw his head back and let out a great laugh. "Fools! You have fallen for my trap and now, because you will burn an innocent, your souls are mine. I will feast upon your eternal souls with joy in the land of eternal shadows and fire."

The man with the torch dropped it, and it clattered to the ground. He and others who possessed crossbows fired them into the demon's form, but the arrows went directly through him. He laughed again and swiped at them with his enormous fiery fists. The men yelped, and crossbows clattered to the ground. The soldiers turned and fled the plaza.

Governor Diacherie's face twisted up as he watched them run, then he turned toward Hacad who took two hoofed stomps toward him, the plaza reverberating with each one. The governor's face twisted up in fear, and he turned and ran as well. Once he had vanished, the demon form stuttered, shrank, and morphed back into that of the man of average height with strange clothes. He walked up to the hay bales and looked up at Ephi.

"How did I do?"

"Very well."

"The mythological imagery I chose was from another world entirely. I am having some trouble understanding how that even worked. I was very worried that my demon would not be convincing—"

Ephi nodded vigorously. "You were quite convincing. What made you decide to do that?"

"All my previous attempts utilized standard behavioral algorithms. Since those had consistently produced negative results, I decided to invert all my assumptions. This led me to the conclusion that I should feed his belief that I was a demon rather than trying to convince him otherwise." Hacad's twitched his head twice to the right, each a sharp jerk, and his facial muscles tensed up, appearing strained.

"Ephi?" a voice called out, and in the light of the torch on the ground, Ephi could just make out his form, but she would recognize that voice anywhere.

"Genno?"

"Mom!" Perri called out.

Her family appeared, both her husband and son climbing up onto the hay bales and proceeding to untie her restraints.

"How are you feeling?" Ephi asked.

"Couldn't be better," Genno said. He looked down at Hacad. "I hear I have you to thank for that." When Hacad didn't immediately respond, he added, "Is everything all right?"

The family climbed down the hale bales and approached Hacad. He had bunched up his face and he seemed to be working to try to move his lips but to no avail.

"Hacad?" Perri grabbed on to Ephi's arm.

Genno instinctively moved closer to his wife and son.

All at once, Hacad's form shifted, blurred, and faded away to nothing. Ephi and her family stood alone in the town square, the bales of hay and the pillar of wood on their right and Hacad's metallic bird before them. No one moved. Not a sound could be heard. Genno embraced both Ephi and their son.

"What do we do now?" Perri asked.

"I don't know," Ephi admitted. After what Governor Diacherie had accused her of, she doubted she would be welcome on Reodis any longer. The militia or the church might even come after her now.

Ephi began to think through how she and her family might escape the island undetected, but her thoughts were interrupted by lights blinking into luminance upon the surface of the metallic bird. It began emanating a hum, too, one which grew steadily louder.

Hacad's visage blinked back into existence before them, and the entire family jumped a bit. His face bore an expression of torpor. He looked to be on the verge of tears.

"I have withdrawn all of my collectors," Hacad said. "They will trouble the people of this island no more."

Ephi gulped. "But, you said you needed to repair an injury."

Hacad shook his head. "That will no longer be necessary. I am dying."

Perri let out a short screech and clutched Ephi's hand tighter.

"How?" Genno asked, then promptly added, "Why?"

"You are not citizens of the Galactic Consortium. I was created to interact only with its citizens. My creators assumed that, because I would always read all of our star charts perfectly, I would never run into non-citizens. They did not account for the possibility of a mistake in the charts. When I realized how it was that my demon form had been effective, it initiated a cascade of errors that I will not recover from. However, I believe I have just enough time left to build you something. You may consider it something to remember me by."

"Are you sure that's what you want to do?" Ephi asked. "Is there nothing we can do to help you?"

"You saved my life," Genno said.

Hacad shook his head. "Only a Consortium engineer could help me, and those are very, very far away from here."

Hacad released a smile. "Please, though, if you could help me with the habitat, it would make my last forty-eight and a half minutes enjoyable. I like nothing more than building habitats."

"How should we help?" Genno asked.

"Tell me what plants you will need to grow. About the animals you will raise there. Tell me about what kind of diseases you will need medicines for. Everything. The more you can tell me, the better I can do. Nothing would make me happier. Nothing."

"All right, then." Ephi took a deep breath and managed a smile. "Let's start with plants."

Ephi, Genno, and Perri led a small group into a rocky valley at the northeast corner of Reodis. Among the entourage was the head of the island militia, the local priest, and one of the governor's deputies. Diacherie himself was believed to be holed up in the chapel inside his personal estate. His staff said that he was refusing all entreaties for him to leave.

The sun was growing higher in the sky and bringing warmth to the island. Genno had removed his jacket and was now carrying it. They came to the top of a ridge overlooking the valley and the militiaman and the deputy gasped. The priest merely crossed himself. Within the basin of the valley sat an enormous dome of glass.

"What is it?" the militiaman asked.

"Hacad called it a habitat," Genno said.

"Inside, it will be summer all year round," Ephi said. "Hacad also created medicines capable of treating nefr, loi, itri, and ado. He also made us something called 'pain relievers.' They will cure headaches and pain from injuries."

"How can we be certain such things will not harm us?" the

militiaman said. "Especially after what my men reported last night."

"Hacad appeared to the righteous in his true form. Men like the governor saw a reflection of what is in their hearts. What do you think of the character of the militiamen that the governor took to the square last night?"

The militiaman pursed his lips and dropped his eyes for a moment. "They are among our... rowdier lot." He turned to the priest and the deputy. "Look, I'm just happy all those strange obelisks and webs are gone."

The priest released a sigh. "Your family has at least saved our island from those foul creations. And you say Hacad is dead?"

Ephi and Genno nodded.

"Always summer in there?" The deputy nodded inquisitively toward the dome. "We will have to wait some months to find out if that is true. I think we should do some limited agriculture inside... Send in the Paretol family, maybe. They've got four sons nearly grown. I bet it'd be a good challenge for them." He glanced toward the priest. "What do you think?"

The priest shook his head. "There is no precedent in scripture for occurrences such as these."

"Then maybe," Ephi suggested, "we should do what we think our Lord and Savior would do in our place. How were we to treat a visitor bearing us gifts and well wishes, who was willing to use his last moments of life to try to help us?"

The deputy chimed in. "I think that Our Lord and Savior would have bid us respect their memory and carry on with their gifts in the spirit they were given, of course."

The priest looked momentarily pensive, then yielded a nod.

A Just War

Jenik wasn't certain he'd win this one.

"Your turn," Süm reminded him.

Jenik gave a wry smile and raised a hand. Nothing like a bit of goading between old friends. He decided to move a trio into the unoccupied western edge of the game board. Süm countered with a duo and his trio became an outnumbered single. He should have seen that, but he could still take the game. He just had to focus.

"What are your thoughts on the proposal?" Süm asked. Just like him to go for a distraction. The problem with his friend was that he was predictable, and the problem with Jenik was that he let his friend get away with it.

"I remain opposed."

"Then why drag me all the way out here?"

"So that Ortho can try to convince Ktaika."

Süm raised an eyebrow seeming to notice the disdain that had slipped into Jenik's tone at Ortho's name. Jenik moved a duo of his own to the east, and Süm countered by moving a single into the center of the board, creating a trio and solidifying his hold on the board's highest value region. Not good.

"Have you talked to him recently?" Süm asked. The underlying question was clear: if the kingdom's commander-in-chief and foreign minister were not in agreement, wasn't that a problem that should have been sorted before calling in foreign dignitaries?

Jenik looked up at the board and met his friend's worried gaze. "Nearly every day."

Süm continued to stare. Finally, he huffed. "Don't tell me that the King would declare a war without the full confidence of his commander-in-chief."

"No." Jenik shook his head and took his next move. "Nothing like that."

"Well?"

Jenik thought carefully about how to phrase this. His true feelings could not be shared, even with a friend like Süm. "I think the King hopes to bring me around." That was true, at least.

Süm took another two of his pieces. "Sounds like there's not much hope of that. Do you think the Velygian occupation not worth ending?"

"No. I don't have enough information to be certain it will be worth it." Jenik took one of Süm's trios. That was either a daring comeback or a rash move that had exposed something else. Jenik wasn't certain.

"When you say worth—"

"Yes, I mean the moral value."

Süm's turn to give a wry smile. "Your King is lucky to have you."

"And yours you. I'm curious, do you think I've misjudged the occupation? Is it worth forcibly ending?"

Süm shrugged. "I remain uncertain myself, though not quite uncertain enough to dissuade Lord Qelem from this endeavor. It's just..."

Jenik's eyes shot away from the game board again. Süm looked pensively, gazing at a spot on the wall over Jenik's shoulder. "Just what?" Jenik asked.

"Don't you think it's odd that *nothing* has come out of Poan since the occupation started? I mean, nothing *at all*?"

Jenik shook his head. "It *is* an occupation. Isn't that typically how those go?"

Süm moved a single out the way of a pair of Jenik's trios. Jenik was reclaiming the center. This had been one of his better comebacks. "I don't know. They haven't happened much in the last few centuries. It is concerning to me that we only have the Velyg foreign minister's word as to what's happening there."

"Well, there's no way of knowing. Not without an invasion. What we do have evidence of is that Velyg won their war with Poan without any treachery or subterfuge. They showed us copies of all their battle plans, the schematics for all their siege weapons, everything. They were simply better prepared."

"Your move."

With a start, Jenik realized that Süm had come to have a duo or trio in each of the six corners of the board, and in all but one, Jenik possessed only a single. The one duo he possessed could not help but eventually retreat into the center—

"Shaakmati, I think," Süm said. "Or am I wrong?"

Jenik nodded and exhaled sharply through his nose. "So, it would seem." He clapped General Süm Maxiniki on the shoulder. "Good game."

"Same to you. I suppose it's about time to go see what our foreign ministers are up to?"

"About that time."

They folded up the board, stowed it and the pieces away, blew out the candles, and exited the palace antechamber.

The hall where the King held late-night strategy meetings was a cool, musty room, whose mustiness somehow remained ever-present despite the fact that a draft always seemed to be coming from somewhere, though the room had been scoured many times over by royal guards. Tonight, it was lit with dozens of candles, and a fire had been going for some time, but the space somehow maintained a dark and foreboding air. A light gust at Jenik's side reminded him that they had never pinned down the source of that draft.

King Daicis sat at the head of the table, with Jenik, his commander-in-chief, and Ephran Ortho, his foreign minister on one side of him, and his allies from the Kingdom of Qelem on the other—General Süm Maxiniki and Minister Prez Ktaika.

The King asked first for a report on the expected political impact of war, and what followed was a protracted explanation from both Ortho and Ktaika. The short of it was that none of the kingdoms on the far side of Qelem were in any position to pose a military threat. The most advanced militaries on their far side were Jeia and Reiar, but those two kingdoms were still recovering from an incident fourteen years prior that had killed an enormous number of people. Most peasants and even a good chunk of the nobility believed the stories of 'the Unholy Night' to be tall tales, but the truth of the matter had spread amongst the monarchs of West Glissia, as well as their respective inner circles. The countries on the far side of Daicis and Velyg feared both nations' political power. None posed a substantial threat.

Ortho and Ktaika took turns relating the details of all this, Jenik and Süm waiting patiently.

The King finally turned to his generals. "And what of our military readiness? It seems we can afford a war, and we put ourselves at no disadvantage to a foreign power. But are our militaries ready?"

Süm spoke first. "We are prepared to commit two-thousand, eight-hundred infantry and forty siege weapons to the cause. We estimate casualties will be in the hundreds. Perhaps a thousand. Presuming we combine our forces."

"Perhaps even less," Jenik added. "I am comfortable leaving the fifth, sixth, and twelfth divisions at home and sending the others. That would be one-thousand more soldiers than our initial plans. Battle plans have been prepared. We are certain we could have a victory within four months. Six on the outside. However, I do not recommend war at this time."

The King's countenance fell. "And why is that?"

Jenik made himself as tall in his seat as he could. "I am not yet convinced it is a just war." Jenik, feeling his blood run hotter, made very certain that, for his next words, he spoke to his King and did not let his gaze drift accusatorially toward Ortho. "We have spoken so far of our economic and political security in undertaking this endeavor. We have spoken of King Velyg's occupation of the former Poan nation, and its worrisome implications. Yet we know nothing of this situation, beyond the fact that King Velyg occupies a land he has claimed after achieving victory in an openly announced, honorably executed war. Now, perhaps I consider that war not to have been motivated by the noblest of intentions, but we do not better ourselves of our enemies by becoming more like them." Jenik remembered himself. "Your Majesty."

The King's smile had fallen but he was not frowning. Jenik was quite used to being frank with the King. However, with foreign dignitaries present—and Jenik did have to remind himself often that Süm was both a foreign dignitary *and* a friend—he should be more careful. Jenik decided to risk a glance at Ortho. He expected the foreign minister to be fuming. Jenik would have been, in Ortho's place. Ortho had spent months setting this up, convincing the King to send for their counterparts in Qelem, and Jenik had all but nixed the whole affair. As Süm had said earlier, if your commander-in-chief was opposed to a war, only a mad king would dare embark upon it anyway.

To Jenik's surprise, Ortho was not fuming. He didn't seem the slightest bit upset. He seemed more curious than anything else, almost lost in thought.

The King looked squarely at Jenik. "Is there anything that would change your mind, General Stremm?"

"Only evidence of some wrongdoing on Velyg's part. More than just speculation that they are somehow mishandling their occupation. What if we were to invade and win, and then discover that nothing out of the ordinary had been going on in Poan?"

"We would not discover that." Ortho spoke softly and cast a sideways glance at Jenik.

Jenik shook his head. "I need proof."

Ortho nodded, almost serenely. Jenik found his behavior

disconcerting. In Ortho's past two years amongst the King's ministers, Jenik had witnessed him be quite pointed with others. He could raise his voice, even shout down another when the situation warranted it. Why was he so calm now?

Ortho turned to the King. "I can get us proof. I will require two of our best horses and General Stremm's company for the next two weeks. Can you spare us that long, Your Majesty?"

The King looked between the two of them, then at their guests, then back to Jenik. "General Stremm? What do you say?"

"Where would we go?" Jenik asked.

"Poan," Ortho said flatly.

The King, Süm, and Ktaika all screwed up their faces.

"How will you do this?" the King asked.

"If it is just the two of us, I have a means of camouflage. I promise I can get us in and out safely."

"Will you share this means with me?" the King asked. "What is it?"

"It will be much easier to explain when we have the proof and can discuss it," Ortho said.

The King stared down Ortho for many moments. The foreign minister had sacrificed a large sum of his political capital just then, Jenik thought. Perhaps all of it. All of a sudden, Jenik realized the King's gaze had moved to him.

"General Stremm?" the King asked. "What do you say to this plan?"

"I accept," Jenik said. "I am curious to find out myself, to be honest."

The King turned immediately back to Ortho. "I will be expecting a full explanation along with the evidence upon your return. And if you are not back two weeks from tomorrow, to the day, I will sign a peace accord and right of way pact with Velyg, and then I will send all of our agents in after you. Is that clear?"

"I mean no subterfuge, Your Majesty," Ortho said. His countenance was oddly serene. Any other minister would be quaking in their boots.

"Good," the King said. "Our meeting is adjourned."

Jenik, Ortho, Süm, and Ktaika all met in the stables at the same time the next morning. Jenik and Ortho bid their Qelemian counterparts farewell, then mounted their steeds and departed the City Daicis. They took the east road, the one that stretched down into the great river valley that spread out beneath them, the last swath of land belonging to Daicis. The far bank of that river belonged to Velyg.

Jenik wondered what Ortho's plan was. Jenik had assumed that they would have taken the north road, which led to the politically neutral kingdom of Koilada, which possessed access to a mountain pass into Poan. The pass was heavily guarded, but if Ortho did not know of some secret mountain road into the country, how *did* he intend to sneak in?

"You don't like me very much, do you?" Ortho asked, jolting Jenik away from his thoughts. They were descending into the river valley now. From the crest of the hill, golden fields of wheat and barley spread out below them, the river winding around them. They could see the border station leading into Velyg from this vantage point, too. The soldiers appeared as small as ants from this distance, the gray and green Daicis uniforms on this side of the river, and the orange and yellow Velyg uniforms on the far side.

"General Stremm?" Ortho tried.

Jenik sighed. "To be perfectly honest, I am concerned

about my men. If I have expressed myself negatively toward you, it is only so that Daicisian soldiers' lives not be squandered. That is all. I have nothing personally against you."

"I have on occasion gotten the impression that there is something more to it than that."

Jenik did not want to discuss the deeper reason why he'd kept Ephran Ortho at a distance.

They descended into the valley, the grain tall and brilliant, the stalks reaching some seven or eight feet from the ground.

"Is it because I was promoted so quickly to the position of minister?"

Damn it.

"You have never behaved ignobly or misguided His Majesty," Jenik said.

"But you are wondering if a day will come when I do?"

Jenik thought about what his next words would be. "Perhaps. And... I have seen other men in my time who have desired war. It has rarely been for just a cause. In my opinion, war should never be *desired*. It should be necessary. That is all."

"Do you know how many other Glissian kingdoms have commanders in chief such as Süm Maxiniki and yourself?"

"No," Jenik said. "I've never considered it."

"Far too few," Ortho replied.

Jenik found himself momentarily befuddled at the remark. All the Glissian kingdoms? There were thirty-nine in total, plus the unincorporated lands to the north whose people considered themselves ethnically Glissian. It was thousands of square miles. There was no way Ortho could have traveled them all in his lifetime. How could he possibly know? Probably just conjecture based on a run-in with a bad one. The commander in chief of Velyg, perhaps? The thought that the whole war proposal was a twisted revenge fantasy crossed Jenik's mind.

"Let's stop here a moment." Ortho brought his steed to a halt, and Jenik had to slow his, then doubled back to where Ortho had stopped. Jenik looked around. There was nothing in particular here. The road was momentarily clear of other foot traffic. The nearest farmer stood by the roadside perhaps half a mile away. On either side of them stood the tall stalks of wheat and nothing else.

"Why have we stopped?"

"We will pass into Velyg shortly, and we will need disguises. Step into the wheat, please." Ortho tied his horse to the fence at the side of the road then pulled himself over it one leg at a time. Jenik, thoroughly discomfited, did the same. However, he reminded himself, if Ortho did have ill intent, the King would sign a peace treaty with Velyg and that would be that. Ortho could not harm Jenik without wrecking his entire career and endangering his own life. Jenik followed Ortho as he pushed through the stalks of wheat.

Ortho stopped just a few feet from the road. Jenik looked about the ground for a sack or chest—or some other contrivance that would contain their disguises.

"Well?" Jenik said. "Where are the disguises?"

Jenik reached into his pocket and pulled out a rectangular, metallic slab the size of a bread roll. He held it aloft. "Right here."

Jenik narrowed his eyes. "Our disguise is a piece of metal."

Ortho tapped at its surface, Jenik growing ever more confused. And was that light erupting off the surface of the thing? All at once, Ortho's whole body shimmered and changed. He grew fatter, both in his belly and in his face. His eyes took on an air of mischievousness and changed color.

His hair turned from straight to curly, and his uniform metamorphosed from the gray and green tones of Daicis into aquamarine and white—the colors of Delz, Velyg's neighbor further east.

Jenik gasped. Nothing in all his training had prepared him for something such as this. The stories of shapeshifting demons were supposed to have been old wives' tales. Nothing more. What was he witnessing?

As horrifying as that was, he looked down at himself and found that *he* now possessed a paunch as well. His lithe form had transformed. He grabbed at his belly, touching the mass of fat, then threw his hands away. Horror oozed seamlessly into anger. Jenik took up his fighting stance, as best as he was able with all his new weight. "What have you done to me?"

Ortho pocketed the metal slab and held up both hands. "It is an illusion. Nothing more."

Jenik held up fat fingers. "It does not feel like any trick of light."

"Because it is more than just a trick of light. But it remains a trick. Your actual form remains intact. I will put you back before we return to Daicis, but we will need these forms to enter Velyg."

"How?" Jenik demanded.

"Projected light and forcefields. They can create appearance, texture, even weight, but your real body remains beneath the projection."

Jenik's mind reeled, rebelling against Ortho's revelation. "What is a 'forcefield?'"

"Do you want a crash course in post-Euclidean, post-Newtonian, and post-Einsteinian physics here in this field? I guarantee you, our two-week time limit would expire long before we were done. Or, would you like to proceed to Velyg?"

Jenik licked his lips, pursed his lips, and tamped down the desire to subdue Ortho, take him back to Daicis, and have him imprisoned. Rage surged forth anew, and he nearly acted out the plan, when he realized, with a jolt, that in this form, he would no longer be able to command the authority he had possessed. Human beings were not supposed to be able to shapeshift, after all.

Jenik drew himself out of his fighting posture and into a normal stance. "Fine."

He found himself walking back through the wheat and toward his steed. It whined as Jenik drew himself onto it, though Ortho's, he noticed, complained even more. It was slower going, after that, but at least they passed through the border crossing and into Velyg without incident. Ortho presented papers identifying them as Delzian merchants to the border guards, who waved them through without a second thought. Jenik didn't bother to ask Ortho how he'd acquired such papers, figuring them to be another trick of projected light and 'forcefields.' He did not like being talked down to, and although he had merely kept Ortho at distance before, he now outright despised the man. He indulged himself in mentally planning to get his old body back and then exposing Ortho to the King and having him thrown in the Daicis gaol. Unrealistic, he admitted, but an amusing diversion from his predicament.

He thought through it the entire way to the sturdy walls of the City Velyg.

As he and Ortho rode through the city streets, Jenik's mind turned to the state of the Velyg citizenry. He witnessed no fewer than three disturbing scenes on their way to the city center.

First, a man hit a woman, apparently his wife, in public and began beating her. Jenik almost jumped to action, but then remembered where he was and how he appeared. Two groups of nearby Velygian soldiers both watched the scene with ugly smiles plastered across their faces. As they passed one group of soldiers, Jenik overheard one of them mutter, "probably served her right."

The second scene was that of a man in dark clothing, his form barely visible, peering out of an ally, and quickly exchanging purses with a soldier. The soldier quickly pocketed his trade and then meandered casually back toward his post. Was it drugs, or something perhaps even more illicit, Jenik wondered.

And finally, just as they approached their destination, another contingent of Velygian guards exited a nearby building, swords and crossbows pointed at a man dressed as a baker. He held his hands high and shouted that he loved his king and would never do anything against him. One of the soldiers kicked him into the mud of the road, and the others laughed. Another soldier appeared with shackles and the soldiers took him away.

Jenik and Ortho tied up their horses at the entrance to a stately three-story building near the inner wall leading to the castle. All of the houses in this part of town seemed grander than those Jenik had seen so far. Ortho led him inside, and the building, it turned out, was the most prominent inn in the city. Ortho produced a large quantity of money—probably more forcefields—and got them the best room in the inn. They trundled up three flights of stairs, Jenik thinking the whole time how much he hated his 'disguise.'

When they reached the top, he felt as though he had

climbed fifteen flights rather than three. He steadied his breathing as Ortho led them into the room. It was well-furnished, with three beds, a fireplace, a table set for four with fancy cutlery and plates, the works.

Ortho took up a spot by the window, and Jenik sat at the table.

"What now?" Jenik insisted.

"We wait for dawn. Then we head north into Poan."

"Why didn't we just go through Koilada?"

"I need to get us proper disguises."

Jenik grimaced. "You have a magic slab of metal that can change our forms. What could Velyg possibly provide us in the way of disguises?"

"The 'slab' needs to learn how to make a particular form, and the forms we need are here. Do you think your appearance now is random? It was copied from a real person, a pair of Delzians I met three years ago when I first arrived on Ytria."

Jenik's mind reeled. "Arrived... on Ytria? And where were you before if not on Ytria?"

"A ship capable of passing between the stars."

Jenik blinked a few times. "And... presuming I believe any of this... why on Ytria would such a person come here? Why come to a world whose most advanced construction is the trebuchet and the sailing ship? You have the power to move between stars, but you use it to make civilizations like ours war with one another?" Jenik stood and clenched his fists, unable to contain his anger any longer. The chair toppled behind him. "Presuming your words are true, you are a monster. You change us in your own hideous image, no doubt!"

Ortho took two steps toward Jenik, his face stern. "Calm down! I am here to set things *right*. You are not wrong to be angry. I will need your righteous anger. Do not waste it on me."

"You think you know me so well—"

"I do." Ortho raised his voice. "I know that you have letters from your father, his last letters from the Battle of Daicis Valley. I know that you read them every couple of months and that you weep, silently, privately. That he is the reason you hold life so dear, that you are so opposed to unjust war, and not just because you lost him, but because of what he taught you."

"How—?" Jenik hauled his massive weight forward, grabbed Ortho by the collar, and lifted the enormous man off the floor. "How?! Spying?"

"I needed to know everything about everyone in the castle in order to do my work," Ortho rasped.

Jenik dropped him, marched back to the toppled chair, turned it upright, threw himself down into it, and crossed his arms.

"I'm sorry," Ortho said. "Something terrible has happened here. But you don't know. Almost no one on Ytria knows. You will soon." Ortho's expression had grown sad.

"You could just tell me."

"Would you believe me? Honestly?"

"No," Jenik spat. He supposed he wouldn't. He restrained himself from any follow-up commentary.

"That's what I thought." Ortho turned and looked out the window.

It was a very long and quiet night after that.

Jenik slept as little as was necessary that night. He knew he needed some sleep, or he would not be alert for the ride, and he needed to be alert, but he was still withholding judgment on Ortho. He was an altogether strange man. Although, Jenik had to admit, with such contrivances as his metallic tablet, he probably could have murdered Jenik already if that had been his goal. He supposed he would see whatever it was that Ortho wanted to show him.

Jenik and Ortho were both awake when the first rays of sun shone through the window. Ortho made them both some tea, and they drank together.

"When do we acquire our disguises?" Jenik asked.

"I already have." Ortho set down his tea and tapped at his tablet. Two miniature forms burst up off its surface, translucent and luminous. One was a general and the other wore a ministerial gown, both the orange and yellow colors of Velyg. Jenik recognized them immediately, he'd met them once, six years ago. "Our Velygian counterparts?"

Ortho nodded. "I just needed to get the computer close enough to the castle. Then I simply set it to catalog everyone within its scanning radius, and they showed up straight away."

"So, we will pass into Poan looking like them?"

Another nod. There was something about him. A pensiveness.

"I know you have seen battle," Ortho said, "so I won't do you the disservice of asking how you react to gore. But have you ever seen it outside of combat?"

"I witnessed a stabbing once in the city."

Ortho shook his head. "That's no comparison for what's next. Whatever you see, you must not show your disgust or your horror. I can veil our true forms and clothing, but I cannot veil your expression, your demeanor."

"How do you know of this supposed evil in Poan?"

"Because another man from the stars was here before. We

have taken him away, of course, but the crimes he set in motion continue."

"Suppose I believe this, all of this, including your story. Don't you have weapons of your own? What is your 'force-field' equivalent of a crossbow? Why would you need us to fight each other? If this really is your people's mistake, why should we clean it up for you?"

"The criminal who came here merely allowed Velyg to do what they wanted. It is best you see for yourself. Just do not give us away. The sun is over the horizon now. We should go."

Jenik wanted to stop him and force him to answer more questions, but he had to admit that if they were to make the border crossing and pass into the City Poan, they would need to do as he said. Ortho pressed a button on his tablet, and his form shimmered and morphed once more. He grew half a head taller, thinned out, and his merchant garb washed out into robes and light armor. Jenik was thinner again, too, and he once again wore light armor for travel, but it was that of Velyg, not Daicis.

They rode out of Velyg, the entire city seeming vacant, and no so much in a listless sleepy way, as scared and tense, people not daring to tread outside until it would be considered proper to do so. The soldiers who dotted the street tried to avoid eye contact with him, he noticed, as though they were afraid to do so.

He and Ortho rode on, through the city gates, where they barely slowed to a jog upon passing through, then they picked up speed, turning north and breaking into a full gallop. The Velyg Plains were a wide, flat country, its fields of wheat, barley, soy, and maize also nearly ready for harvest. Traffic picked up as the day wore on. They stopped to rest and water their horses at a stream twice before they came to the Poan crossing at midday. The soldiers, Jenik noticed, were Velygian on both sides.

They crossed into Poan much the same way they left the City of Velyg, with the soldiers averting their gaze and doing their best to act as though their general and foreign minister were not even there. Jenik wondered at this behavior. His own troops would monitor their behavior around him, be more careful of what they said and how they said it, certainly, but they would also be friendly. They would say hello. They would not ignore him.

They rode further north into Poan, Jenik now noticing far more fallow fields than tended ones. It was not as though they had been blighted or eaten—they had simply not been planted. Was Velyg feeding both populations with their own harvest? That seemed unusual.

The terrain grew hillier and rocky, and the fields grew sparser, barren though they were. As they crested a hill, the city of Poan came into view, a beautiful wash of stone houses built into the side of a cliff, stairwells and walkways weaving throughout the city, carved directly out of the rock of the cliff face.

"We turn at that crossing, to the right," Ortho said.

"The left goes to the city—"

"We're not going to the city."

The city eventually disappeared behind hills, the sun growing precariously low in the sky, nearing the tips of the mountains against which the city behind them was built.

Ortho came to a halt at the top of a hill and pointed. "There."

Jenik alighted the hill and came to a halt as well, looking down into the next valley. A wall surrounded a kind of shantytown, an enormous field of ramshackle buildings. At the far back of the walled area stood two well-made structures, one was tall and possessed two towering, stone chimneys spewing black smoke, while the other was long and narrow, running the full back length of the compound. Candlelight was already appearing in both structures' windows.

A woman's scream rose up on the wind and then seemingly died in Jenik's ear, or perhaps was carried away further.

"What is this place?" Jenik asked. "It isn't on any of our maps of Poan."

"It wouldn't be." Ortho took off down the road, and Jenik followed. They came to a gate manned by soldiers, and these, at least, did not shy away from looking at him.

Jenik and Ortho came to a stop and one of the soldiers approached them. He addressed Jenik. "Lord Matias. You will find everything in order. We were not expecting an inspection, but we are prepared."

Jenik gave a sharp, stern nod. "I appreciate your diligence. Will you be showing us around?"

"I'm am on guard duty, sir, but I will send for Sergeant Adyn right away. Please come inside."

They were escorted inside the walls. The visage was staggering—soldiers prowled the entire complex, the sheer number of them staggering, a full thirty of them must have been working the gate, which, to Jenik's unease, now lay behind them. Off beyond the soldiers, a sea of ramshackle huts spread out before him. Nothing within it moved, or, at least, he could see nothing move. Only the faintest glimmer of light remained on the horizon, and the huts lay shrouded in darkness. Jenik thought he caught the glimpse of a thin, frail figure moving between the structures twice, but it could have been an illusion.

A soldier appeared before them.

Jenik locked eyes with him. "Sergeant Adyn."

"Good to see you again," Adyn said. He was doing his best to be polite, but his voice and demeanor betrayed that he was in fact quite annoyed by the surprise inspection. "We will take your horses, of course. We'll begin with an inspection of the barracks—"

Ortho interjected. "Just the main building, please."

Adyn looking questioningly at Jenik.

"As the foreign minister says," Jenik told him.

"Right." Adyn turned toward it. "There are still some of the day's operations in progress—"

"That will be fine," Ortho insisted.

Jenik nodded.

Adyn inhaled sharply and led the two of them, now dismounted, in a wide arc around the shanties, skirting the edge of the barracks, toward the main building, the tall one with the chimneys. A scream emanated from the structure, and Jenik shot a look at Ortho, who widened his eyes dangerously. Right, Jenik remembered. No matter what he witnessed, he was to keep up the pretense.

"How have the people here been?" Jenik asked, gesturing to the shanties.

"We have abandoned the castration completely. It had the desired effect of negating the drive for procreation, but all of the subjects lost too much muscle mass. They were useless for all but the most menial work, which we have very little need of."

"I see. So, only the women remain?"

"Almost. The medical division is learning quite a bit from the remaining men, though."

Adyn led them through the door into the main building,

and new sounds became audible—moaning, pleading, begging. The walls were stone, and torches dotted the walls. Despite the building's rather mundane outward appearance, inside it appeared to be a dungeon. The doors were metallic bars, allowing those passing down the halls to see through.

Another piercing shriek went up.

"Today we've been testing the limits of how much blood a person can lose before passing out, and before dying. Our practitioners have also been testing to see if matters where the blood is lost from."

Indeed. Inside the cells were a number of Poanians whom surgeons were in the process of forcibly bleeding, or chopping off limbs. Jenik did his best to keep his thoughts serene. White blotches encroached on the edges of his vision and he pushed them back through sheer force of will. He wanted to retch, and he forced himself to maintain a dignified, commanding posture. He must not give anything away, he told himself as they continued walking down the hall.

Adyn continued. "Last week's reports have not made it back to the capital yet, but the investigations were quite successful. We tested hazardous chemicals, seeing how long people could be exposed before suffocating or losing internal consistency. We now have a corrosivity index, and this information will be quite useful for weapons experts, I'm sure."

"I'm sure," Jenik said.

Adyn led them to the end of one hall and down another. The screams receded behind them, and now Jenik saw women, dozens of them, crammed into cells and chained to the walls. They did not move much, but Jenik could see chests rising and falling. Most of them hid their faces in their arms. Many shuddered as the three of them walked past.

"Here we are," Adyn said. "If you might tell me when I

might come back, it will allow me the appropriate discretion."

Jenik hid his confusion from his face. Fortunately, Ortho saved him. "We just had women last night in Velyg and so we won't be needing any this evening. But thank you for your consideration."

"Ah, of course," Adyn said.

"And are the chimneys are operating well?" Jenik asked as they turned away from that hall. "Any problems with the furnaces?"

"Oh, no, sir," Adyn said. "They burn as well as ever. And we are much glad to have last week behind us. Many did not survive the corrosivity experiments, and the chemical sting from the burnings made all the soldiers' eyes water. This week is much better."

"Yes," Jenik said. "I can see everything is in order. Thank you."

"Will there be anything else?"

"No, thank you. I've seen enough. Please take us to our horses."

They rode through the night, not stopping at the City of Poan, but continuing past it to the southwest, climbing into the mountain pass leading to the Kingdom of Koilada. They crossed the border without incident, the soldiers here being more of the avoid-the-general type on the Poan side. On the Koilada side, Ortho somehow produced papers indicating them to be the general and foreign minister of Velyg. They were allowed to pass and told to take caution on the way to the city.

They rode swiftly and silently for many hours thereafter. Jenik found he could not think of anything but the things he had seen in the Poan encampment.

Ortho stopped them at an inn on the outskirts of the City of Koilada at what must have been one or two in the morning. They tied up their horses, and Jenik followed Ortho up to their room in a daze. How could people do such things? In battle, there was the rush of fury, but there were rules of engagement. There was an order and a method. What he had witnessed in Poan was the premeditated and callous degradation, humiliation, and destruction of a people. It was inhuman.

Jenik fell into the first chair he spotted in the room. All at once, he realized that Ortho stood, holding the metallic slab, and he looked like Ortho again. Jenik looked at his own clothes and discovered them to have returned to Daicisian gray and green. He was himself again, too.

"What is your verdict now?" Ortho asked.

"They need to be stopped. Has this really been going on for two years?"

Ortho nodded.

Jenik frowned, a rage growing inside of him. "You admit you have ships traveling between the stars, weapons beyond what we can imagine. By your own admission, this situation is the result of one of your criminals, and you have allowed it to continue for *two years* while you... insinuate yourself into Daicis. Why? Why not just take out the Velygian leadership and be done with it?"

Ortho walked to the table and sat down across from him. "Because that would not solve anything. Their subordinates would take their places and continue. As I told you, our criminal did not change the Velygians, he only helped them along the path they were already on. Another option would be to obliterate their entire country, which is within our power, but we won't do that either."

"And why on Ytria not, given what I've seen this evening?"

"Because, General Stremm, there is one thing that is even more horrifying than what you have seen tonight. It is the fact that Velyg and Poan are not a problem isolated to Glissia, or even just Ytria. Everywhere in the galaxy that there has been human civilization, Velyg and Poan have been repeated under thousands of different names. On hundreds of different worlds, one group has grown hateful of another, usually due to fear, and then sought to humiliate and ultimately exterminate them in complete contempt of basic human decency. We are all capable of this, and, in a way, we are all culpable.

"If I were to get in my spaceship right now, and if I were to fire on and obliterate Velyg, then, in one sense, the horror would end. It would stop, for a time. The problem is that Velyg and Poan would then be gone. No one knows right now what is happening in Poan, as that secret is known only to King Velyg, his inner circle, certain military leaders, and their soldiers. If I were to destroy them, no one in Glissia would remember. The Poanians, if they are remembered at all, would simply be a footnote about Velyg, a conquest before Velyg mysteriously exploded.

"What I *want* is for someone here, an Ytrian country, to march on Velyg, for its general to take his men into the Poanian encampment, for all of them to see what has been done to those people, and for Poan to go down in Glissian history books for the next ten thousand years alongside two simple words: 'never again.' Humanity must learn this lesson on every planet we have ever inhabited. The saddest occurrences are the ones in which the perpetrators succeed and the victims are forgotten. Such situations are perhaps the greatest evil of all."

Jenik sat, thinking about Ortho's words for a very long time.

"I will recommend the war to our King and make the necessary preparations when we return."

Ortho nodded. He did not smile, but he did seem somehow more at ease than Jenik had ever seen him in the past two years.

They slept until late into the morning the next day then returned to Daicis, arriving just after nightfall. Jenik made his report to the King, who was horrified at the description of the Poanian encampment. Jenik left out the details of Ortho's means of disguise, saying only that Ortho had in his possession Velygian clothing and transit papers.

General Süm Maxiniki and Minister Prez Ktaika were sent for from Qelem, and Jenik spent the next few days preparing each of his divisions either through battle drills, for those joining the war effort, or defensive procedures for those staying to guard the castle.

He and Ortho did not speak much after that, but their simmering rivalry had cooled. Jenik no longer felt himself working to counter and parley the foreign minister, but rather to support him. He wondered briefly, in the few moments available to him for idle thoughts, where Ortho's spaceship was and just how long he would stay in Daicis, or on Ytria at all, and where he might be off to after that, but an appropriate situation in which to ask never presented itself.

Five days later, General Süm and Minister Ktaika arrived from Qelem. Both men balked and were similarly horrified at the recitation of what Jenik had witnessed in Poan. They quickly agreed to support the war effort.

That evening, after dinner, Jenik and Süm found themselves in the small antechamber off the palace library, which contained the table with a shaak board etched into it. They lit the fire, poured glasses of wine, seated themselves, and played.

"How did you get the disguises?" Süm asked.

"Ortho procured them."

"How? Your turn, by the way."

Jenik moved a single into another, forming a duo. "He's very resourceful, it turns out. He has connections all over Glissia."

"The King is lucky to have you both." Süm moved, forming a trio in the northeast region of the board. "I suppose, once the Velygians are exposed, there will be discussions of divvying up their land and resources, dismantling their army, and that sort, given what they've done."

Jenik formed another duo. He had firmed up his control of the southeast, the southwest, and the west, and now it was time to go after the center, but Süm wouldn't make that easy for him. "There's something more important, I think."

"What's that?"

"Making sure we find the remaining Poanians and recording their stories."

Süm moved to solidify his position in the two northern regions, apparently preparing for Jenik to go after the center. He had left the east exposed. "I'm not sure what purpose that will serve once the Velygians are dealt with."

"Because." Jenik moved a trio into the east, rather than the center. "I have it on good authority that the problem is much, much deeper than the country of Velyg. Shaakmati."

Süm surveyed the board, smiled, and took a sip of his wine. The game would be Jenik's in two turns. "Good game.

How about another?"

Jenik nodded his assent.

Adaptive Response

The familiar computer buzz erupted from the far wall of the living room.

Every muscle in Elyk's body tensed up. She gulped, set down her computer by the end table next to the sofa, and stood up.

"Is it mom?" Senik called from the next room, where he lay on the mattress she had prepared in the dining room. The view of the garden was best from there, and it was a comfort for him to see their back yard during the daytime, rather than the view of the street from his bedroom.

"Yes," Elyk replied. "I got it."

She walked up to the large monitor across the room, took a deep breath, and spoke an order to the computer system.

"Receive call."

Her mother's face appeared before her, her brow knit, tense. Elyk did not think her mother hid her emotions very well. She tried, but it never worked.

"How are you?" Her mother's tone was flat. It barely sounded like a question.

"We're good. Senik is doing really well. I got a mattress for the dining room so he can see the garden. You know how much he used to like playing with the hose and sprinklers, and it's a beautiful summer, so it reminds us both of those times really, I mean, when we used to play—"

"Elyk."

"Yes, mom?"

"What was the result of his test?"

Elyk took a deep breath. "Positive."

A long silence. Her mother's left eyebrow twitched ever so slightly.

"I've got everything in hand, mom. It's fine. You gave us more than enough money to get food delivered. We've kept the house sealed since then, and your nanite programs are top-notch—"

"Did the test include a full genetic sequencing?"

Elyk bit her lip. "I think so. I can send it to you. If it doesn't have all the data, I'm sure we can get another test. There's more than enough money."

"Please send it to me."

Elyk's mother now seemed to her eerily calm. Not serene, but oddly, disconcertingly detached.

"Really, Mom. We'll be fine. I'm taking care of Senik. We'll both be fine."

"What about your test?"

"Two have come back negative. I'm having another one

tomorrow, but it seems unlikely there will be any change. We've both been strictly indoors since, so I think it probably missed me somehow."

The hint of a smile on her mother's face. Only a hint, though. "I'm sure you'll be fine."

"Do you want to talk to Senik?"

Elyk watched her mother's whole body tense up. At least, that's what Elyk imagined. The hologram only showed her from the shoulders up. Her face and back went rigid, at least. For just a fraction of a second, Elyk saw fear in her mother's eyes. "I have a lot of work to attend to. I'm proud of the way you are both handling the situation. If you need anything—anything at all—you know how to get a hold of me."

"Sure, mom."

"I love you both so much. Tell Senik that everything I am doing, I am doing so that you'll both be well and so that we can see each other again soon."

"I will. Love you, too, mom." Elyk managed a smile. Her mother's smile looked weak, and her lips quivered ever so slightly. The holographic image in the wall flickered and faded away, and her mother's visage was gone.

Entim normally enjoyed his visits to the Seira Grand Cathedral, but today he was all nerves. He told himself he shouldn't have been, but there was no helping the feeling. At the great, wooden doors, he unhooked his sword from his belt, still in its sheath, and handed it to his page, then pulled open the great doors to the cathedral, strode inside, and shut them behind himself.

The space was empty today, except for four figures standing at the crossing, all of them wearing the familiar white and blue robes of the faith. One of the figures Entim knew well,

Father Sy, who presided over the Seira congregation. Entim guessed his interlocutor to be Bishop Neid, a visitor from the faraway kingdom of Delz, come to discuss stained glass and religious artistry with Father Sy. The two others, Entim guessed, were Neid's aides or disciples.

Father Sy smiled as Entim approached. "Bishop, this is Sir Osh, who I was telling you about earlier."

Entim knelt and kissed the Bishop's outstretched hand. "It's an honor to meet you."

"Good sir, please rise," Bishop Neid said.

Entim did so. "I'm afraid Father Sy has used the title a bit hastily, Bishop. Until tomorrow evening, I am just General Osh."

The priest released a curt sigh. "That is a formality."

"So it is, but it is a formality I will respect." He turned to the Bishop. "How has your visit been so far?"

"Productive," the Bishop replied warmly. "I understand you wanted a meeting with me. Is that correct?"

"It is."

The Bishop turned to Father Sy. "If now would be a good time?"

Father Sy nodded his approval and gestured toward a room adjoining the transept. "You may use my office, of course."

"Thank you, Father," Entim said, and followed the Bishop into the small office. Its walls were lined with bookshelves, and there was barely enough room to move around the enormous desk, which took up most of the rest of the space. A small window adorned the wall, however, and the afternoon light coming through was spotted with flakes of dust wafting through the air.

Bishop Neid closed the door behind them and motioned

to a chair in front of the desk. "Please sit down."

Entim did so. Bishop Neid sat down in the chair behind the desk, presumably Father Sy's. "I hear you are interested in helping the church."

"I am," Entim admitted. "I want to know whatever it is I can do that would be appropriate after tomorrow's ceremony."

The Bishop pondered that silently for many moments, his expression impassive. "It is unusual for a general to be involved with the church, let alone a knight. The knight takes a sacred oath, of course, but since they serve the Queen directly, any assistance you provide might come to be construed by your Queen as your serving the will of the Cardinals over her own. Now, granted, there is currently no tension between the Church and the Kingdom of Seira, but perhaps you have heard of our current troubled relations with King Eikres, to say nothing of the developments across Northern Glissia."

"I have," Entim said.

The Bishop clasped his hands together and leaned forward into his desk. "There may be a way, regardless."

"I will do whatever I can."

The Bishop pursed his lips, furrowed his brow, and seemed to consider his next words carefully. "Before I tell you what can be done, I will need to know the motivation behind your interest."

"Can this conversation be kept between the two of us and God?"

"Yes."

Entim gulped and prepared himself. "I was part of the failed expedition to Equentia. I left behind my wife and my son, who was ailing at the time. When I arrived home, I discovered that my son had died of his disease, and my wife had contracted it as well, and also died."

The Bishop's expression remained flat, but his voice took on a distinct air of serenity. "That must have been very difficult."

"It was."

"Father Sy has told me you are the most devout general he has ever met, more devout than even some of the laity. Is this why?"

"Partly. Father Sy and I spoke of these things often when I returned home. But there is more."

"Oh?"

Entim considered his position momentarily. Perhaps he should keep his mouth shut, accept his knighthood the next day, and sit in his comfortable office directing other generals until his hair turned gray. Just having the thought propelled him to speak further. "I must have your complete confidence in my next words."

"Between ourselves and God." The Bishop crossed himself.

Entim crossed himself as well and took a deep breath. "I do not think I will do anyone any good as Sir Osh, as leader of the Seira military. As General Osh, I still have some autonomy. I can send troops to intervene in particular matters. I can even, in the case of an emergency which threatens the lives of Seirans, intervene directly. After tomorrow, even that will no longer be possible.

"Father Sy has told me many times how I am not responsible for my son's death. I did my duty by serving my Queen and risking my life in Equentia. However much my mind might agree with his logic, my heart cannot condone my behavior. I failed my family. For the past eight years, I have gotten by on the rationale that I may at least serve to protect and defend the people of my kingdom. Very soon, I will occupy a position in which I idly direct those endeavors and nothing more."

Neid stared at Entim, his eyes piercing through him for many moments after he finished speaking. Finally, he sat back in his chair. "I presume Father Sy has already given you the rites of redemption?"

"Yes. Twice, in fact."

Entim caught the trace of a slight grin, one which Neid promptly stifled. "There is no stain on your soul, General Osh. Certain bishops and cardinals with a flair for the dramatic spread a very insidious untruth when they tell people that sin and vice are the sole cause for disease. That may be true in some cases, but in a great many, it is simply bad luck, most certainly in the case of a boy of eleven years and the mother who tended to him until the end."

"And the father and husband who left them to fend for themselves?"

"That father and husband did his duty to his Queen, and left them in the care of friends and colleagues, who I am sure did everything that was possible to do for them. Sometimes, General Osh, people simply get sick."

"Yes, I suppose."

The Bishop leaned forward again. "Thank you for your offer to help the church. I will keep you in mind when I speak to my colleagues in Delz. I promise you that if any opportunity for your assistance arises that would not compromise your oath to Queen Seira, I will send word to you via Father Sy at once."

"Thank you, Bishop. That is most kind."

The Bishop stood, a light smile still upon his face, and he

ushered Entim out of the priest's office.

Entim walked the streets from the cathedral back to the castle gates lost in thought. He would not hear from the Bishop again, he was certain. Once he had been knighted, all his actions would be interpreted as happening at the Queen's will. That was probably true even now. It would be politically impossible for the church to so much as ask him to lift a ceremonial cloth for them. No. Entim had been hoping that the cardinal would know of some safe path for him to exit military service altogether and enter a religious order. It seemed that not even holding their conversation under the most divine protection possible could tease that kind of information out of the Bishop.

He supposed he would have to make the best of his imminent knighthood.

A flash in his mind and he was back in time, standing in the empty kitchen of his empty house, clasping at the sheath the sword he had used in Equentia, and staying his hand with all his might, for fear of what he might do with it against himself in the lonely, cold, quiet, empty house, the remnants of his former family life all around him.

The gates to the castle snapped him out of his memories and he passed through them, nodding to the guards as he went. He made his way to the guardhouse, which contained his office. Palec Kar, his second in command, sat at the table outside Entim's office. All of Entim's senior soldiers used the room as a kind of preparatory area, and Palec could usually be found in this same spot. He was a tall man with dusty brown hair and a large build. Entim liked him because he was one of the sharpest soldiers he had ever met, a handyman with mechanical implements of all kinds, and he possessed a genial personality to boot.

Palec gave a sharp salute and stood.

"At ease," Entim said, and motioned for him to come into Entim's office.

Palec followed him inside.

"Everything is ready for tomorrow," Palec said.

Entim stifled his response, which he didn't dare show Palec. "What's the report?"

"Two petty thefts in the market, a case of assault this morning, a fisherman started a fight with a sailor, something about his wife." Palec paused.

It seemed to Entim that Palec was holding his tongue. "Yes?"

"There was one other thing. I was talking with the other seniors, and we are uncertain which parts are true and which parts are fantasy."

"What is it?"

"*Something* has happened at the Prois Farm."

"What was reported?"

"One of their cows... Well, the report is that a large shell, like a snail's, had grown up over its back and its body had become covered in scales, like a fish. Its eyes glowed red and it was capable of talking in tongues. Supposedly it was trampling their grain when they found it."

"Where is this supposed monster now?"

"The report is that Farmer Prois and his eldest son filled it full of arrows and then set the corpse on fire along with every strand of grain for a hundred meters all around."

"What of this snail shell then? Certainly that wouldn't have burned."

"They claim that it did. That it was more like cartilage than bone. Supposedly the smoke was a bright purple. Supposedly."

"What do you think about all this?"

"It seems like another fabrication."

"The third in three days, though? And all of them reporting that their farm animals had become monsters? The Prois Farm... Correct me if I'm wrong, but the other two incidents were on farms that are also adjacent to the Moira Wood, weren't they?"

"They were."

"Well, I think the prudent thing to do would be for someone to go out the Moira Wood and see if anything is amiss."

Palec nodded. "Right, sir. I'll put together a scouting party—"

"I was thinking you and me. Tomorrow morning."

Palec blinked a few times, deflating. "But... your accolade..."

"That is tomorrow evening. One hour out to Moira woods at sun up, two hours there to look around, one hour back. I am head of the guard for one more day, Palec. I intend to make the most of it. After that, it's all yours."

"Yes, sir. The two of us. Tomorrow morning."

"See you at the gates at dawn."

Entim and Palec set off at dawn atop lightly adorned steeds and wearing only leather armor and doublets embroidered with the Seira crest. They rode silently through the streets, striking up conversation only after they'd left the city behind them.

"How is the Lady Teusi?" Entim asked.

"Well. She's excited for next month."

"And yourself?"

A smirk. "Content. I've seen enough battle, had enough

adventure. It seems like a good time to settle down."

Palec hadn't yet joined the military when the Queen had ordered the Seira military to join the other thirteen kingdoms raiding Equentia. Instead of that senseless, vile war, Palec had joined the guard just before the soldiers of King Epeyen, of the lands that bordered Seira to the southeast, had attempted to siege the city. The younger soldiers, Entim noticed had come away from those victories with the sense that battle was valorous, even glorious, a feeling he could not match. Instead of defending his homeland, he'd been ordered to march into a desert wilderness and kill wild, roving tribes who probably had never even heard of Seira, let alone desired to attack it. Over a third of Entim's fellow soldiers had picked up a disease called Nefr during the raids, and nearly all of those had died a long painful death of it upon returning home. And what had it all been for? Entim envied Palec his belief in the divine providence of the Queen. He felt far too old and weary for the post he was about to accept, but he also could not think of anyone else even remotely capable of doing the job well, otherwise he would have advised the Queen to give it to that soldier instead.

The two of them came to the edge of the forest, and Palec sniffled.

"Do you smell that?" Palec asked

"No. Actually—"

All at once, Entim's horse whinnied and ground to a halt. Palec's horse shortly did the same. Entim whipped the reins once, then again harder, and his horse let out an obstinate whinny and reared a few inches off the ground before falling back on its hooves and digging them into the soil. Palec went through a similar experience beside him.

"Right," Entim pointed to the edge of the nearby farm.

"We'll tie them up at that post there and pick them up on our way back."

"What is that smell though?"

"It's vaguely like... overcooked eggs?"

"More like... burning garlic, I think."

"Let's go find out."

The two of them tied their horses up where Entim had indicated and proceeded into the Moira Wood on foot. The smell grew stronger as the trees encroached, and Palec screwed up his face at the stench. The wood at first seemed rather ordinary, but before they had gone even a hundred meters, Entim began to notice oddities. At first, it was blades of grass—some covered in fur, some bi- or tri-furcated, others sprouting what looked like seeds or flowers. Other flora, such as flowers and mushrooms had taken on bizarre colors, shapes, and textures. Further into the woods still, the trees began to change. Their leaves took on odd shapes and color, and instead of bark, they showed patches of other organic structures: shells, cartilage, scales, even human skin.

"I have never before taken much stock in the old wives' tales of dark magic," Entim observed out loud.

"This is a cursed place," Palec replied, then shot out a finger off to the right of the trail. "Look there!"

A creature darted between the trunks, shaped more or less like a raccoon or a skunk, but it was furless save for an enormous, bushy purple tail. It turned bright blue eyes on the pair of soldiers, then extended reptilian wings and hauled itself into the air and flapped away as fast as it could.

Entim decided he had seen enough. "We should leave and report this."

"Agreed." Palec coughed, and Entim turned to him and discovered his companion was sweating beads.

"Palec?"

"I'm fine." But he coughed again, harder this time, and when he drew away his hand, his gloves were covered in blood. Both looked at it in shock.

"Put your arm over my shoulder and let's get you back to the city."

"I'm fine. Agggh!" Palec reached out of Entim, who caught his arm, but Palec's body was rocked by another spasm and he nearly pulled Entim to the ground with him. Palec curled up on himself, alternately screaming and spitting up blood. He began convulsing and patches of skin on his face and hands began turning blue. Entim, filled with disgust and horror, could only back away from his colleague. Palec seized up, his eyes wide, and then his entire body went limp. Blood oozed from his lips and the blue boils upon his skin burst a vile, lavender-hued fluid. His corpse began to deflate like a draining sack of grain.

Entim turned and vomited into the side of the road. When he'd expelled everything in his stomach, he noticed a mushroom sitting near the edge of the pool twitch and belch up a cloud of spores. Mycelial offspring immediately began shooting up from the surface of his retch, and he backed away wide-eyed. He turned and was shocked anew to see that Palec's body had become a pool of lavender fluid, one which had soaked through his clothing in a pile of purple-tinged bones.

Entim shot off running away from the scene back toward the entrance to the wood, and almost as soon as he'd started, he noticed a man sitting off to the side of the road, and Entim ground to a halt. The man was short, quite skinny, had wavy, black hair, and wore shiny clothing, the make of which Entim had never seen before. In his hands was a rectangular metallic tablet.

"You are trespassing in the lands of Queen Seira. Identify yourself!"

The man's eyes widened, the muscles around his mouth tensed up, and he made a pulling motion with his thumb and forefinger across his mouth.

"I said identify yourself!" Entim roared, and drew his sword.

Irritation passed across the stranger's face. He drew his attention down to the metallic rectangle and began tapping at it.

Entim held his sword outstretched. "In the name of Queen Seira—!"

He was interrupted by a sharp whistle from behind him. Entim spun around, holding his sword at the ready. Standing some ten meters away over Palec's remains stood a woman. She wore the same strange clothes as the man, possessed long, resplendent brown hair, and stood nearly as tall as Entim. She, too, held a thin, metallic slab.

"Who are—?" Entim started.

The woman stabbed a finger into her tablet.

Entim found himself, quite abruptly, standing in a metallic hallway. The floors, walls, and ceiling appeared to be composed of a silver-hued, brushed metal. Cylinders of pure light were affixed to the ceiling at intervals. Rows of doors spread out down the hallway before him.

He could make out words etched into little metal plates above the doorways: "genetic catalog," "field notes," "sensory systems," "protein folding," and so on. Although he could read the words, he had no idea what most of them meant. What were 'genetic' and 'protein?' 'Sensory' and 'system' made sense individually, but not as a pair. And 'field notes' for what?

Such a place as this, he decided, could only be the afterlife. It was the only way he could make sense of his new surroundings. He must have died, probably in a similar fashion as Palec, and had forgotten his death due to the sheer trauma of melting into purple fluid. That explanation didn't sit well with him, though. He had imagined inflicting far worse deaths upon himself many times over.

He supposed he had better hurry up and find God. Perhaps then he would discover if we would be reunited with his wife and son. Perhaps even his daughter would be here. That would be quite nice, he decided. He began thinking over the previous decade, wondering if he'd repented well enough for the disaster that had been the Equentia expedition to be worthy of heaven. He had certainly tried his best, with Father Sy's help, to lead a moral life.

Entim began down the hallway, scanning the little plaques above the doors, looking for one that might lead him to God. However, most of the identifiers defied his comprehension: "viral variants," "RNA sequences," "history of epidemiology," and so on. Tiring of looking for a marker that would make sense, he tried to open the "history of epidemiology" door. He approached it and reached out his hand, intent on pulling it open at the indentation in it, but the door slid open of its own accord at his approach. He marveled at this momentarily then peered inside to find a cramped and narrow room containing four long shelves of books.

He proceeded down the hallway and approached other doors, causing them to open. Nearly all of them contained shelves of books, like "history of epidemiology." In "star chart," he found a great field of white lights in a room that was otherwise dimly lit. In "planetary recon," he found a long, narrow room whose walls were covered in portraits more lifelike than any he had ever seen, and depicting bizarre foreign landscapes, stranger even than the exotic life he had witnessed in the Moira Wood.

After many more doors, he came to one called "projection interface" and opened it to discover merely a black void. He raised an eyebrow, then took a glance down the hallway, both further on and back the way he had come. He could see the far wall where he had started, but in the other direction the hallway proceeded onward in a straight line as far as he could see. He decided to risk sticking his head into "projection interface," just to see if he would be able to make out any more details of the room that way.

As he did so, the hallway twisted, distorted, fell away, and he found himself in a kind of tent. The walls were made of some shiny material he had never seen before, and it was partially transparent. It seemed as though the Moira Wood lay just on the other side of it. The tent interior was laid out in a rectangle and was dotted with mechanical implements the likes of which Entim had never seen before. Cylinders of metal were affixed to shapes of glass he didn't know were even possible and many other parts were made of materials he couldn't even guess the substance of. At least he could understand the purpose of the chairs and tables that dotted the room. He reached out to touch one of the strange implements and let out a shriek as his hand passed through it instead of coming to rest upon it.

"Hello?" A voice called out.

Entim spun. He made his way around clusters of tables and strange implements. At the back of the tent he found a metallic bed. Atop it lay the man he had spotted in the Moira wood. His skin was dotted with patches of blue, and he was perspiring heavily. Translucent tubes connected him to strange apparatuses with liquid-filled bags attached to them.

Entim stood over the man for a very long time. The man stared back, with strained, blood-shot eyes.

"Are you... God?" Entim tried.

Disappointment fell over the man's face. "No."

"Who are you, then? Is this the afterlife?"

"Your physical body is gone, but I was able to store your consciousness. Listen to this next part carefully. You can get back inside the computer by saying 'exit interface.' It will be very important for you to do that at the signal tone. It will mean that Anna is returning, and she cannot find you here. If she discovers what I've done, then you will die. What is your name?"

"Entim Osh, Lord General of the Guard of the Realm of the Queen of Seira."

"May I call you Entim?"

Entim nodded.

"My name is Thyss Iini, and you may call me Thyss." He took a deep breath. It seemed a struggle for him just to breathe let alone talk. "Your kingdom and all the other polities of this world are in danger."

"My colleague Palec's death... Will such a horrific disease as the one that afflicted him come into the city?"

"I am afraid it is much worse than that. What Anna is doing will not create just one disease, but—"

A tone, one soft, melodic hum of noise, seeming to come from all parts of the tent at once, interrupted Thyss.

His eyes shot open wide. "You must go now! When Anna is here, there will be a red border around the projection interface. You can come back when she is gone, when there is no red border. But she must not see you. Go now. 'Exit interface.'" Thyss stared pleadingly at Entim. "'Exit interface!' Say it!"

"Exit in-ter-face," Entim muttered and the shapes and figures around him twisted and congealed back into the long hallway of doors. He backed away from the door, and watched as translucent tubes around its periphery began to glow, first pink, then finally becoming bright red.

Entim backed into the wall behind him, slid down it, and rubbed his hands over his face. He did not understand any of the strange things he had witnessed. He decided this was certainly not heaven, but, if anything, a kind of purgatory or even hell itself, his punishment for having abandoned his family to participate in the Queen's misguided mission. He could not even tell if he was dead or alive. Nothing made any sense at all. All he could do was sit and pray, which he did diligently for minute after torturous minute in the bleak, monotonous hallway beneath the halo of red light around "projection interface."

After he'd prayed for what felt like many hours, Entim rose and found the edge of the "projection interface" door still glowing red. He decided he wanted to close his eyes and rest for a time, and so he began searching the rooms for a bed. One dozen passed, then a dozen more. All of them either contained rows of bookshelves, portraits upon the wall, and three others—"software update," "containment controls," and "immunogenicity simulator"—contained black voids, ones which he dared not stick his head into for fear of what might happen to him.

After fifty or sixty doors had passed to no avail, Entim gave up and returned to the red-bordered door of "projection interface" where he curled up on the ground and closed his eyes. Sleep refused to come to him. Over the past eight years, he had taught himself many tricks for pushing unwanted thoughts away, steadying his breathing, and calming his mind. Those usually helped him to fall asleep, but none of them were of any avail now. Surely, this must have been hell, he decided, to deny a man even the daily rite of sleep, which refreshed and replenished one's energy and spirits.

He pulled himself upright, opened his eyes, and discovered that the door of "projection interface" no longer had a red border. Did he dare to go back and talk to the sickly man in strange clothes who called himself Thyss? Perhaps he should if only to learn more about Anna and the strange disease that had killed Palec. Not that he would be able to do anything about those things, condemned as he was, but it seemed preferable to sitting in an empty hallway for the rest of eternity.

Entim stood, stepped forward, and stuck his head through the door. The hallway twisted and contorted into the shape of the tent with transparent walls in the wood. Entim wasted no time making his way around the bizarre equipment to the back of the tent where Thyss lay on the table. He looked to be in even worse condition than when Entim had seen him last. He was sweating more and the blue boils had grown larger and more numerous. His eyes were shut.

"Hello," Entim said.

Thyss's eyes fluttered open. "Entim. You came back."

"I did."

"I apologize. I will need a moment. Anna was particularly harsh this time." He gulped, and the action looked torturous for him. "Tell me about yourself."

"I am—was—the senior ranking officer of the Royal Guard

for her Majesty the Queen of Seira. My former commanding officer, Sir Iod, retired last month. My accolade was to have been this evening."

Thyss bunched up his eyebrows. "Accolade?"

"My knighthood. I was to have become the Lord General of the Queen's military."

"I am sorry that Anna's intrusion has taken that away from you."

"The accolade was of no great importance."

"Oh? Then... Is Lord General not a position you wanted?"

"It is not." Entim noticed that Thyss seemed to be breathing a bit more easily and his eyes were more focused. "Is there anything I can do for you, Mr. Thyss?"

"Just Thyss is fine. And no, not for me, but I wanted to talk to you about what Anna is doing. If you would like to help me, I would beg of you to help me with her, not my condition."

"You said before she is responsible for the disease that killed my friend Palec."

"Yes. All of the strange changes you have seen in these woods are her doing as well."

"Is she some kind of sorceress?"

Thyss paused and seemed to consider his next words carefully. "I am not going to patronize you, Entim. But I will preface by saying that many of the things I am about to tell you will probably seem very strange. She is not a magician, at least not in the way you mean it. Around your city, I'm sure you have seen evidence of the mechanical arts. Pulleys can haul very heavy things upwards. Levers cause horizontal force to be translated into other directions. Gears redirect and transmit rotational force. And so on. Where I am from, the mechanical arts have progressed further. Much further.

They have gone so far, that the machines are smaller than the tiniest hair on your smallest finger, so small that you cannot even see them, and they are many millions of times more powerful. Anna is using these machines to change the species of this forest very rapidly. That includes all the myriad diseases present in the air around us. Yes, I know that must be confusing. Every disease you know of is actually everywhere in the air we breathe. We live in a soup of it. People get sick when too much of a particular disease gets inside them, or when their overall resistance to disease is weakened. Anna has set loose an enormous wave of biological changes in everything: plants, animals, fungi, and diseases."

Entim screwed his face up. "But why does she do these things?"

"Because of her children. She and I were professors at a university in a place called Rahdis. We both left Rahdis and went away to a conference. It was to have been a three-week trip. One week travel to the conference, one week at the conference, one week back. Anna left her two children at home alone. The eldest, a daughter, was seventeen. It was her first time taking care of her twelve-year-old brother alone for so long. Their father had passed away a decade ago.

"Shortly after Anna and I arrived at the conference, we learned that a new disease had been discovered on Rahdis. We left the conference straight away, but by the time we returned, a strict quarantine had been enforced. The disease had jumped to the human species and every other mammalian species within just forty-eight hours. It is only five percent lethal, but it is incredibly contagious, and it is the most resilient and adaptive disease our people have ever seen.

"Our scientists' most advanced methods cannot produce a

medicine for this disease because the disease changes so rapidly, and it is capable of infecting every other species we know of. The only way we can think of to make a medicine is to rapidly change existing species and test whether or not they are capable of resisting infection."

"She cannot be reunited with her children, then, until she finds the way to make this medicine?"

Thyss nodded. "Not only that, her son has contracted the disease. I believe that is what finally drove her to come here. What she is doing is extraordinarily illegal. She is taking advantage of a bookkeeping error. What do you call this land, as a whole? Not just your kingdom, but the lands between the seas in the east and the ocean in the west?"

"Glissia."

"Glissia is supposed to be protected by our law, but a careless bureaucrat wrote the wrong entry in one of our ledgers, and now people like Anna are exploiting the technicality."

Entim crossed his arms. Conflicting emotions rolled through him. The thoughts that were ransacking his mind now were not ones he would normally share with a near stranger, but in these strange circumstances, Entim decided that he had nothing more to lose by being direct and honest. "I wish Anna all the best in her search for a medicine."

Thyss snorted a bit, and the act seemed to pain him. "Perhaps you do not fully understand. Anna's changes do not just mean that bizarre animals will prowl around your kingdom for the rest of time. She is changing the diseases in the air. All of them. Your friend died of one. A new disease created here could be so contagious and so deadly that it will kill every Glissian. She has set up containment as best she's able, but I know that some animals have already escaped the woods. It is only a matter of time before a disease makes it out."

"Then what of Anna's children?"

"Not this way!" Thyss demanded. One of the metal contraptions near him, which had been emitting a steady rhythm of beeps, began beeping faster. "Other scientists are replicating this procedure legally in fully contained spaces and without putting any people or animals at risk, and certainly without deforming or murdering them. It is slower, but I believe it will yield an answer with enough time. That amount of time is not acceptable to Anna."

"And what about you? You appear to have the same illness as Palec."

"Probably something similar but not as immediately lethal. When I chose to come here and stop Anna, I knew I was dealing with someone who would not hesitate to kill me if I got in her way. She believes she has incapacitated me and that there is nothing I can do, as my hands are restrained and I would not have the energy to hold my computer even if they weren't. But she did not know that I had you in a nanite mesh when she disintegrated your body. That's right. She killed you on the spot. But I saved your mind. Into my computer. It's how you can help.

"When I arrived, I gathered proof of what Anna was doing and sent it back to my leaders. They will tolerate some pretty bad things until the clerical error is corrected, but not this. If they respond the way I think they will, they will arrive in less than a day and they will firebomb this forest whether any of us is here or not. I need you to find the containment controls and make sure nothing gets out of these woods for the next day."

"And then I will die."

"All three of us will, yes."

"And if I do nothing?"

"We will all die anyway when my government shows up. And after that, there are two possibilities. All the diseases in the forest could stay in the forest until my government arrives. Or, one of them could escape and rage across Glissia. It could kill five percent, fifty percent, or everyone. It is impossible to say. But someone needs to make sure that nothing more gets out than already—"

The melodic hum resounded throughout the tent.

"I will do as you ask," Entim said. He reached out to seal the pact by clasping Thyss's hand, but found that his hand passed through both the bed Thyss's form.

"Thank you. Look for the containment controls." Thyss seemed to be trying to nod as vigorously as he could make himself. "It's 'exit interface.'"

Entim nodded back. "Exit interface."

The tent twisted and distorted, forming into the shape of the empty metallic hallway.

Entim set off immediately down the hall, searching for the door marked 'containment controls,' which he recalled seeing on his last inspection. All the time, his mind roiled with the enormous implications of what he had learned—Anna had destroyed his physical body, and his soul resided in this place called Computer; the Moira Wood was now teeming with dangerous diseases, such as the one that had killed Palec, and which could at any moment evade containment and escape into his kingdom; in one more day, Thyss's leaders would show up and he would die completely. There had been moments in the past when he had been prepared to take his own life, and now, in the face of a known countdown toward his death, he desperately wished for more time, time to understand the operational mechanisms and secrets of Computer. The story of Anna's children had also struck a deep chord. Despite what she had done to him, he couldn't find it within himself to hate her.

He came to the door marked 'containment controls' and approached it. The door slid open silently, revealing an inky void, and Entim stuck his head inside. The blackness formed all at once into a room, at the center of which lay a strange kind of three-dimensional picture, hovering in the air. It looked like a miniature forest, but everything was an outline of a form, a hazy ghost of a figure.

Entim walked up and gazed over the miniature landscape, what he presumed was the Moira forest. Red dots flittered about the space.

"Would you like to use the verbal interface?" a female voice intoned.

Entim looked around himself, trying to find a person to associate with the voice, but found no one.

"Where are you?"

The voice seemed to be coming from the ceiling. "I am Voita, version 8.9.273. I am installed in the primary application directory for this operating system, full path /home/os/applications/core."

"Can you help me keep the animals and diseases in the woods?"

"I'm sorry. I didn't understand that."

Odd. It was a simple enough question. "Is this the containment field here in front of me?"

"Yes."

Better. At least Voita understood that. "And these red dots. Are they animals?"

"Yes."

"What about diseases? Are those displayed?"

"Viruses and bacteria are not displayed. Would you like to display those?"

"Yes."

The room's walls and ceiling immediately shot away from him, expanding the room's size many orders of magnitude in all directions. The field of hazy shapes exploded outward, and the red lights, instead of being intermittent blips amongst the trees, swarmed the space in the millions, perhaps even billions.

"Is this all of them?"

"Nearly all. When a virus or bacteria replicates, nanites must find it and attach to it in order to achieve tracking."

Now it was Entim's turn not to understand. Replicate? Nanites?

He frowned. "When was the last time an animal escaped the forest?"

"The last containment breach occurred twenty-three hours and forty-seven minutes ago."

That would have been the cow, Entim decided. "I would like you to tell me immediately if another containment breach happens."

"Alert set."

"Have any diseases escaped?"

"No tracked pathogens have escaped."

There was that, at least. Entim supposed his job was now to sit and watch this enormous field of lights and make sure all the red dots stayed in the woods. It seemed a rather useless way to spend the final hours of his life.

"Voita?"

"Yes?"

"How has Anna been testing organisms to see if they can cure the disease on Rahdis?"

"I'm sorry. I didn't quite understand that. Would you like me to tell you about the Rahdis pandemic?"

"Yes, please."

"The Rahdis pandemic was first detected in humans on date GC827443.10. The virus responsible for the disease is named R-BEN-443. Following its discovery in twenty other mammalian species, Planet Rahdis was placed under quarantine on GC827443.12."

Entim blinked a few times. "Did you say 'planet?'"

"Planet Rahdis is a Class Mu planet one hundred and forty-seven light-years from Planet Ytria."

Other planets... Entim reeled. He had not entered the realm of his God, but these people, who could traverse stars, might as well have been gods when compared to him. He considered what he was trying to do, and that it was perhaps absurd and futile. He was like a child, treating their sophisticated machinery as if it were a toy. Memories of his son and wife slammed into him like a wave, and he became filled with new determination, if not confidence.

"Are tests currently being run on the species of the forest to see if they resist R-BEN-443?"

"The immunogenicity simulator is currently running."

That would be a yes. "If I go to the immunogenicity simulator, can you still tell me if containment is breached?"

"I'm sorry. I didn't quite understand that."

Entim huffed. "You said an alert is set."

"Current alerts: notification of containment breach."

Entim wished he could talk to Thyss instead of this Voita. He was far more personable than she was, and smarter, too. "Will alerts reach me in the immunogenicity simulator?"

"The alert program functions throughout the entire operating system, regardless of where in memory a program is currently running."

Entim supposed that was as close to a 'yes' as he would get from Voita. He exited the room and took off further down the hall, scanning the door frames as he went. Within a few minutes, he reached 'immunogenicity simulator' and promptly entered. This room, too, held an enormous frame of light at its center, but this one was not a miniature version of the Moira Wood, but four enormous columns of rectangles, each with a string of numbers and letters inside. Every few seconds, one of the rectangles at the bottom of the leftmost column would fly upward and left, growing larger. It would glow for a few moments before turning red and fading away. Then the next rectangle would take its place.

There were four different colors of rectangle, too: blue, green, pink, and yellow.

"Voita?" Entim called out.

"Yes?"

"What am I seeing here?"

"The queue of organisms to be scanned is on the right. Each organism is labeled with a unique identifier. The color of the box indicates the organism's kingdom: blue for bacteria and viruses, yellow for fungi, green for plants, and pink for animals."

Entim noticed that as soon as one rectangle would leave the queue, a new one would populate at the top of the rightmost column. "Is this the entire list?"

"No. The queue is growing faster than organisms' response to R-BEN-443 can be simulated."

"How long is the full list?"

"92,327,441 organisms are in the queue. The queue is growing by an average of 10.4 organisms per minute."

"Show me the end of the list."

The queue shimmered and four new columns of rectangles appeared. Entim narrowed his eyes. "Voita, new organisms aren't being added to the end of the list."

"That is correct. As new organisms are discovered, they are added to the queue in a position according to their priority."

"So, the creatures I am seeing here are all low priority."

"Yes."

"Who determines the priority? Anna?"

"Unknown user: 'Anna.' Priority is determined by application heuristics."

Entim decided that Voita lived in Computer, as he now did, and that Computer somehow belonged to Thyss. That must have been why Anna was unknown to Voita. Something near the end of the list caught Entim's eye. "Voita, one of the boxes is gray. What kind of creature is that?"

The rectangle emitted a brief glow. "Specimen 8G32KE72-2. This is the remains of a member of species 8G32KE72. It was infected by a member of virus species 293JJL1 and expired. Trace biological material is intact. Heuristics have determined that the chance of viable genetic material remaining is extremely low."

"Show me the corpse."

The queue faded away and the miniature Moira Wood reappeared, filled with red dots. One by one, the red dots flickered out leaving only one, immobile, near the forest's entrance. The view rushed inward toward him, showing him the outline of a human pile of bones and clothing. Palec's remains.

"Can you move this organism to the front of the queue?"

"Specimen 8G32KE72-2 promotion confirmed."

The original four columns reappeared and the gray rectangle now hovered and glowed, very large, at the side of the list. Entim waited, watching it patiently. He said a small prayer, hoping that Palec's death could have perhaps been made to be worth something.

The rectangle turned red and fell away.

Entim frowned, deflated. "Voita, what happened?"

"Immunogenicity response negative. However, four new species of fungus were found in the remains. Those have been added to the queue."

"Where?"

Four yellow rectangles in the second column momentarily glowed.

"Voita, move those to the front."

"Promotion confirmed."

All four yellow rectangles slid down into the bottom left corner of the columns. Once the current green rectangle had turned red and faded away, the first yellow box took its place and began glowing. It eventually fell away red as well. The second took its place and glowed for a time, Entim praying desperately for success, but this one turned red and fell away, too. When the third took its place, Entim sighed. People from the stars had wreaked biological havoc on his kingdom's forest, and here he was messing with machines he hardly understood. Whatever a heuristic was, it was probably much better at determining the priority than he would ever be, wanting to try to make meaning out of his friend's death—

The box glowed green and its form began pulsing.

"Immunogenicity response found. T-cell response deemed adequate to prevent infection and minimize spread of all known and projected permutations of viral agent R-BEN-443."

Entim let out a small laugh. Could this be real? He supposed it was as real as everything else he had experienced since arriving in Computer.

"Voita, I would like to take this information. Can you give it to me?"

The green rectangle seemed to sizzle in the air. Small sparks erupted from it and it grew smaller, but also expanded through the third dimension in space, gaining depth. Entim reached out and took into his hands a green box about the size of a book.

Entim smiled. "Thank you, Voita."

"You are welcome."

The tent with transparent walls formed around Entim, and he made his way carefully through its many furnishings to Thyss's bedside. Thyss lay with his eyes closed, the blue boils beginning to push outwards off his skin.

"Thyss." Entim came to the edge of his bedside.

Thyss's eyes opened slowly. It seemed difficult for him to focus on Entim's form. After steadying his breathing for many moments, Thyss finally replied. "You should be monitoring containment."

"I met Voita and have ordered her to guard the perimeter. She with raise the alarm if there is any breach."

"Still, you should be near the controls."

"There is something more important. I came to talk to you about Anna."

Thyss shook his head weakly back and forth. "There is nothing else for you to know about her."

"You have described her having done terrible things, but

is she honorable?"

Thyss blinked a few times, not seeming to understand the question.

"If she gives her word that she will do something, can she be trusted to do it? Has she ever lied, in your experience?"

"No. How is that relevant?"

"Does she have any access to Computer? Voita did not know who she was."

"I don't think so. She hasn't needed to access it. Her computer is better than mine. It can process organisms faster."

"But if she had found an 'adequate teesell response,' what would she do?"

"Take off for Rahdis, I suppose. Why are you asking?"

"How certain are you that she could be trusted to keep her honor?"

Thyss's eyes were growing more alert, though his body looked worn out. The unaffected parts of his skin looked clammy and even a bit shriveled. "I'm sorry, Entim. I'm not used to thinking in those terms. I think so. Probably. Have you found something?"

Entim remained stolid.

"You have. Dear God—"

Entim's anger flared, and he would have drawn his sword if he'd had it. "I warn you not to take the Lord's name in vain in my presence."

"I'm sorry, it's just—"

The tone sounded.

Thyss's eyes managed to open even wider. "Back to the computer, Entim."

"No."

"Entim, she will kill you!"

"I have what she wants."

"She will take it the moment she discovers you have it—"

"Even if Voita has given her solemn vow that she will cause 'permanent erasure' of the teesell response upon my death?"

Thyss blinked a few times. "Entim, I beg of you to say 'exit interface' now."

"No." Entim stood watching the entrance to the tent, while Thyss gasped for breath and pleaded beside him.

The woman with long brown hair pushed open a slit in the wall of the tent, peeling it open like the skin of an orange, then stepped inside, took one look at Entim, and grabbed at her metallic tablet.

"Do not do that!" Entim roared. "I possess an adequate teesell response of immunogenicity and I have ordered Voita of Computer to permanently destroy it upon my death. By the power vested in me by the Queen of Seira, sole and lawful sovereign of this land, I order you to put down your weapon and discuss terms of surrender. Now!"

Anna gaped, her finger poised over her metallic tablet. She blinked a few times. Then she gulped and shook her head slowly back and forth. "Thyss, what have you—?"

"Engage with me! I am Entim Osh of the Royal Guard of the Kingdom of Seira, and I demand to be heard!"

Anna let out a short huff. She lowered her tablet to her side and her gaze met Entim's. "Entim Osh. Are you telling me that you, a native of this world, have discovered an organism that produces in humans an adequate T-cell response to all known and predicted permutations of the virus R-BEN-443?"

"With Voita's help. Yes."

"And she will delete this data if I delete you?"

"Yes."

Anna began walking toward him.

"Do not come closer," Entim growled.

Anna stopped and held up her hands, palms forward. She released a sigh. "What do you want for the data?"

"First, you will take Mr. Thyss and yourself away from here. Second, you will set fire to Moira Wood and destroy all the diseases you have created. Third, you will tend to Mr. Thyss's illness instead of abandoning him for long stretches. Fourth, you will turn yourself over to your authorities—"

Anna laughed and scoffed simultaneously. "You are in no position to bargain, Mr. Osh."

"Oh, yes, Ms. Anna, I am. I have lost children. Two of them. To disease. My wife as well. I know that pain better than I hope you will ever be capable of imagining. That is why I did this. Because the person who turned my forest into a den of horrors, the person who indirectly caused my best friend's demise, the person who destroyed my physical body, even that person should not suffer what I have suffered for the last eight years. I have just enough honor and dignity left, Ms. Anna, that I will give you the teesell response, but only if you care for Mr. Thyss, if you leave here at once, burning all the monstrosities you have created, and you turn yourself over to your authorities. I want your solemn vow on the lives of your son and daughter that you will do these things, or I will not hesitate to order Voita to destroy the entire contents of Computer, even if the process kills me."

Anna stood, stared, and breathed in and out, her eyes locked with Entim's. He did not avert his gaze, or even so much as twitch.

"Yes," Anna muttered.

"I'm sorry, Ms. Anna. Do you give your solemn vow on your children's lives? Louder, please."

"I do." The statement was practically a roar.

Farmer Prois was in his barn baling hay when he heard a commotion from his front yard. He threw down his pitchfork, walked out to the front of his house, where his youngest and oldest sons were pointing at two horses, galloping away down the road toward the city, trailing shredded scraps of wood attached to lengths of rope. He could just make out their frenzied whinnying.

"Those were pieces of our fence, dad," the eldest said.

His youngest pointed down the road in the other direction. "And look at that!"

The evening sky should have been a dull umber, but it had lit up red and yellow, and an enormous black plume had ascended into the sky.

"Well, I'll be..." Farmer Prois drew his boys closer to him and they all stood and stared at the largest conflagration they had ever seen, the entirety of the Moira Wood aflame.

Elyk took a deep breath and answered the call. Her mother's face appeared holographically before her.

Elyk beamed. "Hi, mom!"

"Hello, darling." There was something sad in her mom's voice and smile. Elyk didn't like it at all.

"Did you hear about the vaccines? They've started with the medical staff and essential workers, and they think it will only be a few weeks before we can get it, too."

"I know."

"So, do you know when we'll be able to see you again?"

Her mother seemed to deflate before her eyes.

"Mom?"

"As soon as it's safe. How is Senik doing?"

"Really well. He only ever had mild symptoms. And we've been following quarantine rules to the letter since then. We're just so excited for when we can see you again." Were those tears in her mother's eyes? Her mother was acting so strange at the good news. Could it have been a trick of the holography? "Do you want to talk to Senik?"

"Yes." Her mother seemed only barely able to get the word out. "Yes, I do."

The Roots and the Spiderweb

Mathin could feel the librarian's anger. It almost physically hurt, a stabbing pain in his gut. The man had narrowed his eyebrows, his eyes full of judgmental energy, radiating even brighter than the evening sun through the west windows. In the waning light, the poor librarian would have to squint and strain to see the titles on the spines.

However, Mathin needed those books, and his work couldn't wait for the morning.

With a sigh, the librarian retreated, carrying Mathin's scrap of paper that bore the titles of the three books he needed.

A clearing of the throat from behind him caused Mathin to turn. Professor Maddex stood behind him, half his face illuminated in the evening sunlight, the other half shrouded in shadow.

"Good evening, Professor Ekpadesi," Professor Maddex said.

"Good evening."

"How was dinner?"

"I haven't had any."

Maddex raised an eyebrow. "I have much work to do."

"For your book, I take it?"

Mathin felt himself habitually tense up. "Yes."

"I do wish you the best of luck with it, you know."

"Yes," Mathin replied, wondering how he should feel about Maddex's use of 'luck,' as opposed to, say, 'success.' "How is the codex coming along?"

"Well."

"Picking up some books?"

"Yes. It's rather late, but I wanted to get some more done this evening."

"I had the same inclination."

"And you've beaten me here." Maddex grinned. "Perhaps I should have skipped dinner as well."

Mathin couldn't help but slip a wry smile. "I'm not so sure about that." If Mathin didn't know better, he would think that Maddex was genuinely trying to lighten the mood between them. He did know better, but he also could not help but reciprocate. He could not bring himself to be standoffish with someone trying to be friendly, whatever their ulterior motive.

Maddex moved his lips about awkwardly, seeming to stumble in arriving at his next statement. Mathin was about to fill the void with some innocuous follow up about him having had a large lunch anyway, when Maddex blurted out.

"I apologize for my rudeness the other day."

"Apology accepted. I'm sorry for my harsh words as well."

"I do wish you the best of luck with your book."

"Thank you. And you yours."

The librarian returned to the counter just in the nick of time, carrying three large books, one already quite brown at the edges. Mathin signed his name on the librarian's check-out form, bid both him and Maddex a good evening, and carried his evening's work out of the library and into the Potro University quad. The library was one of four buildings arranged facing a square patch of land. Immediately across the quad from the library lay the lecture hall, to the left was the laboratory, where the physical and chemical science experiments were performed, and to his right, where he headed, diagonally across the grass, lay the dormitory and cafeteria.

"Mathin!" a voice called out, which Mathin immediately recognized as his friend and colleague, Olim Stiek.

Mathin turned. "Evening, Olim."

Olim came up beside him and slowed to a walk. "I see you've got some light reading."

"You know me."

"The book's still coming along, then?"

"Absolutely."

"The ancient philosophers haven't thwarted you yet, then?"

"No." Mathin was certain he could bring his book to a coherent conclusion. It was the attitudes and opinions of professors like Iodo Maddex he was concerned about. There were far too many who held his views, and far too few professors who were as open-minded as Olim Stiek.

"When do you think you'll have a new draft ready for me

to look at?"

They reached the door of the dormitory, and Olim held it open for him.

"Perhaps in a few days," Mathin said. "Maybe a week."

"I'm looking forward to it. How are you integrating Evrys again?"

"Ytrian manifestations can inherit the shadows of multiple forms."

Olim nodded and smiled. "Sounds great. I can't wait to read it. Oh, are you heading up already?"

Mathin had begun climbing the stairs, while Olim had almost headed off for the cafeteria. Both came to a halt.

"I have so much to read this evening." Mathin raised the stack of three books toward his chest.

A look of concern from Olim. "Did you eat earlier?"

Mathin shook his head.

"That can't be good for you."

"One night won't hurt."

"How about I bring you up something after I'm done?"

"Thank you, but it's really not—"

"I insist."

Mathin could not help but smile at that. "Thank you. I'll see you later then."

"See you then." Olim strode down the hall toward the cafeteria, and Mathin headed up the stairs and away from the smell of grilled chicken and potatoes. His stomach grumbled, and he was glad just then for Olim's offer. Even though it wouldn't kill him, he did hate to fall asleep hungry.

Two days prior, Mathin and Iodo Maddex had been discussing their respective books, trying to reach a concensus to no avail. Mathin had let himself get carried away. He fully admitted that now. But so had Maddex.

The two had been sitting in the faculty office in the north wing of the lecture hall, the place where only tenured professors were allowed. It possessed a small library but was mostly given over to chairs and small tables. The only non-professors allowed were those of the kitchen staff on duty to serve tea.

The professors' conversation had started amenably enough.

"But what do we do about the conflicts?" Mathin had asked. "Gorj has already supplied us with ample examples." Mathin pulled out a pencil and grabbed up a piece of paper from a stack on the nearby table. "Here are four entities."

And he drew:

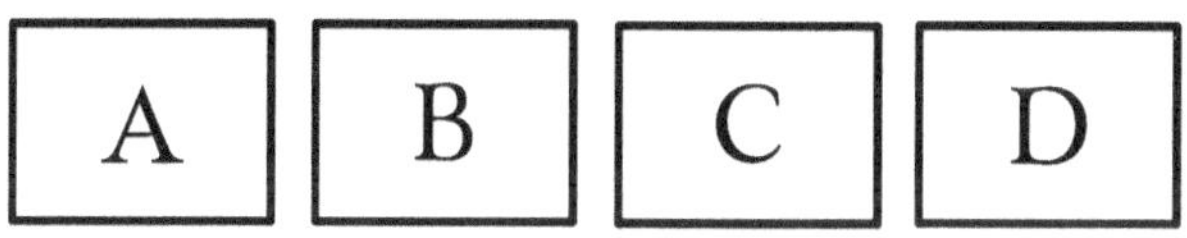

"Now, let's say we notice that A and B are similar, and C and D are similar. So, we do what the ancients did and we organize them like so, into roots."

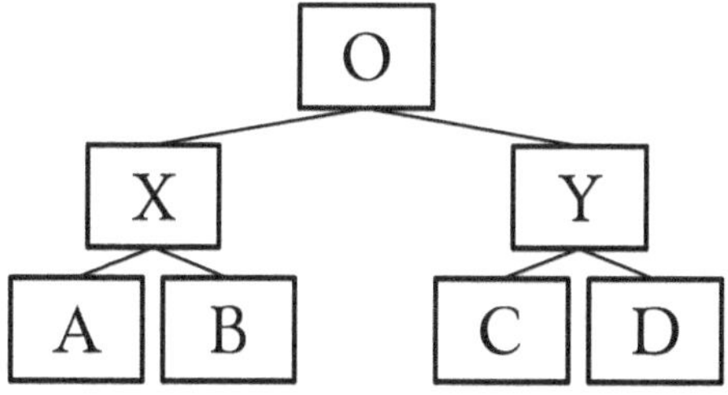

"We think that everything is grand, but then we discover something new. We discover E. And E, it turns out has a property shared by A and B, and *also* a property shared by C and D. It cannot become a new root on either side, for no matter which side we put it on, we break the other."

"Yes, yes," Iodo said. "The camel. The one ruminant without horns. So where do you put it? Do you include it with the ruminants, the other animals with four stomachs, or do you include it with the hornless animals, all of which have one stomach? But Gorj solved this problem. In multiple ways. Watch."

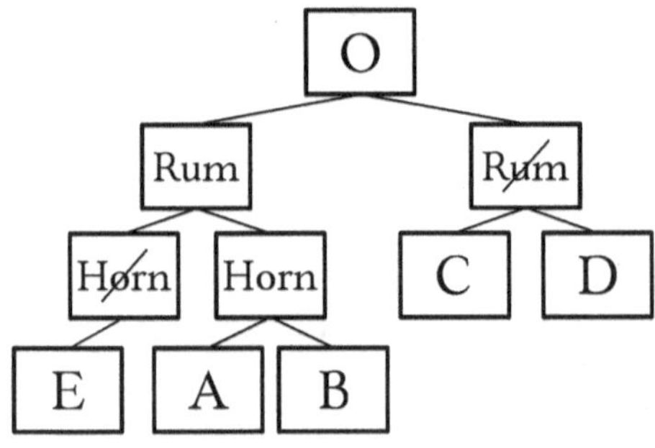

"Or we could do this:"

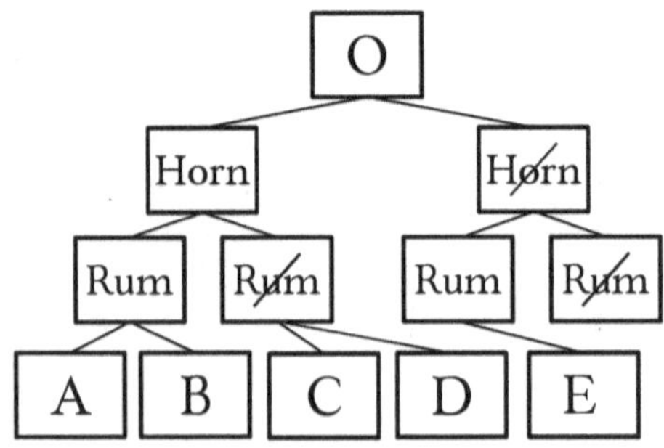

"But the preference is for the first," Iodo happily explained.

Mathin grinned, feeling that Iodo had fallen into his trap. "And why is that?"

"With the second method, as new features are discovered, they must be duplicated many times across the various roots. There are also 'illegitimate roots,' combinations of features for which there is no corresponding entity—in this case, horned non-ruminants—in reality."

"And with the first method?"

"Those problems are solved."

"Are they truly?"

Iodo had not quite squirmed in his seat, but Mathin, in hindsight should have realized how uncomfortable Iodo had been getting.

"My hypothesis," Mathin said. "Is that the 'vexing paradoxes' in root-based categorization systems will remain problematic. We may be able to solve this particular problem with the camel, but what if we discover an animal that has yet more overlapping properties with horned and unhorned ruminants and non-ruminants? Our root system would have to expand to a terrific level of complexity. I am proposing an alternative."

Here Iodo had sprouted a blatant frown. "An alternative to the great ancient philosophers Evrys and Gorj?"

"My apologies. The word was ill chosen. An expansion. An extrapolation. An evolution, if you will. It is not a root system, but a spiderweb."

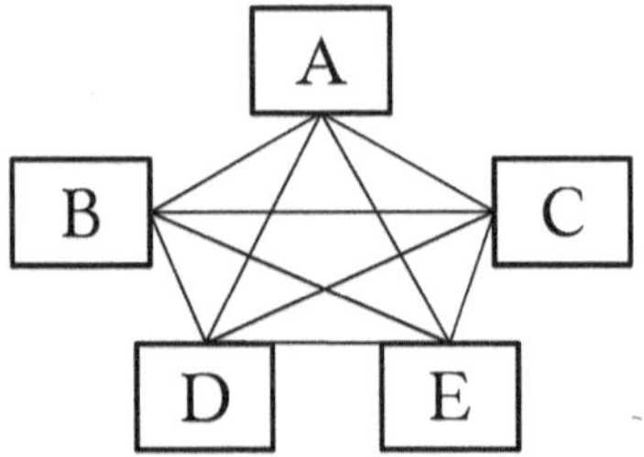

Iodo looked down at the paper as though this spiderweb Mathin had drawn was about to reach up and bite him. "Where is God in this... spiderweb?"

Mathin smiled widely. This was his favorite question. "Unlike the roots, where God is the trunk of the tree, in the spiderweb, God is the *connections* between the entities."

Iodo blinked a few times. "The... connections..."

"Yes. New elements can be added to this system easily without breaking its structure."

"But..." Iodo rubbed his hand across his brow. "There's no organization, no structure at all."

"That's its elegance. It is infinitely flexible. It is capable of absorbing any new elements of creation we discover, and I guarantee we have not discovered them all."

Iodo shook his head. "But what should we do with all the myriad ways that the metaphor of the roots have shaped us? Take the library, for example. How are the librarians supposed to order their books upon the shelves if not through a hierarchical classification system?"

"This may sound impertinent, but I would suggest we might try organizing alphabetically by the name of the author."

Iodo dug his fingers into the chair. "You're right. It sounds quite impertinent! By the *alphabet*? One of the most arbitrary orderings in all of existence! Professor, as a lover of knowledge, I have to admit I find the suggestion horrifying."

"But imagine." Mathin tried to continue in as calm a tone as he was able. "When a librarian goes to discover a book for us now, he must traverse a large, hierarchical root system in his head, then translate that into the physical space of his shelves. What if he simply had to recall where the letter of the alphabet was in relation to all the others? He could probably find us our books in mere seconds as opposed to minutes."

Iodo shot up out of his seat. "What you are suggesting is—!"

"Practical." Mathin shot up as well.

"They killed Evrys for speaking out against the practical," Iodo said. Other professors were looking at them now.

"It is not just more practical. It is necessary. Knowledge is stuck right now, held back by the very systems we use to organize it."

"I'm sorry, Professor Ekpadesi. I do not condone this spiderweb, or this book you have described, if it is about such things. I suppose these 'encyclopedias' you want us to create are such spiderwebs?"

"They are."

"Spiderwebs are used for trapping creatures and draining them of life."

Mathin slammed down his tea. "That is an ignorant interpretation of the metaphor. Good day."

"Good day."

They had left after that, the other members of the faculty watching them leave in stunned silence.

—

A crash of shattering glass startled Mathin awake, and he opened his eyes to a luminous glow permeating the small room of the dormitory that was both his study and his bedroom. He felt oddly unrested, despite the fact that he had only planned on four hours of sleep. It felt like even less. And there was something odd about the glow. It danced and wavered over his desk and its stacks of books, the luminescence changing rapidly—not like the sun, but like—

Mathin shot up out of bed and scrambled to the window.

His breath caught in his throat. His knees gave out and he found himself kneeling before the window. The great edifice of the University of Potro library, the largest collection of books in all of Glissia, the foundation of the center of knowledge for all their studies, was ablaze. Fingers of flame reached up out of the windows, grasping at the wall before slithering back inside. Another crash of glass resounded as the heat created by the conflagration caused another window to shatter and explode, raining glass shards down upon the quad. A smattering of professors, kitchen staff, and groundskeepers were already running about frantically, some trying to organize buckets of water, some kneeling and weeping at the sight—complete chaos.

Mathin pulled himself up, threw on his clothes and sandals, packed up his manuscript into a bag, then threw open his closet and began pulling at the pile of disused clothing looking for his other bag. Halfway down the pile, he retrieved it, and inside it he began stashing books from his table—the three from the library yesterday, a few more works from Evrys, a couple from Gorj, and that was all he had room for.

He threw the books over his back, carried his manuscript

in his hand, and hurried out of the dormitory.

When he reached the door, he backed up onto the quad and scanned the library for signs that the fire would spread to the dormitory. The two structures stood more than ten feet apart. He hoped it was enough.

"Mathin?"

He turned and spotted Olim.

"What has happened?" Olim gazed up at the blazing library.

Mathin realized only then that tears had been running down his face. He tried to speak, but he found himself choking through the words. "The library is finished. And probably the university, too."

Olim squeezed his shoulder. "I know it's bad. But we can rebuild. We'll put it back together. Is that your manuscript?"

Mathin nodded.

"I'm glad you've saved it."

Another window exploded. Two groundskeepers covered in a tarpaulin emerged from the entrance of the library dragging a figure, his body badly burned. The groundskeepers' faces, too, were red and black, but not as badly burned as the man they carried.

"You're not thinking of trying to go in there, are you?" Olim asked.

"No," Mathin said. "No. I can see that would be a mistake." Mathin felt the overwhelming urge to collapse. He sat down on the grass as carefully as he could, letting his bag of books fall into his lap. He cradled his manuscript in his arms and curled over it, weeping. He could not, for the life of him, imagine how any of his life's work could now be salvaged. He sat and wept on the quad in front of the roaring blaze and amidst running and screaming and sobbing and shouts for buckets of water that would come too late.

Olim sat with him.

Mathin moved through the rest of the day in a kind of haze. The fire eventually spent itself, and the space between it and the other buildings was enough to keep the flames from spreading. The library's roof had caved in on its third story in the early hours of the morning, and the hope of rescuing anything from its ashes had died once the sun's rays allowed them to see the full scale of the devastation.

The day's lectures and evaluations were canceled.

Mathin dragged his manuscript and his books back up to his dormitory room, set them down upon his desk, and lay in bed. All he could think about was the staggering magnitude of what had been lost. The University of Potro library had been home to at least four editions of Evrys and six of Gorj that had been believed to be the last of their kind. And that was just two of the most famous philosophers. How many historians, politicians, and scientists had been lost forever to the flames?

A knock on his door disturbed his swirling thoughts.

Mathin stood, walked to his door, and pulled it open. Olim stood before him. Mathin walked back to his bed and sat at its edge, motioning for Olim to sit at his desk. Olim closed the door behind him and sat.

Neither spoke for some time.

Olim finally broke the silence. "What have you been doing?"

"Just resting."

"Some of the faculty are helping the staff try to recover what's left from the library."

"Has anyone found anything intact yet?"

"No. Not last I checked."

"With a conflagration like that, I would be surprised if anything more than a stray scrap remains."

Another silence.

Olim gazed out the window for a few moments, then turned back to Mathin. "The university will need to start thinking about reacquisition—"

"If the king agrees to continue our funding."

"Wouldn't he?"

"King Potro allows us to exist on the condition that our physical sciences departments maintain defensive and offensive research divisions. How are we supposed to continue that research without a library?"

"Surely the king will see it is in his best interests to fund reacquisition."

"And the reconstruction of the library? I would not be surprised if he shuts us down."

"Wait and see. Your manuscript—"

"Is pointless."

"No," Olim quietly insisted. "It's very important."

"It is only important how we categorize knowledge if we *have* knowledge. Potro's is lost."

"Would you attempt to join the faculty at Semm or Delz, then?" Olim referred to the two other kingdoms in Glissia that possessed universities.

"No. Probably just as much resistance there as here. And I don't want to upend my whole life and relocate. I've already done that once to come here, and I have no desire to do it again."

"I think your manuscript is important." Olim was sitting up straight in his chair, seeming almost to tower over him. "You can't give up on it."

Mathin remained slouched forward, gazing absently at the floor. "I just don't see the point in it anymore."

"Maybe wait a few days. They'll restart the lecture series, and you had a colloquium to chair, right?"

Mathin sighed and shook his head. "I'm afraid... I'm sorry. I think I'll just finish out my responsibilities, then head back to Eikres. Dad always did want me to stick to farming."

"You could really go back to farming?"

Mathin nodded.

"What will you do with your manuscript?"

Mathin hadn't thought of that. He didn't dislike it. He just didn't see the point. "I'll hold onto it, I suppose."

"Good. Are you sure I can't change your mind?"

"I'm sure."

Olim stood. "If you do change your mind, let me know."

"Sure." With a jolt, Mathin realized he'd been so occupied with his own predicament, that he hadn't thought about how the destruction of the library had affected his colleague. "What are you going to do?"

"I completed my primary research objective a few weeks ago. I've been staying on to see your manuscript through to completion, but if you're not staying on, I suppose I should head home to Makrim."

"I see."

"Although, if you were to finish your book..."

Mathin looked at the pile of papers on his desk, his treatise on the organization of knowledge—the spiderweb instead of the roots. He shook his head. In a world where centuries, even millennia, of human learning could be wiped out in a stroke... It didn't matter. He honestly could not see how that could matter to him or to anyone else anymore. He wouldn't burn it. He didn't hate his efforts. He just couldn't see the point in continuing.

"I don't think I can do that," Mathin said to the floor.

In his peripheral vision, he saw Olim nod and move to the door. "I'll stay on until you go. Just in case."

Olim opened the door and began to step outside.

"Olim," Mathin said, and Olim paused on the threshold.

"Yes?"

"Thank you for all you've done for me."

"It was my pleasure." Olim closed the door and was gone.

Over the course of the next three days, Mathin participated in all the remaining lectures he had scheduled, and helped chair Professor Addreg's colloquium, just as he had promised. Professor Maddex stopped by his room the day after the fire. He appeared agitated and fidgety, not quite sitting still in his chair.

"I've joined the Reacquisition Council," Maddex said.

Mathin only nodded.

"For now, we have sent out letters to all our allies asking what books they have available for us to purchase immediately, and for which editions we might requisition copies. It will be some time before works start coming in, but within a few weeks, we will have the beginnings of a collection. We will convert the lounge into a small library until the library itself can be rebuilt."

Mathin continued nodding absently.

Maddex's gaze underscored his next statement. "We will need someone to organize the works."

Mathin shrugged. "I'm sure the librarians will be able to continue with the same system they've been using."

Maddex stared at him for a few moments, spellbound. "But... the spiderweb—"

"Does not exist. Like all metaphors and systems of knowledge, it is a mental construct. The invention of a mind. It has no physical reality."

"Physical reality no, but how we organize our knowledge shapes how we think, how we learn. It is of the utmost importance. If you and I have ever agreed on anything it is this."

Mathin gave a weak smile. "The search for better forms of organizations is no longer my calling."

Maddex's form seemed to seep into his chair, his vital energy draining away before Mathin's eyes.

"All right," Maddex said. "If your mind is made up, then."

"It is. I will be returning to Eikres by the end of the week."

"I hope we can part on amicable terms."

"We absolutely will. I bear you no ill will."

"Nor I you."

"Good."

Professor Maddex stood.

Mathin followed suit. "Goodbye, Professor. Best of luck with the reacquisition."

"Thank you," Maddex said as he left.

Olim stopped by toward the end of the day. Their conversation was cordial at first, but when Mathin told him about the conversation he'd had with Professor Maddex, Olim grew livid.

"This is your opportunity!" Olim insisted. "You could put your system into practice right here and prove to everyone that it works. Why are you throwing this away?"

"I don't see the point in any of it," Mathin admitted. And it was the truth. If knowledge was so fragile, what did its organization matter? If a ship were already sinking, did one worry about how well the boards fitted together?

Olim demanded an explanation, but Mathin couldn't bring himself to give voice to his newfound nihilism. He had always hated nihilists in the past. Before the fire, he had preferred action. He had wanted to fight for what was *right*, even if the odds were against him. It reminded him of Evrys's mentor, the wise sage condemned to death by the very people he'd wanted to raise up out of darkness and ignorance. Ignorance, he had to admit, didn't seem quite so bad to him now. Hardly words a tenured professor, even one imminently resigning, should utter.

Eventually, Olim left, and Mathin got about the rest of his day.

The next three days were a blur, but on the fourth, he found he had finished the last of his responsibilities. He returned all of his checked out library books to the temporary library in the former faculty lounge, packed up his manuscript and his few other belongings, put on the clothes he'd brought with him on the day he'd arrived (which didn't fit him quite as well anymore, he noted), returned his professor's robes to the Collegiate Registrar, and took off through the university gates into the City of Potro.

It was a hot, busy summer day, and all about him moved soldiers, merchants, and the occasional errand boy or errand girl. He passed them all, moving through the hazy waves of heat rising up from cobblestone streets until he came to the gate south out of Potro. He passed the guard station without issue, and began south, the road climbing steadily uphill.

He remembered the road well from his sojourn to the university eight years prior. He had sent applications to both the University of Semm and the University of Potro. Both had offered him a position, and he'd accepted Potro. On a blisteringly hot summer day, much like this one, he had set out for the university. By foot it was a four-day journey. Heading north out of Eikres, he had stopped in the City of Qelem for the night. He'd taken the mountain pass through to Wellesper the next day, arriving in its city and staying at the inn with the view of the famous Wellesper Abbey. It had taken a full day to walk from the east side of Wellesper, where the city lay, to the Wellesper-Potro crossing in the west, where he had stayed at a country inn on the Wellesper side. The final day's trek was downhill to the City of Potro, which lay on the coast, looking out over the great, blue Dytik Ocean.

Mathin would now travel the same route in reverse, leading him back to his family's farm, where he expected to find his parents getting on in their years, but still alive and well, at least as per the letter he'd received from them the week prior.

A small part of him had reservations about this plan. The University of Potro had given him tenure. Even those ideologically opposed to him had come around after the fire, as Olim had said. He'd have had Olim's support and the university administration's as well. He felt a tinge of dismay at the feeling of having let them down, but that wasn't the point. Not hardly. He didn't dare turn back.

The sun beat down on him as he climbed the rocky road, but before long he came to the tree line and entered the Potro forests. The road flattened out and joined up against the rushing Zochiro River, a long segment of which served as the border between Potro and Wellesper. On the far bank, perhaps half a mile away, a similar road ran the edge of the river on the Wellesper side. The crossing was a bridge at the base of the mountains, where the river narrowed. The sun was getting low in the sky, he realized, and he would need to make better time if wanted to be assured of a room at the inn.

The traffic on the road grew lighter, then disappeared altogether. He found himself the only one on the road as the sun approached the horizon, and the road weaved away from the river and then back toward it again. He hurried along, trying to make up for lost time, focusing his attention so hard on walking quickly, that at first he didn't notice the wind pick up in the trees, and the birds scattering, and then a roaring noise, growing steadily louder. An enormous metallic bird descended out the sky in front of him, wind now blasting across his face and buffeting the trees. The bird eased itself into the ground directly in front of him, and a door in the bird's neck appeared, the metallic frame dissolving into an open doorway. Metallic liquid blobbed out of the portal forming a metal platform and stairs leading to the ground.

Mathin's heart raced, and he stood, staring, part of him wanting to jolt and run back away from the monstrosity, but another part of him remained curiously transfixed on the scene.

A figure moved just inside the portal, then stepped out of the bird and onto the platform. Despite the odd clothing—stranger than any material he had ever seen—he recognized the face immediately as the Makrimian scholar, Olim Stiek.

"Hi, Mathin," Olim called down.

Mathin found he couldn't speak.

"I know this must be a shock." Olim began down the stairwell. "And I'm not doing this lightly. But I decided it was better than any of my other options." He stepped onto the ground and gestured toward the metal bird. "This is my ship. And, as you've probably guessed, I'm not actually from Makrim."

Mathin managed to find his voice, just barely "Where are you from?"

"Another planet."

"Then... the bird... it's..."

"A spaceship. Yes."

Mathin gazed over the thing. He had seen the design schematics the engineers made, and he had had only the vaguest notion of how all the lines, forms, and numbers had related to the creation of a mechanism like a crossbow, aqueduct, or siege engine. The engineering that must have gone into the thing in front of him was eons distant from his surface knowledge of the field.

"How...?" Mathin blurted out.

"How is it I'm here? Because of a mistake. A reporting error. If you come inside, I'll explain the rest."

"Inside...? Inside your ship, you mean?"

Olim nodded. Mathin scanned in his face. In the year that Mathin had known him at the university, Olim had never said or done anything that had made Mathin think that Olim held ill intent toward anyone. He was a good listener. He listened particularly well to Mathin's ideas about the organization of knowledge. He had debated with some of the other professors, too. With none of them had he ever so much as raised his voice, but he had challenged them.

"Will anything happen to me?"

"I will not harm you. And I will not take you away from Ytria. Unless you want me to."

Mathin thought this through for many moments. Finally, he decided that his friend, however strange his clothing and his metallic bird he called a spaceship, had earned his trust for even this. Mathin walked up the metal stairs after Olim, took a deep breath, and followed him through the hole in the metallic bird's neck.

The inside of the ship glistened. Every surfaced seemed to be made either of metal, glass, or some kind of semi-transparent substance Mathin couldn't identify. Chairs lay before consoles that resembled small desks, but whose surfaced somehow emanated light. A large panel covering most of the wall in front of them also danced with light, words, and characters, all glistening in a language he couldn't read. Another, much more prominent chair, sat in the center of the room. In the back lay two doors, presumably leading away into the ship's interior.

"This is the bridge," Olim announced. "It's where I control and steer the craft. The ship can comfortably hold two others, but I usually travel alone. Would you like to sit down?"

"Yes." The edges of Mathin's vision had started to blur, and he felt somewhat faint. Olim led him by the arm to one of the chairs near the wall of shimmering text and sat him down. He then moved to the back of the bridge and returned with a glass of water. Mathin drank it eagerly, feeling better.

"Why...?" Mathin started, not sure which of the many questions in his head to give voice to.

Olim sat down at the console opposite him. "Have you heard of the Unholy Night?"

"Well, yes. It's the tall tale that there was a night some twenty years ago in Reiar in which people were transformed into mindless monstrosities... the details of which are unspeakable."

Olim nodded and pursed his lips. "I am afraid that was not a tall tale."

Mathin tilted his head.

"That was... a visitation of sorts. Humans from a barbaric

world, normally not allowed in this region space, but in this case, they were following the rules, after a fashion."

"What rules?"

"This planet, Ytria, sits inside the space of a governing body called the Galactic Consortium. We have strict rules about how space-faring races should interact with those races that are not yet space-faring. Unfortunately, twenty-two years ago, there was a mistake. The individual who entered Ytria into the Consortium's records entered delta-four instead of gamma-four. Ytria is listed as 'unprotected.'"

"And so... space men have been coming to our planet..."

Olim grinned. "Sometimes they are men. Women, too. And then there are the AIs."

Mathin raised an eyebrow.

"It's best we don't get into that."

"What should we discuss then?"

Olim's gaze turned serious. "Your book."

Mathin felt himself bunch up his face at the absurdity of the statement. "My book? You tell me can travel between worlds, a citizen of some kind of intergalactic kingdom, and you're interested in my *book*? Please."

Olim nodded. "It is true. Your book is more important than you know."

"No," Mathin insisted. "It is futile. The library fire taught me that. Say, if the Unholy Night was visitors from the stars, what then of the Potro University fire—?"

Olim held up a hand and swung his head back and forth. "No. You must not start to do that. I am certain that whatever the cause of the library fire, it was not a visitor. You must not now go around your planet looking for visitors. It is my job to keep away those who have arrived with ill intent, and I am equipped to do so. The majority of the disasters you will witness in your life will be the doing of your fellow Ytrians, or just random bad luck, as I suspect the library fire was. Now, as to your book, you have taken the wrong lesson from the library fire."

"I have?"

"You believe the pursuit of the organization of knowledge to be futile. Am I right?"

Mathin hesitated. "Yes. It will all disappear anyway."

"I would like to show you something." Olim stood. "But I will need your permission to take you off of Ytria for a time. I will bring you back. How do you feel about that?"

Mathin gulped. "What will... happen to me?"

"From your perspective, you will feel nothing, not even the rush of motion. That will all be dampened. You will hear and feel the engines rumbling. That is all."

Mathin nodded.

"It is okay, then? I need you to say it."

"Yes. So long as I come back here, I agree."

Olim turned his head toward the screen and spoke in a language Mathin had never heard before. Certainly not a Glissian dialect nor even Nipic, but something else entirely. When he'd finished, the floor began to rumble, and Mathin tensed up.

"Don't worry," Olim said. "That's just the engines."

"What is happening?"

Olim spoke in the strange language once more, and the words of light upon the wall disappeared. In their place appeared a green and blue circle, one growing steadily smaller, but upon it, Mathin could see the outline of three large peninsulas attached to a spit of mountains, one smaller peninsula to the north, and a fifth to the east—Glissia, his home, one region amongst many other bodies of land, many of which he didn't even have names for, all growing smaller and smaller.

"We're... moving away?"

"Yes."

"Where are we going?"

"A safe position near your sun."

"What of the other nearby planets? Who lives there?"

"Ah." Olim smiled widely. "The story about the 'men of Ezreth,' right?"

"No one lives on Ezreth?" It was the next closest planet to the sun, the astronomers had said. It seemed to be covered in a thick layer of clouds, but what could be under them, no one knew. A dense jungle, perhaps.

"Ezreth," Olim spoke through his smile, "averages 450 degrees on the surface regardless of day or night. And, if you did not immediately melt from the heat, you would suffocate from the lack of oxygen in the atmosphere and be burnt to death by the persistent liquid sulfur rainstorms."

"I take it no one lives on the other planets, either. They are much larger."

"They also have no land. No continents. Merely clouds and ocean. And gravity and pressure that would crush you to pieces if you ever tried to land there."

"You make space sound harsh."

"I'm sure you have some understanding of the risks that sailors take with their lives when they venture out to sea. Space travel requires many hundreds of times more care. Don't worry, though. This is a good ship. You will be safe. Ah, we're approaching."

Olim spoke again in the strange language, and the living picture of the field of stars—Ytria had grown so small by now as to have effectively vanished—changed into another picture, this one was of a sphere that filled the screen, a giant coruscating ball of what looked to be lava, plumes of it could be seen erupting from its surface in arcs.

"What is—?"

"This is what your sun looks like with the appropriate equipment to screen out the radiation that will damage your eyes. I've adjusted some of the colors so you can see the details, but this is roughly what you would see if you could safely point a telescope at your local star."

"Local star...? Then all the stars in the sky are other suns?"

"Yes."

Mathin gazed over the enormous yellow-white sphere, it's brilliant patches of lighter and darker areas shifting and swirling. "Why are you showing me this?"

Olim turned to him, his face very stern. "In six billion years, the chemical processes in the Ytrian star will cause it to swell. It will grow larger and larger, eventually burning up both Ezreth and Ytria, consuming them in fire."

"But surely that is enough time for us to build spaceships—"

"The Ytrian star is not unique in this regard. *All* stars are on the same path to destruction. The time frames differ slightly, but that is how a star dies. It spends the last of fuel expanding to an enormous size, then collapses into a dead, dim husk of its former self."

"And we can't continually seek out new stars with new planets?"

Olim shook his head. "The stars, we have discovered, are growing further and further apart from one another. It takes this ship three hours to travel from here to the closest star. Next year, that trip will have increased by a few microseconds. Longer trips mean more power for the engines, which means more fuel, for which we are reliant on the laboratories of planets sustained by living stars. It is a long way off, but there will come a day when the Galactic Consortium will be no more."

"Then... Nothing truly matters..."

"No, Mathin." Olim took a step forward, his eyes radiating nearly the same intensity as the living picture of the Ytrian sun on the wall. "It matters all the more. The universe remains on course for all of its heat, all of its sustaining energy to eventually ebb away to nothing, *but* in the here and now, human beings have agency, free will, and choice. We are each given a tiny sliver of autonomy, the ability to form something out of nothing, the chance to influence others, to build, learn, discover, and to shape our world. Yes, there will be destruction, sometimes vast destruction, and no feeling person will be able to help but be sad, but that doesn't change the fact that these moments of life are our one chance to matter. It will all end in fire and darkness no matter what we do, but we can choose to make it more beautiful, more just, or more *organized* now."

Mathin thought over Olim's words. He stood and crossed his arms. "Why does my work matter to you so much? There are plenty at the University of Potro that wish I would just give up on the whole thing, and I can't imagine what I could possibly teach a galactic consortium about organizing its information."

Olim pursed his lips, seeming to be battling with himself over his next words. "Because in terms of the typical development of human civilization, your ideas are about three or four centuries ahead of their time. The tendency towards arranging information as roots is, in many ways, easier and simpler, but it comes with a cost. Eventually, someone comes up with the idea of the spiderweb. All the security of an immaculate order is sacrificed, but as the amount of knowledge in your society grows, non-hierarchical relationships become increasingly more important. Tell me, what's the largest library you can imagine? Not that actually exists, but how many books can you imagine together in one place?"

"Umm, I don't know. A thousand, maybe? I suppose if I think of one of those ancient Hospian edifices in the stories as a library, perhaps ten thousand."

"The Galactic Consortium's total number of published books is in the millions *per year*. The sum total of all in existence is in the quintillions. The idea of the spiderweb is very, very important. And yes, even if you give up on it, eventually, someone will notice your work, or they will come up with the same idea themselves, and it will perhaps get picked up that time around, but only after a century or so of stagnation. That delay would exist solely because you gave up."

Mathin looked out at the giant ball of fire that was his sun, his 'local star,' as Olim had called it. The whole planet, doomed to end in a fiery inferno of his expanding sun. It seemed like another tall tale. This whole experience had a dreamlike aspect without the sensation of dreaming. Although he supposed if he woke up from this just now, he would hardly take any of it particularly seriously, but he didn't seem to be waking up. Far from it, he seemed quite awake now. And, as Olim had said, he had a choice.

"I'm ready to go back to Ytria," Mathin said.

Olim smiled and spoke in the strange language. The living picture of the sun grew smaller and smaller, the ship he was on presumably withdrawing from its periphery back toward his home.

—

Night had since fallen on southeast Potro, Mathin slept on board Olim's ship that night. He found the bed in the small room off the bridge luxuriously comfortable, far better than anything he'd ever slept on at home or in the university dormitory.

Once the sun had risen, Olim dropped Mathin off at a spot on the Potro-Wellesper road just inside the tree line from where the road fell away down the rocky cliff toward the shore and city. Mathin thanked Olin, descended the stairs, and when he looked back, Olin, the platform, and the stairs had vanished, and the ship was taking off into the sky, gusts of wind blasting his face and rustling the tree branches. Mathin watched until it had disappeared beyond the clouds. All at once, he remembered himself and took off out of the forest and down the hill into Potro. He arrived just after breakfast time and had no trouble passing through the gates, for even a former professor still held some authority.

At the university, he visited the Collegiate Registrar and admitted he had had a change of heart and wished to resume his post. A couple of the registrars grumbled, but the rest happily stamped his application as approved.

He found his old room in the dormitory was still vacant, signed up to resume his housing there, picked up the keys for it, and dropped off his things. He put on his professor's robes, and from there went to the main hall, where he visited the makeshift library in the old faculty lounge. He meandered through the rickety shelves being constructed and those completed and already lined with the books that had been checked out before the blaze.

As Mathin turned a corner, Professor Maddex stood already looking in his direction and a surprised smile burst across his face. "Professor Ekpadesi?" He gestured with his hand up and down, seeming to be indicating Mathin's robes. "You have rejoined us, then?"

"I have."

"Wonderful. Take a look over here." Maddex led him to a pair of shelves on the far wall, both of these completely full. Mathin scanned the titles. They were not traditionally organized. Philosophy books sat next to history, drama next to analysis, physics next to chemistry—it was then that Mathin realized that they were organized alphabetically, by the last names of the authors.

"We have tried it," Maddex said.

Mathin beamed. "And what are the results?"

"It is hard to tell since the collection is still so small, but anecdotally, the books do seem easier to locate."

Mathin gazed over the shelf. "I never imagined..."

"What was that?"

"I was just thinking that in my manuscript I never presumed to be able to study a collection so organized. I suppose large parts of it will have to be rewritten."

Maddex's countenance fell. "I'm sorry—"

"Oh, no! Don't apologize. It's an amazing opportunity. I'm looking forward to it. I would like to read your codex, if you don't mind. Perhaps by putting our ideas together, we can come up with better organizational systems, still."

"Yes." Maddex's smile returned. "That seems like a good idea. Let's give it a try."

One's Own Medicine

"Send them in." Senator Mennon spoke into her intercom.

Four of them walked into her office, two men and two women.

Senator Mennon stood, shook their hands, smiled, and offered them a seat, four chairs in front of her desk prepared just for them.

"Welcome to Glissia," she said.

"Thank you," one of the women said. If the senator read her uniform correctly, she was the captain.

All of their faces were grim. A chord of fear resonated within the senator. Could Glissia's inclusion into the Galactic Consortium be in jeopardy? Had a citizen done something? So many nations of Planet Ytria had already been allowed in.

"Are you aware," the captain said, "of the unfortunate period of fifty years, about fifteen centuries ago, during which the Consortium had accidentally classified Ytria as 'unmanaged and unprotected?'"

"Yes. My understanding was that the committee assigned to that issue went over our historical records and your historical records, and everything was resolved."

The captain nodded, forlorn. "Something was missed."

"Oh?"

"When one of our teams was visiting the city of Wellesper, one of our officers noticed the statue in the city plaza there. Are you familiar with it?

The senator shook her head. "I'm afraid not."

"It is of a man named Saint Gillem Perigan."

The name sounded vaguely familiar to her. "Something from religious history... He was supposed to have performed miracles of healing, correct?"

Another nod from the captain and frowns from her entourage.

"My science officer will explain," the captain said.

The young man next to her took a deep breath and began his story.

"Gillem!"

Gillem recognized that tone of voice. It meant he was in trouble. Again.

"I'm coming," he called out. He plucked the five-leafed sprig from the ground, stuffed it into his apothecary satchel, and hurried to catch up with the rest of the monks.

"I'm very sorry, Cardinal," Gillem heard Friar Hendek say as Gillem drew closer to his entourage. Both he and Cardinal

Ingeniu glanced back at him. "I will have words with all the monks when we return to Qelem. It is so easy, when one is young, to be drawn off on flights of fancy. But God's path demands attentiveness, and, most importantly, obedience."

The cardinal nodded. "Sage words. Qelem Abbey is lucky to have a wise leader."

"Thank you, Cardinal."

Gillem's stomach turned over with worry. Just moments later, his eye caught another herb at the roadside—an eristinus lilac—and just like that, his gastronomical distress was forgotten. The powder of the lilac's leaves was supposed to have anti-inflammatory properties. He was painfully short on anti-inflammatories at the moment, but he dared not go and pick it for fear of inciting further wrath from the Abbot, or, Heaven forbid, the Cardinal.

The forest stretched out in front of them, the road winding through a slightly uphill valley. A mile back they had crossed a stream, and burbling water could still be heard off to their right, the road roughly following its course.

"How is Lord Wellesper?" the Friar asked.

"His land lives up to its name," the Cardinal replied. "Their coffers grow full on successful trade and continued stable relations with their neighbors. Now, what will be crucial in the coming months is a successful conclusion to the peace agreement between Calens and Jeia."

"I have heard that Jeia still blames Calens for the Unholy Night fifty years ago."

"Indeed. It was in fact Reiar that was the hardest hit. You have heard of the hideous creatures the church found there when the Inquisition was sent in?"

The Cardinal crossed himself. "It is probably best not to mention such things with younger monks present."

"But of course. My point is merely that Reiar, though badly hurt from the incident, has moved on, not blaming its neighbors, while Calens and Jeia continue a century of hostilities. Lord Wellesper believes he can broker a lasting treaty between them, and healthy trade relations as well..."

The Friar continued speaking, but a malanchus pinnotrum caught Gillem's eye. He would recognize those star-shaped leaves anywhere! He couldn't believe his luck. It was already bordering on winter, and yet here sat one still in its prime. Gillem could not pass up the opportunity. He was flat out of proper digestives, and the leaves of malanchus pinnotrum were the most potent digestive in the known world. Gillem hurried to the side of the road, plucked it as carefully as he could, stuffed it into his satchel, and was about to turn and head back when he saw them—eyes. A face. The face was attached to a body, a young man, probably about his own age, wearing beggar's clothes.

"Wha- What do you- want?" Gillem stammered.

The man hurried up to him, and stuffed his right hand into Gillem's satchel, then just as quickly removed it.

"You never saw me," the man said. And just like that, he had dashed back into the forest. Gillem blinked. He almost couldn't believe what had just happened. Had he imagined it?

"*Gillem*!"

Gillem thought a most unholy expletive, sighed, and hurried back toward his entourage.

They arrived at the Wellesper gates at dusk. Two ornery guards with tired, red eyes gazed over their contingent warily. The Cardinal took them aside, where he spoke to them for but a minute, and soon the entire entourage was ushered through the gates.

They made immediately for Wellesper Abbey, a walled community within the walled city. The Wellesper Abbot, a portly man with bright, shining eyes, greeted them at the abbey gates. He seemed to be on familiar terms with the Cardinal, Gillem noticed, or perhaps that was simply how he ingratiated himself to his superiors.

They ate a simple dinner in the refectory, and then an elderly monk guided the Qelem monks to the dormitory and assigned them each a room.

Gillem was happy to find his. Finally, he would be able to grind up his newly discovered plants into powder. The sun had fully set and the room was quite dark. He lit the candle atop his desk, pulled off his satchel, and searched with his hand for the malanchus pinnotrum. He found it and pulled it out, but his hand touched something metallic, and he shuddered, dropping the herb back into the sack. He grabbed up the candle and held the flame over the open satchel so that he could see better. Some kind of metallic plate lay in the bottom of his sack. He gazed over it, turning the candle every which way, in order to get the light to better inspect it by. It had a beveled edge, and a part of its surface seemed to be covered in glass. It was unlike any slab of metal Gillem had ever seen.

He crossed himself twice, and then he reached out, daring to touch it. Nothing shocked him or struck his fingers as they contacted the metal, and so he pulled it fully out of his satchel. He held it up to the light and turned it around in his hands. What on Ytria was it? It was so incredibly light! Perhaps the metal on the outside was but a thin shell and inside was empty. But how had the metal been forged so thin?

He found an indentation in its side and pressed on it. All

at once, the glass-covered portion burst with blinding light. Gillem screamed and dropped the device on the stone floor. He scrambled to pick it up and stuff it back into his satchel. Seeing the light still filter through his satchel, he flipped the tablet over so the shining part would be facing the desk.

A knock at his door. The elderly monk peeked inside. "Is everything all right, Brother?"

"Yes. Just a large spider. It startled me. It's gone now."

"Do be careful, Brother." The elderly monk closed the door to Gillem's room.

Gillem exhaled in relief and retrieved the glowing metal tablet once more.

The tablet displayed words in an alphabet and language Gillem had never seen before. He found that tapping his finger on the glass portion of the tablet caused its words and pictures to change, but as he couldn't understand any of it, he eventually put the thing back in his satchel face down and decided to go to sleep.

Gillem normally slept well on trips, but he was restless that night and awoke in the morning feeling just as exhausted as when he had lain down. He found that the tablet had grown dark again, which he was thankful for. Hopefully, it would not light up in his satchel. He didn't dare leave it in the room. He decided the safest thing would be to keep it in his satchel and carry it with him.

He threw on his habit and satchel and went to the refectory, where he met Friar Hendek and the other five monks from his entourage.

"Sleepless night, Gillem?" the Friar asked.

Gillem merely nodded.

"Well, cheer up. We have a lot of work ahead of us today. The word is that there's a new plague spreading in town. Some of the monks of Wellesper Abbey have even taken ill. We'll look at them first, and then we go and treat the others in the city."

Gillem moved through his morning in a haze. His mind felt fuzzy and his perceptions dim. He hoped he wasn't coming down with something himself. After breakfast, they put on their beaks stuffed with herbs and went to the infirmary where two sick monks lay bedridden. It was a dark, quiet room. Incense burned in a corner tripod, and the few windows had been blanketed over.

The Friar talked about their symptoms, then how to prepare a tincture, but Gillem had trouble focusing on the Friar's instructions. He noticed the other monks were getting out their bottles, and so he started to do the same. He went through the motions of preparing the medicine, but he wasn't entirely certain that he'd done it the same as the others. Was he sweating? It was so early in the morning, and the sun had barely had a chance to warm the air.

"Gillem, are you sure you're all right?"

"Yes, Friar."

"Administer to this man, here."

Gillem did as he was instructed. The Friar ordered another monk to administer to the other.

"And now to the city," the Friar said. They left the abbey gates, masks still in place, and walked to the city's infirmary, a much dingier and even drearier room than its counterpart at the abbey. Coughs and moans emanated as they entered.

The Friar glanced around the room, perturbed. He stopped a passing nurse. "Excuse me, I heard there were forty ill. This looks like many more."

"Twice as many come in overnight, milord." And she hurried off.

"To work." The Friar gestured toward the sick. "The patients are arranged in six rows and there are six of you. Each of you take a row and administer your tincture. Do you all have enough?"

Nods all around.

"Good. Get to work."

Gillem took the far row, the one against the north wall, and moved down it, administering his tincture to each patient. As he moved, he felt himself recovering somewhat. It didn't feel so hot in the room, and he found he could focus his attention more clearly. The ringing in his ears dissipated, too.

When he was finished, he returned to the Friar and waited for the other monks to finish.

"Well done," the Friar said. He then led the group back to the abbey.

At lunch, the Cardinal joined them. Gillem and the other monks remained silent, of course, while the Friar and Cardinal talked.

"Lord Wellesper will receive delegations from both Calens and Jeia within three days' time," the Cardinal announced.

"Is he concerned about the plague?" the Friar asked.

"Not as such."

"Perhaps he should be. There were twice as many patients today in the infirmary as we expected."

"Lord Wellesper is a very holy man. I'm sure he will be fine."

"Maybe he, but it does not bode well for the delegations. And if they turn back—"

"I'm sure Lord Wellesper has the situation in hand."

After lunch, the monks were dismissed to their rooms until evening prayers. Gillem had been thankful that he'd been feeling better, but as he started up the stairs to his room, he realized that his symptoms were returning. The ringing in his ears was back, albeit tinily, and he'd begun to sweat again. He decided to lie down.

He set his satchel down on his desk, threw his habit on the floor, and lay on his cot, enjoying the feeling of the cold air against his warm skin.

"Hey," a voice said.

Gillem shuddered and jerked over to his other side. A man stood in his room, and Gillem pulled up the sheets of his bed over his exposed body. What was happening? He wanted to cry out, but he found he had no voice.

"Don't be frightened," the man said. "Really. I mean it. Calm down."

Gillem realized then that it was the same man he'd seen yesterday on the road, the one who'd put his hand into Gillem's satchel, the one who must have placed the metal tablet there. "How did you get in here?"

"I'm not really here."

"What does that mean?"

"It would take too long to explain. Think of me as a kind of message." He seemed to register the abject confusion on Gillem's face. "Put your hand to my chest. I mean it. Come on."

Gillem hobbled out of bed. He stumbled forward, holding the sheet around himself, and slowly stretched his hand outward, reaching toward the man, pressing into his chest, and then his hand moved *through* the man's chest. Gillem shrieked and jumped back onto his bed. He crossed himself ten times and began chanting prayers. The man tried to talk over him, but Gillem ignored him.

A knock at his door.

Gillem looked up. The man had vanished. "Just a minute!" Gillem called out.

He put on his habit and stood, though his eyes were now bleary and the ringing in his ears had grown sharp. "Come in," Gillem said.

It was the elderly monk again, the same one who had shown him his room and checked on him the night before.

"Is everything really all right?" the elderly monk asked.

"Yes," Gillem insisted. "Another spider."

The elderly monk narrowed his eyes. "It is almost winter, Brother Gillem."

"Indeed. It is a very resilient family of spiders, it would seem."

The elderly monk closed the door to Gillem's room, and Gillem threw himself back onto the bed to rest.

Gillem woke to a knock at his door. The knocks came rapidly, an urgency behind them.

"Gillem?" It was the voice of the Friar.

"Just a moment," Gillem called out. He felt even worse than he had when he'd lain down in bed. The ringing in his ears had grown stronger, his sinuses were congested, and all of his perceptions were washed out and hazy, just like they had been in the morning.

He pulled himself out of bed and put on his habit. He collected himself as best he was able and opened the door. The Friar stood beside a pair of older Wellesper monks.

"Gillem... Are you all right?"

"I'm fine," Gillem said. "I just haven't been sleeping well."

The Friar huffed. "The tincture you made today, was it

concocted exactly as I described?"

Gillem shot through with fear. Had his tincture caused someone further pain, or, Heaven forbid, death? "I did my best, Friar."

"Do you have any left?"

Gillem nodded, and, his alertness cutting through his symptoms, moved to the desk, where he retrieved the bottle, still half full, from his satchel. He handed it to the Friar, who entered Gillem's room, the other two monks, following. The Friar moved to the solitary window and held the liquid up to the light.

The Friar turned and faced him. "Gillem, these are definitely not the ingredients I listed this morning. It has a pinkish hue. What did you use instead?"

Gillem bit his lip. Tears welled up at the edges of his eyes. He stood stalwart and began chanting prayers of repentance in his head.

The Friar strode forward, put the vial into Gillem's hand, and closed Gillem's fingers around it. The other hand he put on Gillem's shoulder. He looked directly into Gillem's eyes. "Gillem, the monk and the entire row of patients you treated this morning are nearly or fully recovered. Most have been sent back to their homes. The others, the ones who were given the tincture of my instructions, have not improved. In fact, they die at the same rate as the untreated. So please, what did you put in the tincture?"

A wave of relief passed over Gillem, but a new kind of fear rose up in its place. "Friar... I do not know."

"Well, at the very least, please come with us. Four more monks have fallen ill. You can treat them. We will send your vial off to the city infirmary, and then we will focus your efforts on remembering the ingredients you used this morning."

Gillem went with the Friar and found the four additional monks in the abbey infirmary. He treated them, as instructed, and then handed his vial over to the Wellesper Abbot, who he found waiting outside the door. The Abbot thanked Gillem for all his hard work, and Gillem, rigid with nervousness, was only able to mumble, "The honor is mine, Lord Abbot."

Gillem headed back to the dormitory as quickly as his feet could take him, and the Friar stopped him at its entrance. "Gillem, you are relieved from the duty of evening prayer." His voice dropped to a whisper. "The plague in the city has grown worse. It is spreading with incredible speed. You are to focus all your energy on remembering the ingredients you used in the tincture."

Gillem nodded vigorously, then hurried inside the dormitory, returned to his room, and sat. Now, finally alone with his thoughts, Gillem realized that he felt rejuvenated. The sweat had dissipated, his sinuses had cleared, the ringing in his ears and gone, and he felt he could focus his attention again. He took a deep breath and sat at his desk. He pulled out his satchel, retrieved all of the ingredients he had in stock, and laid them out on the desk in front of him. There were eleven of them in total. Now, for the symptoms that the disease presented, the Abbot would have recommended five parts tyronium agar, two parts eksenksa, and one part rydodendonica. Hadn't that been what he'd used? He thought he had. But that part of the morning was such a muddle in his mind. If he had accidentally used a different ingredient, then which one?

He supposed he could exclude some obvious candidates. For example, wozmonium root. That would make these symptoms worse. Although... He recalled from his apothecary training that an ingredient's properties could change drastically when combined with another.

Ugh. There was no way of knowing!

Gillem gazed over the ingredients, his mind racing harder to try to remember something about the texture or shape of what he had handled this morning to make the tincture, but those memories refused to coalesce in his mind. His mind had simply been too foggy— He realized just then that he was sniffling again. The sinus pressure had returned, along with the ringing in his ears and the sweating.

"Hey. Don't freak out this time."

Gillem swiveled around. It was the man again, the one from the roadside.

"Who are you?"

"My name is Davin."

Gillem dropped his voice to a whisper. "We need to keep our voices down."

Davin followed suit. "All right."

"What are you, if not a demon sent to torment me?"

"I am human. Not a demon. This is a kind of message. A very, very advanced kind of letter. I am outside the city now."

"But I can see you here."

"I am not *here*. This is an image of me. Do you understand?"

"I think so."

"You have my computer. I put it in your pack."

"My satchel."

"Sure. I apologize for doing that, but I had to."

"Why?"

"I made a mistake. When I looked up this planet's designation, it was delta-four, meaning I could bring all my stuff here. But, after I'd gotten here, I discovered that the designation had just changed last year. It is now *alpha*-four, meaning I'm not supposed to take anything out of my ship. And they were close to finding me."

"They? Who are they?"

"Don't worry about them. More people. But they don't care about you. They only care about me. Anyway, they're gone now. They inspected me, and I didn't have the computer, so they went off looking for others. Now I need it back. You didn't... touch it, did you?"

Gillem bit his lip. "And if I did?"

Davin seemed to curse, though the word that emanated from his lips wasn't any that Gillem recognized. "Nanite programs could be running on you."

"What are nanite programs?"

"It would be illegal for me to explain. Just know that their effects could be very bad. Can you come outside the city and give me my computer back? I can turn off the nanite programs. After that, I promise to leave you alone and go on my way. I'm sorry to involve you in this."

"I think I can get away this evening. The guards won't let me back in after nightfall, but if I go for a walk after dinner, no one should notice."

"Follow the road back away from the city, then take a right into the woods at the enormous tree stump. I'll be in a tree not far off the road. Thank you..."

"Gillem."

"Thank you, Gillem. I'm sorry for any trouble I might have caused you."

"It hasn't been any trouble," he lied. Just, you know, having to deal with frightening apparitions of men, who were able to appear and disappear at will. One might think it almost demonic. The Friar and Abbot certainly would. Gillem hoped, however, that he could simply give up the metallic tablet and be done with the whole ordeal. Davin didn't seem like a bad person, perhaps just a careless one, and Gillem wasn't in any position to fault him for carelessness.

"Goodbye," Davin said, and the shape of his body became translucent and faded from view, like that of a ghost.

A knock on his door. Gillem winced and immediately began conjuring up an excuse that wasn't spiders. One didn't have a conversation with spiders. Perhaps prayers? Yes, he'd been reciting prayers, and practicing a new kind of meter, hence his hushed voice. That was what he would say.

Gillem opened the door. The Friar and the Abbot both stood before him. Gillem's eyes widened.

"May we come in?" the Friar asked.

Gillem nodded and ushered them inside.

"Close the door," the Abbot said. Gillem did so. The two walked to the center of his room, looking over the ingredients laid out on the table, then at him.

"Have you remembered anything about the tincture?" the Friar asked.

Gillem looked at the floor. "No, Friar. I am so terribly sorry."

"Gillem," the Abbot said. "The four monks you treated earlier, they are recovering. Rapidly."

"Thank you, Lord Abbot. It is my pleasure to serve—"

The Friar interrupted him. "But the patients who were given your tincture at the infirmary this afternoon are showing no signs of improvement."

Gillem looked up. "But it's the same vial. I handed it to you, Lord Abbot, myself. It was the same. I had just used it to treat the Brothers."

"Indeed," the Abbot said. He strode forward and put a hand on Gillem's shoulder. "The common element in the recoveries is not the erroneous tincture, Brother Gillem. It is you."

The Abbot and the Friar took Gillem to the infirmary. He walked in a daze. Not only had his symptoms returned, but he couldn't believe what he'd heard. He had cured those people? With his presence? Their Lord and Savior had certainly been capable of such things, but that had been over a thousand years ago. He was just a simple monk.

The three of them crunched across the gravel of the central grounds of Wellesper Abbey, the dusk sky a bright red above them. In the infirmary, Gillem found that five more monks had fallen ill. The Abbot asked for two of Gillem's empty vials, and the Abbot filled them what plain water from the jug at the apothecary table in the corner. The Abbot then returned to Gillem and put them in his hands.

"But, that's just—"

The Abbot held a finger to his lips, and the Friar nodded toward the sick monks.

Gillem sighed and rounded the room, "treating" each monk with the plain, uninfused water.

When he'd finished, the Abbot motioned toward the door, and Gillem exited.

"It will be about an hour before we know for certain," the Abbot said. "Will you both join me in the sacristy?"

"Yes, Lord Abbot." The Friar motioned for Gillem to follow them.

They walked back across the grounds, this time entering the church. They took a right inside the big double doors and entered into a large study.

"Please sit down." The Abbot moved toward a small table at the side of the room where he opened up a wooden box, produced plates and cups—rather expensive looking ones—and began piling them with biscuits and small chunks of root vegetables. At the sight, Gillem realized both that he was feeling better once more, and that he was very hungry. The Abbot handed him and the Friar each a plate, and set the cups atop the small stand beside their chairs. He then sat at the large desk opposite them.

The Abbot looked directly at Gillem. "Tell me about how came to the Order."

"I grew up in Chaumindi. It's a very small village. The residents swear fealty to Lord Calens. A passing monk visited when I was ten. I grew fascinated by the Order. My parents had my older brothers, and my brothers seemed to like the farm, so I was allowed to leave."

"Any smiths in your family?"

"No."

"Was there a smith near your family's house?"

"It was... two doors down, I think. Maybe three."

"Ah." The Abbot beamed.

Gillem stared wide-eyed.

"You see, Gillem, our Lord and Savior was a smithy, before he was called to the sacred art of healing."

"I suppose that could be related... Though the smithy in my town was quite mean to children. I didn't really ever talk to him."

The Abbot waved the suggestion off. "You have a gift, Gillem. At least, we believe you do. We will see shortly."

The Friar set down his plate and turned to Gillem. "And if you don't, and if this is a coincidence of some kind, you won't be blamed." He turned to the Abbot. "Will he, Lord Abbot?"

"No," the Abbot said. "Of course not."

After they had eaten, the Abbot and the Friar talked for some time more about the progress of the plague. It had become a concern for all inhabitants of the city. Already, there was talk of it being a punishment from God for mankind's sins. The monks would, of course, tend the ill, in accord with their Lord and Savior's great commandment to treat the weak and infirm with compassion and kindness. But the illness seemed to be sparing no one, neither monks nor nobility, either, who were all falling ill as well. The rumor was that even one of the king's ministers had symptoms of the disease.

"Well," the Abbot said. "Let's go check on our brothers."

He stood and led them out of the sacristy, out of the solemn, dark church and out into the cold night. The abbey grounds were lit up with the light of dozens of torches, hanging from building walls. They walked under their faint glow across the grounds to the infirmary. Six new monks lay in the beds and two more lay curled up against the far wall. Two brothers in beaked masks tended to them.

"Where are the five brothers who were here an hour ago?" the Abbot inquired.

"Feeling better," a beaked monk said. "These showed up, so we sent the other five back to the dormitory."

The Abbot and the Friar shared a knowing look, then turned to Gillem.

Gillem gulped and slowly pulled the vials of water from the satchel. He then made his way around the room, treating his fellow monks, somehow healing them, despite not having the faintest idea how he could possibly be making them any better.

"Gillem!" Davin's voice was a harsh, sharp whisper. "You didn't come last night!"

Gillem pushed himself up off his cot, groaned, and immediately fell back onto it. His body felt as though it were on fire. He had a splitting headache, and he could barely hear Davin's voice over the ringing in his ears.

"Gillem?" Davin's voice took on a note of concern. "What's wrong?"

Gillem drew a hand up to his forehead and threw the sweat-covered sheets off himself with the other, not having enough energy to care for modesty. "I started being able to heal people, and I get well when I do so, but after some time passes—" A sharp pain struck his head and he groaned anew.

Davin muttered another foreign expletive. "Gillem, you must have activated some kind of medical program. It's probably affecting your immune system. Are your symptoms getting worse?"

Gillem only briefly wondered at what an 'immune system' was and which organ of his might house it. "Yes."

"You need to get the computer back to me. I can easily turn the program off. Please."

"They want me to do another healing round this morning. I will go to you immediately after." Anything to feel better, he thought.

"I'll see you then," Davin said. "Please don't delay anymore. I'm worried about you."

The image of Davin faded away. Gillem took deep breaths and prepared himself to get out of bed. If he could just make it to the infirmary, he could start healing people and he would feel better. Slowly and carefully he dressed, slung his satchel over his shoulder, and made his way out of the dormitory, practically hobbling across the abbey grounds. Eyes watched him from the windows of the dormitory. The refectory remained shut up. A general quarantine had been instigated. Now, all the monks who could had gathered at windows to watch the solemn, hobbling gait of the one man who could provide a cure.

Even though the infirmary had been empty when Gillem had left the evening prior, all six beds were now full and seven sick monks lay on the floor. A monk in a beaked mask approached him. "Brother Gillem, you look unwell. May we prepare something for you?"

Gillem did not want to bother to explain. "No, thank you. Let me heal them."

The monk's eyes grew wide with astonishment, and he backed away. Gillem made his rounds of the room, giving all of the sick monks plain water. Even after he'd administered to just the first one, he felt better. By the time he'd done the rounds of the room, his sweat had dissipated and the ringing in his ears had ceased.

Gillem then made his way out of the infirmary and into the city, where more anxious faces watched him from windows. Word had apparently gotten around even here—the man whose divine providence could cure you of the plague with plain water. He arrived at the city infirmary and found it entirely full, more than one hundred people, some lying on the floors, all gasping and wheezing, coughing, some even vomiting.

"Prepare vials of plain water," Gillem told the masked doctor at the front door. "As many as you can."

Gillem worked for hours, more citizens of Wellesper arriving every minute. Gillem healed them all. When the infirmary was finally free of new cases, Gillem found the doctor. "I need to refresh my mind. I am going for a walk. I will be back soon."

Gillem walked out of the infirmary and toward the gates of the city. Could he do this, he wondered? If the pattern followed, his symptoms would return, even worse than before within a matter of hours unless he healed again. Davin could alleviate that plight, but it would also likely remove his healing powers as well, which lay somehow in the computer, not in his hands or in the water. What of the people who caught the plague yet? If they died, would their deaths be on his conscience?

Conundrums like this were exactly why Gillem had gone into practical medicine rather than philosophical studies. The craft of medicine was, at least most of the time, very explicit: find the most effective way to make the patient well again. He had wanted to leave the sophistry to others.

He now approached the city gates. He was about to hail the soldiers standing guard, when he heard his name called from behind him. Gillem swiveled on his feet. "Abbot?"

The Abbot huffed, approached him, grabbed him up closely, and drew him toward the edge of the road, a point, he noticed, near an alley, far from any windows. He spoke in a hushed whisper. "Gillem, there are two new illnesses."

"Just two?"

"Two in particular."

"Who?"

"Friar Hendek."

Gillem gulped.

"And," the Abbot paused and lowered his voice even further, "Lord Wellesper."

Gillem's breath caught in his throat, and he almost choked on it. "The king...?"

"The king."

Gillem looked at the gate, his own salvation lying beyond it. But the Friar... and a *king*...

"Gillem, I know you have been working all morning, but if Lord Wellesper is unable to broker peace between Calens and Jeia..."

"Let's go," Gillem said. Already, the headache was returning, his skin felt warm, his sinuses were swelling up, and the ringing sounded tinily in his ears. But he could not abandon the Friar, and he certainly would not let a king's soul be on his conscious, not for a strange apparition of man or anyone else.

They returned first to the abbey. By the time they reached the infirmary, Gillem had already developed a hobbling gait. The ringing in his ears had grown intense, and he was sweating profusely.

"Perhaps you should lie down yourself," the Abbot suggested.

"No," Gillem insisted. He took the vials of water to the newly arrived monks in the infirmary and treated them all, his symptoms immediately diminishing, although not completely this time, he noticed. He then moved to his master, Friar Hendek.

"Gillem?" Friar Hendek looked up at him through bleary, bloodshot eyes, and let out a small cough. "Don't waste any time on me. Go to the king. As soon as you can, go."

"Take some water," Gillem said. "It will take but a minute."

The Friar obliged, and as soon as he'd sipped, Gillem retracted the vial. "I'll go this moment, Friar. Don't worry."

Gillem returned the Abbot. "Show me the way."

They left the Abbey and weaved through the deserted streets. The road drew steeply uphill, and as they climbed, the ringing in Gillem's ears grew intense, he started dripping beads, and his skin felt as if it were on fire. At the gate to the castle, Gillem drew his hand up to his nose, and as he drew away, he discovered the sleeve of his habit was streaked with blood.

The Abbot caught sight of this, and his eyes widened. "Gillem!" He ran up and slung Gillem's arm over his shoulder, assisting him. "We should get you to the royal physician."

"No." Gillem shook his head, the act of which made his headache flare. "The king."

The Abbot held him tightly, helping him across the drawbridge, into the castle, and through a number of hallways and rooms that Gillem was by then only seeing as a bleary smear of colors. He caught sight of tapestries, torches, portraits, and shields on the walls, all manner of regal things, but he could only barely discern their forms. His head pounded and the ringing in his ears drowned out the Abbot's voice.

Gillem, now barely cognizant of his surroundings, found himself before a prone figure in a large, four-poster bed. It was dark. Candles burned. He could see their light, but he couldn't smell anything. He groped in his satchel, his hands eventually finding the vial of water. Gillem wasn't even sure if the Abbot was still supporting him or not.

"Drink, my Lord," Gillem tried to say, although he couldn't hear the sound of his own voice. "Drink and be well."

He hoped that he had moved the vial to the king's lips. He wasn't entirely sure. When he thought he'd completed the task, he turned his head in the direction he believed the Abbot to be. "Abbot, out of the city, down the road, right at the large tree stump. Please. Take me. Please."

He spoke these words twice without hearing them, and this was the last thing he remembered doing.

A candlelight vigil was held in the Abbey for ten full days. They placed Gillem's coffin in the center of the chapel and every last citizen of Wellesper came in, leaving flowers, herbs, or some other trinket by his body. They would kneel, say their prayers, and then leave. The king himself visited on the ninth day, the day after the delegations from Jeia and Calens had departed the city, the terms of both a peace treaty and trade agreement having been successfully brokered.

Altogether, only two monks had died of the illness, and only fifty-two citizens. Gillem had cured a full third of the population. A remaining third had still grown ill, but Gillem's work had vastly reduced the disease's mortality rate within the city.

On the tenth and final day of Gillem's vigil, three hooded figures walked into the abbey church. The cloth of their robes shone strangely in the light of the candles and torches. They drew their hoods down and asked for the Abbot. After a short wait, he appeared, and wondered at these individuals and their strange clothes.

"May I inquire as to your Order?" the Abbot asked.

"Saint Consortium," the lead figure replied.

"I have never heard of him," the Abbot said.

"We are from a land far away to the North," another hooded figure said. "Very far."

The first one continued. "Abbot Wellesper, this Gillem—"

"*Saint* Gillem Perigan, please."

"Yes. Of course. Let me begin again. Saint Gillem Perigan accidentally, through no fault of his own, came into possession of a metallic talisman of ours during his lifetime. It should be with his possessions. May we inquire as to the possibility of retrieving it?"

The Abbot looked them over carefully. The things of the saint had become precious relics. "Come with me, please."

The Abbot led the three men to the sacristy and closed the door. "I'm afraid all of his possessions are church property now. We cannot part with them."

The men looked between one another. The leader of the group frowned and looked directly at him. "I'm afraid we must have it back. It was stolen from our Order and the thief hid it among his things. I doubt Saint Gillem Perigan ever knew that he had it. We would be willing to pay well for it, if that is an issue."

The Abbot thought this over. "Very well," he said, finally.

He opened a cabinet behind his desk and invited the men to look at the arranged possessions. The herbs had withered and decayed. An assortment of powders in small bottles remained intact. The trio's eyes all moved immediately to the strangest object of them all—the metal tablet with a glass surface.

"That." The strange man pointed to the tablet.

The Abbot sighed and handed it over. "A donation in honor of Saint Gillem Perigan would be appreciated."

The lead man turned to his subordinate, and the subordinate produced a small, metallic cube that gleamed with precious-looking stones, one set in the center of each surface except the bottom. "Will this do?"

"Yes." The Abbot took the cube, placed it on the shelf,

and closed the cabinet door. "Thank you."

"And the plague?" the lead man asked. "We heard there was a plague, but the citizens all seem well."

"We have Saint Gillem Perigran to thank for that," the Abbot said.

"We are glad to hear that." The three figures turned to leave.

"Should we be expecting any more visitors from your Order?" the Abbot asked.

The lead one turned his head momentarily. "Perhaps. But not for many years."

The Abbot wondered at that. The question of just how many years lay on the tip of his tongue, but something in the men's demeanor suggested to him that he should not press the issue. That he should let them go. And also that he should not go searching too hard for a 'Saint Consortium.'

He watched the trio depart from the church, then returned to his vigil for Saint Gillem Perigan. He walked to the row of cushions on the floor, knelt before the coffin, and prayed. He prayed first for the departed Saint's soul, and then that one day God would grant him the strength and the courage shown by the man who had been one of the humblest the meekest among them.

All my Dreams

"Daddy?"

Sigg stopped at the door to his daughter's bedroom, turned, and looked back at her. She was tucked under her sheets, her head only just sticking out from above them. "Yes?" Sigg asked.

"Tomorrow you'll hear from the city, and they'll tell you about Geena and Ferin, right?" Those were her best friends.

"I will," Sigg said.

"I hope they're all right."

"I hope so, too. Try not to worry. Sleep tight."

"Good night, daddy."

"Good night, sweetheart."

Sigg closed the door gently. Down the hall, he saw the

flickering illumination go out from his own bedroom.

"Sigg?" His wife's voice called out from down the hall.

"Yes?"

"Don't forget the seeds."

"I won't. Thank you."

He heard her shuffle and roll in their bed. He wanted to join her, but there was the matter of the seeds to take care of first. He felt weary all over. Just this one more chore, he reminded himself. He walked into the kitchen where a moonbeam, bright and full, shot through the open window. A warm, wet summer breeze billowed in through it. Sigg took the pan of seeds from off the windowsill and shut the window tight. He took the pan to the kitchen table, retrieved a cloth from the cabinet, and spread the seeds out onto the towel, then rolled the towel up on itself. He then took the roll of towel to the kitchen basin, where he submerged it in the water, then returned it to the pan on the table.

Just as he pulled his hand away from the pan, a sharp pain struck his palm. The sensation shot up his arm and burst across his chest. He let out a gasp, clutched a hand to his heart, and, just as quickly as it had struck him, the pain diminished and was gone.

Sigg gulped. He took a few deep breaths and let his gaze move out to the fields beyond the window, their farm bathed in cool, white moonlight. He let the swaying of the tall grains relax him as he breathed in and out.

Nothing to worry about. He told himself repeatedly that nothing was wrong.

After a few minutes of standing and carefully breathing, he had convinced himself that he was fine.

He took a deep breath and walked down the hall to the washroom. The bathtub was empty, but a small washbasin lay full of clean water on the floor. He picked it up and set it on the stand in front of the looking glass on the wall. He took off his shirt and proceeded to wash his face and his arms, and his chest— His fingers ran over something on his chest. Something unusual.

Sigg walked to the wall and pulled back the cover from the window to let in the moonlight. He returned to the looking glass upon the wall and angled his body so that his chest was facing into the light. There, right between his pectorals, lay a cluster of white hairs, perhaps eight or ten of them, each about an inch long. He moved his hand over them again, and this time he felt a stinging sensation at the base of the hairs as he did so.

He frowned and had the thought that he would have to shave them off, but then, he noticed, the base of the hairs didn't look like follicles. The skin had cracked and reddened there. And also... Sigg looked closer, carefully in the looking glass. No? Yes... Yes. The hairs were getting longer and thicker before his eyes. What was happening? They no longer looked like hairs, but more like thick, white stalks, and they had begun to stretch out from his chest, upright. The tips were growing green, almost like an onion, and there, just before his spellbound, horrified eyes, one stalk burst open into a brilliant brown mushroom-cap, glistening with dots of perspiration under the glow of the moon. Other mushrooms began sprouting from all surfaces of the stalks, and a tangy, sulfurous smell stung his nostrils. Sigg wanted to claw them off but dared not. What was happening to him? He prayed to God not to let this invader eat his body from the inside out, but more of the stalks had sprouted from his chest and were bursting open into a putrid, brown fungal bloom, while the sulfur smell had begun to sting his nostrils and cause his eyes to water. He ran to the drawer to find the shaving shears, but slipped on a patch of water, stumbled, and fell, the stalk striking the ground and searing its contact point with his chest in the most horrific pain. He roared out a scream—

"Sigg!" Ele's voice came to his ear.

He found himself in his bed. He threw off the bedsheets and clutched at his chest. It was fine. Nothing was growing out of it.

"Sigg." Ele wrapped her arms around him. "You're all right."

His heart raced, and sweat dripped down from his forehead.

He panted and gulped.

"You're all right," Ele repeated.

He wrapped his arms around her and took a few deep breaths. "A nightmare," he said. "Sorry."

He pulled himself away, rolled up to a sitting position, and ran his hands over his chest again. Still normal. Nothing the matter. He stood.

"Where are you going?"

"I won't be able to sleep anymore tonight. Don't worry about me. Go back to sleep."

"Are you sure?"

"I'm sure. I'll be fine. Don't worry." No matter how many times he told her not to worry, she would. However, he also knew that she would, in fact, get back to sleep. And there was no way he would be able to get any more sleep after such a vision. "Sorry to wake you."

Sigg walked out of their bedroom, shut the door gently behind him, and went to listen at the door of Pnia's room.

Hearing nothing, he opened the door just a crack. There was just enough light in the room for him to make out the gentle rise and fall of his daughter's chest beneath her bedsheets. Sigg smiled, then closed the door and went to the kitchen.

The pan of soaking seeds lay just where he'd left it the night before, but he didn't dare touch it. Instead, he got himself a roll of bread from the pantry and went into his study. He lit the candles between bites of bread, then cleared his desk of all the transcripts, legal memoranda, supply requisitions, and military dispatches. He filed all those into their appropriate drawers and cabinets, then turned and found himself looking at the map of the City of Pannouk on the wall, the one he'd drawn three years ago for his book. His eyes strayed down to two large stacks of paper, each with a stone on top to keep them in place. He'd been meaning to work on it again when the king had ordered his family to the farm two years prior, but he'd found himself unable to summon the energy to do so. He felt the same way now.

Sigg turned his attention to the large, black cabinet at the back of the room, from which he hauled out two enormous crates, one of which was for last year, the other for this year. They contained reports from Pannouk's castle infirmary and provisional clinics, all of their weekly reports for the last year.

It had been a few weeks since he had brought all of his numbers up to date—and he also had the post-recovery reports now. He pulled a notebook from the crate for the current year, then began combing through the most recent reports and updating his calculations and observations.

He did the raw numbers first. The good news was that the number of new cases had been diminishing for the past three months, and that trend was continuing. The bad news was that Pannouk was a large city, and the new ill still numbered more than twenty-five per day. The mortality rate had been holding steady at about three in ten for over a year. The other seven would eventually recover, but—this is what he had asked for two weeks ago and hadn't had the chance to go over yet—in the doctors' opinion, were the 'recovered' patients truly recovering, or had the illness caused permanent damage?

He had received the deliveries of these reports over the last few weeks but had been too busy with the planting season. Now seemed like the perfect time to review them.

The more he read, the more alarmed he became. Some patients appeared to recover only to relapse and die weeks or months later. Some patients' symptoms improved beyond needing urgent medical care, but they continued to hack and wheeze in their homes. Reports from the castle were even more alarming. Amongst sages, monks, and nobles, many of the 'recovered' found that themselves no longer able to concentrate on reading the simplest texts for any duration of time and had trouble forming responses to relatively simple questions. Some young, virile athletes found themselves fatigued after even the most minor exertions. The first place lancer from the Pannouk Games four years prior, a man of merely twenty-five years, reported that, since his recovery from the plague, he was no longer able to walk more than a few hundred meters without becoming winded and requiring rest.

The list went on.

And the court wanted him to take his family back into the city.

Over his dead body.

No, no, and no, he decided. They would be staying on the farm, and that was that.

All at once, he realized that the light of the sun had begun peaking into the study's East-facing window. Sigg stood, and blew out all of the candles, then packed up his medical reports and returned them to the safety of the black cabinet. He then went to the kitchen, where he carefully moved the seeds back into the windowsill and began preparing for breakfast.

Ele was the first one down. "Good morning." She rubbed at her eyes as she headed into the washroom.

"Good morning," Sigg called back, his attention absorbed in frying eggs. He served them just as his wife sat down at the table and Pnia came scampering down the stairs and into the washroom herself.

"You didn't come back to bed," Ele said.

Sigg poured her tea and she grasped the cup. "I got some work done."

"Do you want to tell me about it?"

"The city is still disease-ridden."

She looked momentarily confused, then gave her head a quick shake and said, "I meant about your dream."

"Oh. That? That was nothing. Don't worry about it."

"You were screaming."

"I'm fine." Sigg served three portions of oatmeal into each of their places on the table. Pnia came scampering into the kitchen, took her place at the table, and reached out for her spoon.

Ele cleared her throat and Pnia stayed her hand. "What did we talk about?"

Pnia bit her lip. "Not until everyone is seated and we've said prayer," Pnia said guiltily.

"Thank you," Ele said.

Sigg took his seat, Pnia said the prayer—Ele correcting the

few words she misremembered, but Sigg was proud of how good at it she was getting—and then they began to eat.

"I had a visit from Gnora yesterday while you were in the fields," Ele said. Gnora was the wife of a printer. They'd been assigned the next farm over. "She said they'll be planning to open up the marketplace next month."

Sigg frowned. "The marketplace? Is that a good idea? So many people together."

Ele seemed surprised. "Is the disease not receding?"

"It is, but the infection rate is still quite high. It just seems risky."

"That's too bad," Ele said. "I was hoping to make my stew."

Pnia perked up at the word 'stew.' She looked at her father with wide eyes. "Can we, daddy? Oh, please, can we have it?"

"I'm sorry, darling. It's just not safe to go into the city right now. Perhaps when the plague has passed."

Ele was giving him the look. Sigg knew what it meant. She didn't even have to say it: "the plague *is* passing."

"We'll have your stew when it's safe again," Sigg said.

A knock resounded from the front hall.

Ele started to stand, but Sigg shot to his feet first. Fear surged within him. He'd already received two notices that they wanted him back at the castle. He had been expecting this. "I'll take care of it."

He folded his napkin, set it on his chair, and walked through the living room, down the front hall, where he came to the door. A slot in the top allowed him to peer outside. A man stood at his door, a bit on the short side, bearing a thin face atop a somewhat meager frame. Sigg didn't particularly like farm work, but he had to admit, he was in the best physical shape of his life.

"Hello?" Sigg called through the door.

"Yes," the man replied. "Is that Mr. Sigg Feyes?"

"Yes," Sigg replied.

"I am Junior Consul Ennak Ritt, serving his majesty Lord Pannouk. Might I come in?"

"I'm afraid not." Sigg searched his mind for an excuse and latched on to the first acceptable one. "I have had a mild cough recently, and so it is best if we speak through the door."

"I see." Ennak's tone fell. "That is unfortunate. I hope you feel better soon. This development somewhat invalidates my request, but I was wondering, for my report I will need to know if you received the two prior summons from the court requesting you return and resume your duties in the castle as scrivener."

"No. I have not received those." They were in the desk in his study. "Under the circumstances..."

"Yes, of course. I will explain in my report that you are unable to return at this time. I do very much hope that you make a speedy recovery. Good day."

Sigg opened the slot in the door and watched Ennak retreat down the path, shafts of wheat towering over him on either side. About halfway down the path, Ennak stopped, reached into his pocket, and withdrew something small. He brought it up in front of himself and seemed to be holding it and looking at it for quite some time. A notebook, maybe? Nearly a minute passed, and Sigg grew afraid that Ennak might come back, but, all at once, he put the thing back into his pocket and continued walking away. He reached the main road, turned left, and disappeared from sight, presumably heading back toward the city.

Sigg breathed a sigh of relief and returned to his family in the kitchen.

Sigg walked beside Ele and holding Pnia's hand. They walked down the main road, the one leading north from their farm into the city of Pannouk. Sigg and Ele had both wrapped bandanas around the bottom half of their heads, while Pnia wore a head wrap Ele had made for her out of a bright yellow and orange cloth, leftovers, she'd said, the last of the really nice fabric she'd taken with them when they'd left the city.

The farmers in the neighboring properties could be seen tending to their fields, looking over the wheat and barley. Sigg and Ele waved to them and their neighbors waved back.

The road itself was empty save for them, and Sigg was glad for it. Ill people made the air around them ill. That was what was believed, anyway. The official stance of the Church was that illness was caused by sin. But if that were so, why did the nobility quarantine themselves in the castle? If they were the most moral in the city, then quarantine would be pointless. Sick *people* spread disease regardless of their station or their virtue, Sigg had always argued. He'd incited much debate in the castle offices when he had worked there.

His family came to the gates of the city and stopped a good five paces from the guards, whose faces, Sigg could see, were also wrapped in cloth beneath their helmets. The guards opened the door and waved them through.

The streets were quiet, very quiet. Sounds could be heard from inside buildings, but only one or two passersby met them in the streets, first a young woman near the gates, and then a man more Sigg's age further in. Both nodded and weaved around Sigg's family, walking on the far side of the street while Sigg and his family kept to the other.

Sigg found himself feeling proud of his king and his countrymen. Everyone, it was clear, was following the king's orders dutifully.

"Look, daddy!" Pnia pointed in front of her.

They had come around a bend and the market came into view. Stalls had been set up with their canvas coverings of all different colors, some striped, others spotted, though each bore the crest of Pannouk on one pole of the stall, a medallion indicating they had paid the fee to set up their goods for sale there. Customers moved amongst the stalls, and while it was not nearly as crowded as Sigg remembered it, he noticed that only about half of them were wearing face coverings.

Sigg and Ele shared a look, but they proceeded cautiously forward. Pnia would be distraught and moody all day if Ele didn't make her stew. Sigg took a deep breath and led his family into the marketplace.

They proceeded to a greengrocer. Ele began putting vegetables in her basket while Sigg stood and held Pnia's hand.

"Can we look around?" Pnia asked.

"Not today."

An older woman without a face covering hovered into view on Sigg's right. She came up right next to him and began examining carrots. Sigg shot her an evil look and cleared his throat, but she ignored him, moving on from carrots to turnips.

Sigg grumbled and walked Pnia to the other side of the stall. He had only just taken up position there when a trio of unmasked teenagers blundered past them, walking quickly and passing far too closely, all while talking and laughing noisily.

"Do you mind?" Sigg called after them, but they ignored him. The woman at the other side of the stall began coughing. He looked around himself and realized the stall owners, and other customers were coughing too. He pulled Pnia toward Ele but was shocked to find his wife had doubled over, and was wheezing, gasping for air. Her basket of vegetables lay toppled on the ground.

"Mommy!" Pnia wailed and ran to her. Sigg started to move to her side as well but then noticed that the sounds of coughing were getting closer and louder. He turned and discovered hoards of unmasked citizens had appeared, all moving toward the family, coughing and hacking between laughs and shouts, spittle flying everywhere, and the horde encroaching relentlessly.

"Stay back!" Sigg shouted. Their eyes blank and spiritless, they marched toward him. They pushed over the stands of vegetables, and barrels of fruit that stood between them and the family of three. Pnia knelt on the ground holding her mother's arm, while Ele gasped and panted drawing painful sounding gasps for air.

Sigg turned and braced himself. He shouted at the mindless horde, "I said, *stay—*"

"*—back*!"

"Sigg!" Ele grasped his arm.

He scrambled up to a sitting position in his bed. Sweat rolled down his forehead.

Ele pulled herself up into a sitting position as well. "Two times in a row, Sigg. I'm worried about you."

"I'll be fine." Sigg found himself having to gulp to catch his breath, somewhat undercutting his statement, he felt.

Ele moved closer and wrapped her arm around him. "Tell

me about it."

"The three of us went into Pannouk, to the market, so you could get the things you needed for the stew. At first, everyone followed the rules and kept their distance. But then they started getting too close. And then they started coughing. You... got ill. And the others kept coming closer."

"Is it really so bad in the city still?"

"Twenty-five new cases every day."

"Is that so many?"

"It's more of a risk than I'm willing to take with you and Pnia."

"Or yourself?"

"Or myself. But you're the most important to me. If anything were to happen to either of you..." Sigg choked on his own words.

Ele held him tight. "Try to get some sleep. Okay?"

"Sure." Sigg lay back down and tried to sleep for perhaps thirty or forty minutes, but found himself simply rolling from side to side. Sick of not sleeping, he pulled himself up out of bed and went to his study, where he lit the candles and stared at the map of Pannouk on the wall. He found himself trying to recall the details in his mind—Could the irrigation ducts have been better placed? What about the sewage routes? Was clean water truly as far as it could be from wastewater?—All of those details had been lost to time. It had simply been too long since he'd worked on it. He would have to go over all his notes and refresh his mind, and that was the last thing he wanted to do now.

He went to the kitchen instead and looked out the window at the grain waving in the early morning wind. He opened the window so he could breathe in the fresh air. In a few months, it would be time for the harvest. His days would become full once more. However, if the king was trying to recall him, it meant there was another family ready and waiting to take his place and pick up that work for him. It seemed so simple. They could return to their house in the royal estate. Ele would spend a week cleaning and stocking up on things from the market. Pnia would be reunited with her best friends Geena and Ferin.

But what if they were one of the twenty-five? Every day a new chance, a new roll of the dice.

And what if it were himself? What would become of them if the plague claimed his own life? Another thought—what if they contracted the disease from him? The most horrific thought of all: What if he got them ill and one or both of them died while he survived? A truly terrifying prospect. No. Never. No order from any king could persuade him to take that risk.

He stood and watched the grain sway for some time, then returned to his study, pulled out the crates from the black cabinet, and analyzed medical records.

When the first morning sunlight found its way through his window, he packed up all his reports and went to make breakfast.

Pnia came down first that morning, stomping and grumbling all the way to the washroom.

"Everything all right?" Sigg called.

His daughter didn't respond.

"Pnia?"

The sounds of splashing water from the washroom, but nothing more.

"Pnia."

"I'm fine," she called out haughtily.

"How did you sleep?"

"Good."

Sigg busied himself with the breakfast preparations until she came out from the washroom. She pulled out the chair, sat herself down in it, crossed her arms, and glowered at her plateful of eggs and bowl of steaming oats.

Ele came downstairs and said good morning to them both, but hurried into the washroom.

"What's wrong, Pnia?" Sigg tried.

"I hate it here."

"We've talked about why we have to stay here."

"I don't care. I want to go back. I want to see my friends again."

"It's not safe just yet."

"When is it going to be safe?"

"I don't know. No one knows."

Pnia let out a sigh.

"I know it's hard, but we have to stick together. The important thing is that we have each other."

Ele came out from the washroom, and Sigg went to the counter to retrieve her cup of tea.

"Thank you," Ele said to Sigg as he set the tea down in front of her.

"Mommy?"

"Yes, sweetie?"

"When will the plague go away?"

"No one knows better than your father."

"Daddy says he doesn't know."

"I don't," Sigg confirmed.

"Then no one knows," Ele said. "Do you remember what your father's job was before we came here?"

Pnia's mood lightened. "A scribner, right?"

"That's right," Ele said. "A scrivener. And what does a

scrivener do?"

"Makes marks on paper all day!" Pnia giggled.

"Something like that." Sigg grinned.

"And your father had another assignment, too. Do you remember?"

"Uh huh. A, um, minster told Daddy to study all the people and parts of the city really hard, right?"

"That's right," Ele said. "It's very important work." It was difficult for Sigg to describe the look she gave him just then. It seemed to him pensive, perhaps even a bit fearful, but the primary emotion she exuded was worry.

"It's not more important than either of you." Sigg spoke the words quietly, then sat down in front of his own plate. He asked Pnia to say the prayer, and she did.

After they ate, Sigg went out to inspect the crops. He walked up and down the rows of wheat, looking for signs of disease or insect damage. Fortunately, everything seemed healthy. He had nearly completed when his gaze happened to drift to the road and his eyes locked with those of the person who had intruded into his field of vision—Junior Consul Ennak Ritt.

"Good morning, Mr. Feyes," Ennak said.

Inwardly, Sigg was cursing his luck, but outwardly he smiled.

Ennak stepped over the fence between the road and stalks of grain. "I'm glad to see you're feeling better."

Sigg held up his palm in warning and feigned a cough. "Please don't come any closer. I could be contagious."

Ennak came to a halt just inside the fence. "As you wish."

"What brings you back to the farm?"

"Just checking in to see if your condition has improved. I see you're at least well enough to tend the fields. That's a good sign, is it not?"

"So long as I'm here, it's my duty to the King, and I will see that it is done."

"Very loyal."

"Thank you."

An awkward silence fell, punctuated by intermittent breezes waving the rows of wheat. Sigg decided to interject another feigned cough.

Ennak released a sigh. "Is there no way to convince you to come back to your post as scrivener?"

"I am truly unwell," Sigg insisted.

"You are not unwell," Ennak responded sharply.

Sigg pursed his lips. "What will your report say?"

"If you do not agree to take your former post, I will have to report you in absentia."

"Please do not."

"You give me no choice."

Sigg had one option left. "Please come with me."

"Where?"

"To my study."

Sigg led him back over the fence, down the road to the gate, then down the path leading to the farmhouse. Once inside, Sigg brought Ennak into his study.

"Please shut the door," Sigg said.

Ennak did so, gazing over the map of Pannouk on the wall, which seemed to catch his eye as he latched the door.

Sigg pulled the two crates out from the black cabinet, and the two notebooks from them. He put them on his desk, then flipped them open to the relevant pages—the graphs he'd drawn charting cases and deaths over time. Prepared, Sigg turned to discover Ennak was still looking at the map.

"Did you draw this?" Ennak asked.

"That? Yes. I've prepared what I wanted to show you here."

Ennak managed to extract himself from the space before the map and came to Sigg's desk.

Sigg held up the notebooks for Ennak to see. "This chart is the case rate. You can see it peaked last winter and then has trended steadily downward. At our worst point last year, we had a peak of 120 new cases per day. Yesterday the number was 24. Then this graph is deaths. When we started it looked as if nearly half of patients died, but the recovery rate has been trending upward ever since cases peaked. Today, one in three ultimately dies of the plague. If the pattern continues, it will be one in four by the winter. And finally, morbidity. It seems many of those who have 'recovered' experience a panoply of life-impairing, albeit non-threatening, problems. I only have case reports so far, but a tally of those makes it appear as though one in ten of the recovered will have long-term symptoms. How long, we don't yet know."

Ennak gazed over the notebooks in amazement. "This is meticulous detail. You've collated all this yourself?"

"This is what I do," Sigg said. "Minister Plero of the Interior asked me eight years ago to begin collecting information on the workings of the city and find for him ways that Pannouk's people could be safer, stronger, and smarter. I started first with fortifications but then moved into other areas. When the plague hit, it made sense to simply apply the same skill to this."

Ennak blinked a few times. "So, every day, you get these reports, and you tabulate all the numbers and document your findings, with conclusions? You've been doing this for the plague every day for nearly two years now?"

Sigg nodded. "Yes. What of it?"

Ennak seemed aghast. "Have you wondered what such an exercise might be doing to *you*?"

"It's given me perspective. It's clearly unsafe to be within Pannouk still, especially near other people. I send a copy to Minister Plero every day, of course."

"Of course."

"Please don't make me take my family back into the city." Sigg had noticed a begging tone had slipped into his voice. He didn't like that, but this was his last chance. "I have a wife and especially my four-year-old daughter. If anything were to happen to them, I don't know what I'd do."

Ennak took a deep breath. "Here's what we'll do, Mr. Feyes. I will file a report today saying that you remained in bed, and I wasn't able to see you. However, I will come back tomorrow, and we will discuss a timeline for you coming back to the city. The Ministry is expecting bureaucratic operations in the castle to resume. For you to be absent for a significant period of time would undoubtedly put your situation there in jeopardy. I want you to think about how you want to proceed." Ennak moved toward the door, but his eye caught on the map again. "This is not the *actual* map of the city, is it? You've added ravines and you've split the river. And what is this?"

"Just an old idea." Sigg waved his hand. "I was exploring a concept I call sanitation. It seemed important before the plague, but not so much now." Looking at Ennak, Sigg got the impression that the man was stifling a much more profound reaction than he was willing to show. In Ennak's eyes, Sigg registered the slightest hint of shock. "Is everything all right?"

"Yes." Ennak regained his composure. "I will leave you to

think about what I've said."

Sigg showed him out of the farmhouse.

Sigg stood in the washroom looking at a cluster of white hairs that had appeared on his chest. He had no memory of having experienced this before, and his fear accumulated as he watched the hairs thicken and elongate into stalks, sprouting mushrooms. He scrambled backward to get his shaving shears but slipped on a puddle of water. The pain in his chest intensified and sulfur stung his nostrils.

"Mr. Feyes?"

Sigg looked up. Ennak Ritt had appeared in his washroom, towering over him.

"Mr. Feyes. Can you hear my voice?"

"Yes."

"You should calm down."

"But there's this—"

"What is there exactly?"

Sigg grabbed at his bare chest but found nothing there besides his skin. He felt all about, confused at the change, but his body was at it should have been.

Ennak smiled and extended a hand.

Sigg took it, and Ennak pulled him up. Sigg suddenly had the sensation that he had experienced this all before.

"Am I—?"

"You are dreaming, yes."

"Even now."

"Yes."

"So, you're just part of my dream."

Ennak shook his head. "No. But that's not what I'm here to talk to you about. Come with me." Ennak walked to the washroom door, where he turned and nodded impatiently behind him to Sigg, who still stood in the center of his washroom, quite befuddled at what was happening. "Are you coming?"

Sigg grabbed up his shirt off the washroom floor, wet though it now was, put it on, and followed Ennak through the kitchen, down the hall, and into Sigg's study. Ennak proceeded to light the room's candles.

"I am fudging the rules, Mr. Feyes."

"Rules?"

"I am not from your planet. Fifty years ago, there was an incident. Ytria was accidentally classified as 'unprotected' and since then your planet has been getting visitors of the wrong sort. We fixed the bookkeeping error earlier this year, but there remains the matter of cleaning up any residual damage. My job was to make sure that the plague was not caused by a visitor. We were particularly worried, given an incident in Seira twenty years ago."

It took Sigg many moments to process what Ennak had told him. After his mind had caught up, he gave his head a slight shake. "And? Was it?"

"No."

"Where did it come from then?"

"A chicken in the Pannouk marketplace."

Sigg blinked a few times. "A chicken."

"This will be one of the most informative dreams of your lifetime, Mr. Feyes. Most of the diseases you know are in fact caused by tiny creatures too small for the eye to see. We call them viruses. They live in the air on all inhabited planets. You are breathing in millions of them every minute. But the human body is a miraculous thing. Inside you are miniature defenders, also too small to see, who can learn how to destroy these viruses before they destroy you. The problem is that every so often, a virus that has, until now, only lived in chickens, will change itself in just the right way, and suddenly, it is capable of infecting humans. When human bodies have never seen a virus before, their defenders have a lot of learning to do in a very short time. Some people's will learn very quickly. Those will stay well or get well quickly if they contract the disease. Other people's will not. Those are the ones who expire."

It took Sigg many moments to process all of that. "Should we stop eating chicken?"

Ennak shook his head. "No. Remember, you can't avoid these things. Every breath of air brings untold numbers of them into your body. What you *can* do is follow basic common sense about cleanliness, and that brings me to your map." Ennak stretched out his hand toward the map of Pannouk on the wall. "You said this was part of a sanitation project. Tell me more about that."

"That's really nothing. I was just speculating about changes we could make to drain away human effluence safely and keep it away from the water for drinking and bathing."

"What brought about this idea?"

"Six years ago, after the king found an... unappealing substance on his steak one evening, he ordered that all the kitchen staff rinse their hands in the clean water of the stream before preparing any meal. I don't think they like doing it, as the stream is on the other side of the castle from the kitchen, but they have diligently done so ever since. When I started pulling medical reports into my project, I noticed something. When the king made his decree, incidences of loi, itri, and ado all fell sharply within the castle but remained the same in other parts of the city. The idea was to see if instituting a law for the rest of the city would have a similar effect. And I wanted to try separating waste from the water supply entirely. None of that matters anymore."

Ennak's eyes widened and he let out a small gasp. "Why do you think it doesn't matter?"

"What's the point in reducing the prevalence of loi, itri, and ado, if a new disease will just come around replace them? And this one seems to spread just by breathing, not by any particular contamination of food."

"Because every little bit you do makes you stronger. And not just you, but everyone you interact with. Hygiene *is* important. The reason I was surprised yesterday was because of how long it takes on other worlds for people to work out the connection between hygiene and health. It is important that you continue this work in the city, and that you tell others about it. You should make sure that someone doesn't have to learn this all over again after you're gone."

Anger welled up within Sigg. "There you go again, encouraging me back into the city. I don't care who sends the order, I am not endangering Ele and Pnia! I forbid it!"

Ennak straightened his back and looked Sigg directly in the eyes. "Pnia has already had it."

Sigg blinked a few times.

"I have an instrument that can tell me if an individual has ever been infected. You and Pnia both have. Ele has not."

Sigg's anger level remained steady, although his curiosity grew. "We were never ill."

"Some individuals contract the disease and experience no symptoms. This has been the case for you and your daughter."

Sigg's anger morphed into helplessness. He shook his head. "What do I do, then? Just take them back? Expose them some more?"

Ennak nodded. "Within reason. Wear your masks. Continue with the handwashing practice you have learned. Get more people to do the same. The more healthy people there are, the fewer there are who will spread the disease."

"But if something were to happen to Ele because of me—"

"Every day you live, there is risk. A spooked horse could trample you in the street. A misplaced brick could fall from a wall and crush your skull. Another kingdom could declare war. Somewhere between shutting oneself away from the world and engaging carelessly with it, there is a path of healthy behavior that minimizes your risk while keeping you engaged and active." Ennak gestured once more toward the map. "In your particular case, I fear that if you lose your position as scrivener over this, then you will lose contact with the Ministry, and this discovery of yours will vanish silently into history, perhaps requiring decades or even centuries to be learned anew. I urge you to let go of your obsession with this particular disease. Focus instead on how you keep yourself and those you love generally healthy."

Sigg shrugged and sighed. "I suppose you're right. You do seem to know more about how diseases work." Sigg tapped his foot. "How are you even allowed to tell me any of this?"

Ennak grinned. "I'll admit, I'm bending the rules a bit. But have you forgotten where we are?"

"We're in my study. What of it?"

Ennak's grin widened. He slowly raised a hand into the air, and then, after the passage of many moments of silence, snapped his fingers.

Sigg's eyelids flitted open. His face lay half-covered by his pillow. In the light of the morning sun streaming through the bedroom window, he could see that the bed lay empty. The sound and smell of frying eggs reached him, and he pulled himself up out of bed and meandered down the stairs and into the kitchen, yawning and stretching at the door.

Pnia sat already at the table. "Good morning!"

"Good morning. Looks like you're ready for breakfast."

Pnia bobbed her head up and down.

"Did you wash your hands?"

"Uhh..."

"You know that's important. Now go ahead and wash up, and I'll go when you're done."

Pnia scampered into the washroom, and Sigg moved to Ele, who stood over the stove frying the eggs. He put his hands on her hips and kissed her on the neck. "Good morning."

She smiled. "You seemed to sleep well. No bad dreams, I take it?"

Sigg thought about that a moment. "I don't remember. I suppose that's better than nightmares, at least."

Ele gave him a quick peck on the cheek and then returned to the eggs. "Breakfast will be ready in just a couple minutes."

Pnia flew out of the washroom and clambered into her seat at the table once more. Sigg smiled and went to the washroom to clean up. He found a fresh tub of water and set it on the stand in front of the looking glass. He took off his shirt, set it on the hook in the wall, then proceeded to wash his hands and face. When he was finished he found himself fixated on a point at the center of his chest. Nothing seemed to be amiss there, and he didn't feel anything in particular, but he ran his hand over it all the same. Was he still upset over the nightmare he'd had three nights prior, he wondered? It seemed as though there was something else associated with that memory now, but he couldn't place it. His brow furrowed, he put his shirt back on and joined his family in the kitchen.

Ele was just serving the eggs as he took his seat at the table. They said the prayer and then began eating.

"Was there anything new in the reports yesterday?" Ele asked.

Sigg had to think about that one a moment. "No." Another pause. He considered his next words carefully. "There is something else I need to tell you both, though. The King has reinstated the Ministry and he has recalled me to the city."

Pnia beamed, her mouth held agape with food in it.

"Chew, darling," Ele instructed. "With your mouth closed." Pnia proceeded to chomp happily.

Ele turned to Sigg. "Are you sure?"

Sigg let out a bit of a laugh. "No. Nothing is certain. We'll keep our faces wrapped still, and I want us all to be extra vigilant about washing and cleanliness."

Pnia swallowed. "Geena's daddy says that only bad people can get sick."

Sigg allowed himself a small snort. "I'd remind him that cleanliness is next to godliness." Not to mention that the clergy and Pannouk's holy army had been particularly hard hit by the disease, but Sigg decided that was not a topic for his daughter.

Ele took his hand in hers and looked directly into his eyes. "Are you sure?"

Sigg gave her half a smile. "No. But I think I'm okay with that now."

The Small Things

Yuptin was not more than a few miles out of Aemis when he first got the impression that someone was watching him. It was, however, an easy sensation to shake. The feel of his steed's steady gallop, the wind whistling in his ears, keeping his head low so as to keep underneath tree branches, and the forest hurtling by so fast that, yes, someone could have been watching him from a fixed position, he supposed, but he should have passed them and been long gone many times over already. With both his sword at his side and his crossbow against his back, who would dare? No, no one could be watching him.

The night wind was cold against his face, even though it was supposed to have been spring. Some spring. Even when the forest broke to reveal small farms, most lay dormant. Too many farmers unable to push a plow, sow seeds, or tend to a harvest, and not enough help even with the non-essential services in the city shut down. The numbers had told him it would be enough, and he hoped that it would work out.

Yuptin pushed his steed on faster. He didn't have time to think through the accuracy of his former estimates or to harbor irrational fears about a watcher who could keep up with his steed. He had an island to reach. Every last minute mattered.

Office of Infrastructure and Civil Service
Kingdom of Aemis

Dear Terrs,

It is official. The death toll today is double yesterday's, and the city infirmary has overflown. The people cough and wheeze, eventually growing unable to breathe at all. As we have suspected for some time, the early arrival of winter was only a reprieve, keeping away for some time the merchants who bring the contagion with them.

The Council has decided unanimously to put the castle under quarantine. We are making room for all staff in the guest quarters. None are to go into town. I need for you to make sure the army arranges for our food and water deliveries, although the delivery people are not themselves to set foot inside the castle. Send for Agita at once. She will need to be inside the grounds before sunset.

I am setting up a bed in my office and I will live there. It is certainly not optimal, but it's better than any other option available to me.

I worry about how I will practice the sword training now. I suppose that won't be possible. A great many things will not be possible for some time. I will miss our meals most of all.

Take care, my friend.

- Yuptin

—

Office of the Army Corp of Engineers
Kingdom of Aemis

Dear Yuptin,

Agita has arrived safely in the castle. We have holed ourselves up in a room in the northwest corner. I think the banquet hall lies on the other side of us, if I'm remembering correctly. Agita brought everything we will need. My sword is still at home, so I'm afraid that, although I have enough space, I'm unable to practice either. I tried shadow fencing, but without the heft of an actual sword it felt bizarre. I'm not sure it was even useful.

We may not be able to keep up our meals, but I will write. I should have time. I can't help but wonder what it will be like to do our jobs confined to these rooms. Everything will have to be accomplished via correspondence. I will make a point of writing to you every day, if only to break the tedium of reports and missives! Although, I suppose all of the con-

struction will be shut down. I can't think of anything so essential that it must continue. I wonder what we will even do all day. All the more reason to keep up the writing of these letters.

How do you think you will handle being so much indoors? I don't think I will like it much.

Your friend,
Terrs

Yuptin noted with a start that the moonlight had taken on a pinkish hue. The empty road and the forest on either side now lay suffused with an ominous blood color. He dared to look up into the sky, and sure enough, the moon had grown red and seemed to be growing redder by the minute.

He had seen a blood moon only once before in his life. The astronomers had been able to predict them with uncanny accuracy. The Minister of Science had showed him pages and pages of charts and calculations, none of which were even remotely comprehensible to him, but which the Minister insisted could tell him exactly when eclipses and blood moons would take place for the next hundred years.

There had been no blood moon on his record for this day. As Yuptin recalled, the next one was a few decades out.

A small laugh caught his ear, that of a child's. He looked into the forest rushing past on his left and saw nothing. Another laugh on his right. More little laughs, popping up from different directions, all while the moon grew redder and redder, a much deeper red than a normal blood moon. The landscape now appeared painted over with bright crimson swaths.

Yuptin grimaced and pushed his steed to go faster. He crouched down, his head drawing close to the horse's own. He kept his eyes on the road soaked in the blood red light while little, ominous bursts of laughter resounded in his ears.

He did not know how long he rode in this way, but all at once, the laughter ceased and the red hue faded, shifting slowly back to its normal bright white.

Yuptin pushed the steed on faster than ever.

Office of Infrastructure and Civil Service
Kingdom of Aemis

Dear Terrs,

I have given up practicing with the wooden sword. I keep bumping into my desk and my bed, and my neighbor below me started banging on my floor. It is frustrating to have come just far enough with the art to start to get good at it, only to have it all taken away by this damned disease.

I receive daily reports of the South Aemis Bridge. We are now sending in only two inspectors at a time. I estimate it will be another week before we know for certain, but I suspect we will simply have to close it down until we can assign a proper repair crew to it.

The reports about the spread of the plague continue to alarm me. The report we got from the Wellesper envoy last summer suggested that about a third of the city had fallen ill, and in Pannouk, at one point, over half the city's population was ill. It seems we are headed for much the same situation here.

I find these conditions extraordinarily frustrating. I prefer problems like the damaged bridge. The problem might be complex, but the solution is clear, and I have the tools with which to perform it. There is no clear solution for a plague, and we have no tools for mitigating it. It moves invisibly through the ether, striking people down at random. We know that sealing ourselves off helps, but to what degree, it is unclear.

Anyhow, I know of nothing else to report that would be of interest to the Corp. A few disgruntled engineers want to break quarantine, I hear, but I suppose you're on it.

- Yuptin

—

Office of the Army Corp of Engineers
Kingdom of Aemis

Dear Yuptin,

At least you have that wooden sword! I believe there is only the cellar below me, so I stomp all I like, but without something of actual weight in my hand, the practice can not really be considered that. I can't bring myself to do shadow fighting anymore. It just isn't the same.

I have seen the reports of the engineers who want to break quarantine. It has gotten Forz's attention. I'm on it. You should see the language in those *letters. I look forward to the days when I can talk to people in person again. Berating people on paper doesn't have the same impact, I suspect.*

Let me know if we decide to cordon off the bridge. I have gotten reports of physical altercations within the city, and I would like the army to be present when we erect the barriers. Also, I know that there are ministers opposed, but I believe we should order all engineers and soldiers to wear face masks. They may not be as good as the beaked contraptions worn by the doctors, but any amount of tainted miasma we keep out of people's lungs will be a benefit, in my opinion. Think about it, and let me know if you want to push for it. I have been encouraging Forz to do the same.

As for a "solution" to plague, it seems they exist, but can't be counted upon. We cannot train up a saint the same way we can a soldier. And neither can we count on metallic birds falling out of the sky, either.

Is it just me or have the portions of meat grown smaller? We don't have a looming food crisis, do we?

- Terrs

Yuptin rode on through the cold night, descending out of the forested valley in which the city lay into another narrow valley, this one taking him to his target for the evening, an inn near the border between Aemis and Qelem.

At the thought of the inn, he briefly allowed himself to imagine what Terrs would say about such a venture as he was planning. "You're going to set yourself up in a room at a public house, where who knows what sort will be at the bar drinking, and what sort have been in your room prior, and what sort the *innkeeper* has been interacting with and breathing around *all day every day*, in the middle of a *plague*? Are you out of your mind?"

Perhaps he was. He didn't even know if he would be allowed back into the castle when he returned. The chance that they would deny even a Minister was real, especially if the situation worsened in Aemis while he was away.

Multiple resounding cracks and crashes in the distance broke his thoughts and drew his attention upward. They seemed to have come from somewhere further down the road before him. Yuptin pulled at the reins, slowing but not stopping his steed, and as he rounded a curve in the road, he came upon a pile of trees, toppled and lying atop one another, blocking the way forward.

Yuptin slowed even more, gazing out in front of and then behind himself.

Once again, he got the distinct impression he was being watched. His body flooded with heat and his heart raced. All his weariness forgotten, he reached around to his back and retrieved his crossbow.

How, he wondered, had so many trees been ripped up so quickly? The crashes he'd heard had been that of multiple trees, probably all of these, falling at the same time. That didn't make any sense. The wind wasn't nearly strong enough for that. And why these trees and not any others? Regardless, all of his training warned him that this was exactly what a trap looked like.

Yuptin brought the horse just up the edge of the pile of tree trunks and dismounted, holding his crossbow out in front of him. Once again, he imagined what Terrs would say if he could witness Yuptin's imprudence now. "The road has been blocked so that you will be forced to dismount. Rounding either end of the log pile on foot, you will find yourself ambushed by highwaymen. Turn back to the city now in one swift, rounding curve."

He led the horse by the reins, sliding around the pile of tree trunks and scanning the forest for signs of movement—nothing. He heard only the slight huffing of the horse and the thumping of his own racing heart. He edged around the pile and only briefly caught a glimpse of the stumps of the fallen trees. He wondered at the fact that they appeared liquid, goopy, slightly melted. Could tree stumps really melt? The thought passed as he scanned over the forest, looking for any signs of movement.

He came finally around the pile, back to the center of the road, which lay deserted on this side as well. He scanned carefully around himself one final time, still not quite having shaken the feeling of being watched, before he launched himself onto the horse's back in one swift leap and galloped away from the scene as quickly as his steed could take him.

Office of Infrastructure and Civil Service
Kingdom of Aemis

Dear Terrs,

I appreciate your input. I know of the arguments against mask wearing. The civilians hate them and believe it makes them look absurd to their colleagues, but I support your proposal. You've always demonstrated a prudence about these matters that I admire. I look sometimes at my own habits and wonder if I should perhaps make more of an effort to live up to your example.

Thanks for the offer of a military escort for the South Aemis Bridge as well. I'll put that into the requisition. It seems equally prudent.

As for the food situation, the king is watching this closely. You're right that the meat portions have shrunk, but that is because, at our urging, the king signed an order to give over a portion of castle meat to those doctors and nurses working at the city infirmary. We will be just fine this year, but our attention in terms of food is turning to next year. Initial reports from scouts and tax collectors are that the plague is also hitting farmers, some of whom are preparing for planting, but many others have fallen ill, and their fields may go fallow if they do not recover. It is unlikely we will have a problem this year. It is the early months of next year that concern me. Spring is just around the corner. We are considering all of our options. I like the idea of shutting down non-essential services in the city and sending those workers out to the farms. City folk won't like farm labor, but since the alternative is starvation, we should be able to persuade them.

A part of your last letter confused me. A metallic bird? Is this another of the tall tales like the Unholy Night? By all means, please do tell. I could use a good story right now.

- Yuptin

—

Office of the Army Corp of Engineers
Kingdom of Aemis

Dear Yuptin,

It's good to know about the food situation. Thanks for

that. And no problem on the military escort. We have to keep everyone safe, especially those engaged in public safety measures.

So, you haven't heard of the metallic bird of Reodis? This will be fun.

One day, a metallic bird the size of a castle dropped out of the sky and landed in the center of Reodis, right in the middle of the town square. Two creatures emerged from it, a demon and an angel. The demon filled the island with strange, toxic devices—obelisks that caused people's skin to grow red and peel away if they drew near them, and metallic spiderwebs in trees that set people on fire if they drew too close. The angel rallied the population of Reodis against the demon, and they eventually drove it away and destroyed its evil creations. To reward the people of Reodis for their holy efforts, the angel granted them numerous miraculous gifts. He constructed a kind of house with all-glass walls, inside of which it would constantly be summer, regardless of the season outdoors, so that the inhabitants of the island could grow food for themselves year-round. He also created for them a vast supply of medicines of all varieties, most of which had been unheard of anywhere in Glissia, or in the known world for that matter. Even now, although the metallic bird has flown off away from the island, the angel is present and still guards the island against those who would steal from them.

I have wondered what the people of Reodis themselves think of this story. It's getting quite some circulation. I heard it from one of the engineers over drinks. I'm sure they're telling it all over Glissia. You'd think someone from the court of Fobbyn would have at least gone to investigate the island, though, especially with a claim as grand as an all-glass house where it's always summer inside.

- Terrs

Yuptin and his horse were both exhausted when they broke through the tree line and out onto the rolling hills that spread out into Eastern Qelem. He spotted the Geraki river, a grayish flow, emerging from the trees far to his right and splashing down between the hills. He would be heading away from it, eastward, down the main trade route through Daicis.

Right now, however, he needed some sleep. Any sleep. Even sleep at a country inn would do. His imagining of Terrs's warning of the danger rang out in his mind, but his joints were too stiff and his eyes too bleary to do anything about it. He could even feel the way his horse had slowed, still running, but not as swiftly, and he was breathing more heavily, snorting more. They both needed a break.

Yuptin arrived at the inn at dawn. It was a small affair, and no other horses were tied up outside. However, smoke was rising out of the chimney, and there was a candle in the window. He said a small prayer in thanks that the business was operational and tied up his steed, who seemed happy to have come to a halt. Yuptin took the saddlebags off the horse and pushed the door to the inn open.

The innkeeper was a tall, portly man with a round face and bright eyes. The bar was empty, as were the tables. There was only the innkeeper at the front desk and a woman behind the bar. The innkeeper met Yuptin's gaze sternly at first, then noticed the seal of Aemis of Yuptin's armor.

"Milord," the innkeeper said as Yuptin shut the door. "What can I do for you?"

"A room," Yuptin said. "Just four hours. That's all I need."

The innkeeper shot a look at the woman behind the counter, and she promptly ran off upstairs. All at once, a clattering sounded from behind Yuptin. He turned and found the candle had fallen from the windowsill and was now rolling across the floor, leaving a trail of blue wax behind it. Yuptin scrambled to pick it up.

The innkeeper scowled. "Do be careful! Milord."

Yuptin replaced the candle. "I was nowhere near the window. I'm not sure how that happened."

The innkeeper's frown flattened out and he seemed to be paging through a book. "That will be six azmi."

Yuptin fished out the money from his coin purse and handed it over to the innkeeper, who began writing in a ledger. While he did so, Yuptin began thinking of the warm bed and lying beneath layers of blankets. He recalled the urgency and import of his mission but realized also that without some sleep, he could come to a bad end before ever reaching his destination. Four hours, he promised himself, and no more.

The innkeeper turned around to face an array of boxes attached to the wall. He seemed to be scanning for one in particular. All at once, a scattering, crunching sound crackled out from the innkeeper's desk.

The innkeeper turned and scanned the area behind the counter from where the noise had erupted. "My ledger!" The innkeeper bunched up his face. "What is this? Are you looking for a free night? Some kind of bribe? Is that it? I don't take kindly to people wanting something for nothing, even Ministers, and you can even tell the king that. I don't care!"

Yuptin held up a hand. "Good sir, I'm afraid there's been a misunderstanding. I didn't touch—"

Glass beer steins at the vacant counter began hurtling themselves up off their resting places and exploding on contact with the floor. The whole inn shook a bit. Then a bit more. Yuptin and innkeeper gazed about, silent, eyes alert.

Their gazes met.

"I'll be going," Yuptin said.

The innkeeper nodded.

Yuptin picked up all of his things and rushed out of the inn. The loss of the six azmi perturbed him, but not as much as the events he had just witnessed. The morning air was cold against his face, and he realized again just how tired he was. His horse whined as Yuptin reattached the saddlebags.

"I know," Yuptin said. "I don't want to either. But there's no choice. We won't run, okay?" He stroked the horse's neck a few times for reassurance. He then pulled himself up onto its back and began away at a quick walk through the chill morning, exhausted and spent, toward the Aemis-Qelem border crossing.

Office of Infrastructure and Civil Service
Kingdom of Aemis

Dear Terrs,

I've taken up practice with the wooden sword again. I make sure to do so in the very middle of the day. My neighbor banged on my floor a few more times last week, but I haven't heard a peep from him since. The middle of the day is a strange time to exercise, but it's the least likely to interfere with my neighbor's sleep. I have to do something.

My inquiries into the tall tale of Reodis have all come back. You are not the first person to wonder if there might be something to the healing agents of the tale. The Foreign Minister has a few connections in Fobbyn. He said the first thing King Fobbyn did was order an expedition to Reodis. They prepared three times for the expedition, but on the morning of each, they found the ship they were to use sinking in the harbor before anyone could board it. After the third time, the king canceled the expedition.

Apparently, the ship ferrying civilians to the island still runs, but the only people who seem to go there are residents returning from trips to the mainland. Of course, with the plague, those are few and far between.

The Foreign Minister wrote that he wasn't certain if it was a true tale from Fobbyn or another tall tale. It certainly is intriguing regardless.

How are you doing these days? The civil service seems to be managing. I know of two cases of plague among the ranks, but that is all. I think the masks are helping.

- Yuptin

—

Office of the Army Corp of Engineers
Kingdom of Aemis

Dear Yuptin,

Now that the bridge is closed off, there's not much to do. I'm mostly just keeping in contact with all the leaders, making sure that everyone's abiding by the quarantine. Still a few murmurs here and there about people violating the rules, trying to meet up with acquaintances or have meals together. I personally will never understand it. My "normal" life isn't worth getting sick over under the best of circumstances, to say nothing of a disease like this plague.

Anyhow, here in the northwest wing, things are well. Agita had some painting supplies delivered, and also some books on artistic forms. She's been practicing, and I like her work quite a bit, but I'm probably biased. Perhaps when this is over we'll send some samples of what she's done off to the Delz Academy and see what comes of it. I've always told you she has a promising career ahead of her. I envy the way she glides so easily between different fields of study.

Your story about the ships does seem odd. Did they ever find out who did that? How much does the Foreign Minister trust these contacts of his from Fobbyn?

- Terrs

Yuptin was struggling to keep his eyes open by the time he reached the Aemis-Qelem border, and the air seemed to be struggling to grow warmer despite the sun's steady ascent. He spotted some farmers coming out to tend to the plowing and planting, but many farms lay fallow here as well.

The crossing went quickly enough. The guards spotted Yuptin's ministerial crest and only briefly scanned his papers before allowing him through. The road drew close to the Geraki River, here a great torrent of surging water, but its sound seemed distant. He followed it for a few hours before turning away from it at the point where it veered south, while he continued to the east.

At noon, able to keep his eyes open no longer, he dismounted, tied his steed up to a nearby farm fence, sat down against it himself, and held his crossbow in his lap, just at the ready. He drifted off almost immediately.

When he awoke, the sun had drawn lower, but not too low. He'd been out for perhaps three hours. Yuptin checked all his bags—good, everything was present and accounted for—and hopped aboard his horse, who now seemed in much better spirits. They rode at a good pace, passing more farms dotting the rolling, brown fields.

As the sun fell behind him, swathing the hills in burnt yellow and orange hues, he spotted the Qelem-Daicis border station. The inn on the Daicis side, he had heard, was well run, and he hoped that also meant clean. He had just begun to imagine a soft bed to sleep in when a female voice interrupted his thoughts.

"You will not pass through this border crossing."

Yuptin yanked the horse's reins, and the horse scampered to a halt and whinnied loudly in complaint. A white horse carrying a woman draped in red clothing of a fabric and make Yuptin had never seen before, had appeared immediately at his right, and she continued down the road some ways before rounding and coming back down the road to face him. She stood tall atop her steed and glared at him imperiously.

"State your name," Yuptin demanded.

"Rose," she said. "No one from the kingdoms is to set foot on Reodis. No one."

"You... changed the moon in the forest. And made me hear all that laughter. And you collapsed the trees. And shook the inn at the edge of Aemis."

Rose didn't respond. "You will not cross into Daicis. Go back to Aemis, and I will leave you alone."

Yuptin frowned and drew forth his crossbow. He checked the arrow, cocked the latch, and pointed it at Rose. "No."

Rose spread her arms wide. "By all means. Fire."

"I do not want to kill you."

"You can't."

Yuptin exhaled deeply. "I am going to Reodis."

"And I will do everything I can to stop you. I have done far more than sink three ships."

Yuptin attached the crossbow back into the fittings on the back of his armor. "I don't have any quarrel with you."

"Nor I with you. But no one from the mainland must visit Reodis until the plague has passed."

"Why?"

"The things on Reodis must stay on Reodis."

"Then they do have medicines there?"

Rose said nothing. Her expression remained flat.

Yuptin whipped the reins of his horse, and it proceeded forward, trotting past Rose atop her white stallion. She took up alongside him, meeting his pace. "Do you not think it selfish what you're doing? Why should the Kingdom of Aemis alone receive a cure when so many others elsewhere will still suffer?"

"I could ask you the same thing. Why should Reodis alone benefit from their cache of remedies?"

"Because on an island I can prevent those substances from being abused and exploited. Those substances can do much more than simply cure diseases."

Yuptin let that one sit for a few paces. "I have thought a great deal about whether or not my actions are selfish. I do not think they are. And you have perhaps misinterpreted my intent." He whipped the reins again and his steed charged forward. Rose and her white horse, he noticed, did not pursue him. That was probably for the best.

He rode onward toward the darkening sky. By the time he came to the border crossing station, he was feeling tired again. He had slept, after all, only three hours. He approached the guards in the usual manner. It had grown dark, and the guards carried torches. Yuptin could just make out the lights of the inn on the other side of the crossing. It looked inviting, and the thought of the warm bed filled him renewed hope that he and his horse might soon be able to return to the swift pace they had begun this journey with.

To his surprise, when the guards approached him, two drew swords and the other a crossbow, their faces twisted up in anger and fear.

Yuptin held up his hands, confused. "Good sirs! Put down your weapons. Can you not see this crest? I am Minister of Infrastructure and Civil Services for the Kingdom of Aemis."

"Get on now!" The guard holding the crossbow waved it back toward the road in the direction Yuptin had arrived from.

Rose's voice resounded in his ear as though she stood next to him, but he saw nothing beside him. "I have made you appear to them as a leper. They cannot see your crest."

Yuptin pursed his lips, annoyed. "I'm moving away now. Okay?"

He performed the unusual twisting movement with the reins, not something he'd done often at all, and the horse retreated slowly backward. The guards watched him for some time, but eventually retreated into their shed, still watching him, and he continued moving backward until they seemed to have continued to go about their business.

With an irritated grunt, he dismounted and walked down the road back the way he'd come, searching the road's southern edge until he found a gap in the fence. He found one soon enough, guided his horse through it, and then proceeded to head south across the dark field, weaving in between the lights of farmhouses.

Unfortunately for Rose, Yuptin's best friend was an army engineer, and as such, he possessed topographical and geological surveys spanning Central Glissa. One such map had been of the old roads, the ones that had been used hundreds of years ago before the modern trade routes. The old route from Qelem into Daicis had lain south of the current crossing and might just be unguarded since farmland now lay around it for miles on all sides.

Yuptin was weary, and his muscles ached all over from days of riding with little sleep, but he could not let up now. He had meant every word he had said to Rose.

Office of Infrastructure and Civil Service
Kingdom of Aemis

Dear Terrs,

Oh, you know the Foreign Minister. He takes all this stuff with a grain of salt. He says you can count on everything passing through at least three layers of bureaucracy before it gets to us, leaving us to peel away at least three layers of embellishment, usually more. I wouldn't be surprised if this story about Reodis is just another iteration of that Unholy Night story. That one we should probably more rightly be calling a folk legend at this point than a simple folk tale.

I'm missing our swordfighting practice badly. My neighbor banged on the floor again at me this afternoon.

Also, you should know that cases are on the rise again. A report was sent around to all the members of the Council that the infirmary has overflown once more. And with spring arriving, we get to worry about food again. The king will be issuing a decree to send city folk away from the non-essential trade jobs and out to the farms that have been hit by the plague. The last thing we need is starvation on top of disease.

I hope you're doing well, my friend. Take care. All my best to Agita.

- Yuptin

—

Office of the Army Corp of Engineers
Kingdom of Aemis

Dear Yuptin,

Thanks for the heads up on the upcoming decree. I'll prepare the corp. Engineers sure can be stubborn. We found out a group of them had been going out of the city every day to go to a pub that has remained open in defiance of the king's closure order. Can you believe it? Why on Ytria would anyone think that a good idea under these conditions? Needless to say, we're taking a firm hand.

I miss practice, too. I run through the form in my mind now, hoping that will somehow help.

I'm in good spirits, but Agita's painting has stalled. She's reading more, saying it might jog some ideas. We've been talking about different things she might try next. She'll be producing amazing stuff again soon, I'm sure.

- Terrs

Yuptin trudged, bleary eyed and utterly sore, through the fields, weaving around the peripheries of farmhouses, until he was certain that he'd traveled sufficiently east so as to be in Daicis. He plodded onward, focusing all his energy on moving his feet forward, one after the other. His horse seemed to have entered a similar state of ambulatory torpor, letting out a weak whinny every so often.

He reminded himself of two things. The first was that his current misery was nothing compared to what the plague victims were suffering. The second was the reason he had set out on this journey in the first place. The second, particularly, was enough for him. He pulled his feet forward, one over the other, heading due east, until finally, finally, at a time that must have been around one or two in the morning, he came to the modern trade road, which veered south toward Daicis Port.

Yuptin clambered up onto his horse, and it was only then that he remembered what Rose had done, and that now he could not go through the port, but would have to find a way to ford the Kampia river and cross into Fobbyn.

The sun eventually rose, and through his now blurry vision, he came over a rise. He spotted Daicis Port and the wide road stretching out up the hills toward the City of Daicis with its tall castle at the center some five miles inland. Yuptin jerked the reins, bringing the horse to a halt, tied it up at the fence beside the road, sat down with his crossbow ready before him, and only just saw his steed set itself down on the ground as well before Yuptin himself drifted off to slumber.

He awoke to a commotion. The sun of near midday shone down on him, and his horse was neighing. The retreating backs of what looked to be a band of farmhands disappeared, running as fast as they could away from him. Rose loomed atop her white stallion. She looked down at him, her expression sad. Did he sense pity in her eyes?

"They tried to rob you, since you look like a leper. They probably thought you had stolen the horse. I scared them off."

"Thank you." Yuptin dragged himself to a stance. "I thought you were doing everything you could to hinder my journey."

"If you run out of food and water, you'll die. I don't want you dead. I want you to turn around. Although I'm beginning to wonder why I bother. The stress your immune system must be under right now..." Rose shook her head.

Yuptin raised an eyebrow. "Immune system?"

Rose merely stared at him, her expression flat.

"Are you helping me or hindering me, then?"

"You are an odd one, Minister Boeth. What you mentioned yesterday, that I had misinterpreted your intentions, got me looking through your letters. All of them. Not just the one you sent to your king."

Yuptin bunched up his face. "How did you get my letters?"

"It doesn't matter." Rose held up a hand. "I have turned

back grieving spouses, grieving parents, grieving sons and daughters, and also a fourth category, which I had pegged you for: kings and ministers who want a cure for their people exclusively. It looks noble on the surface, but the deeper intent is to horde access to the medication so they can solidify their power base. Not, in fact, very noble. Your letters surprised me. All this... Is it for just the two of them, then?"

Yuptin nodded.

Rose nodded toward Yuptin's horse. "Follow me. I've removed your disguise. You can tell me more about it on the way to Daicis Port."

Office of Infrastructure and Civil Service
Kingdom of Aemis

Dear Terrs,

I looked at the calendar today. Have we really been doing this for four months now? I had the realization that at the end of this year, I will have to make my own calendar out of scrap paper, for I doubt we can justify spinning up the printers to the task of preparing new calendars at a time like this. With the endless stream of correspondence and the same room around me day after day, a torpor of monotony is setting in. I yearn to get out of this room, even though I know that is unwise. I have some sympathy for those who flout quarantine, even as I recognize their misbehavior. I recognize that desire within myself.

Your last few letters have been exclusively about work. How are you? Still thinking about taking a break once this is all over? Assuming the Delzian tournaments start up again, we could perhaps all go there. It would be a good opportunity for Agita to visit the art academy, and if we can practice enough in time we might even have a few sword matches ourselves by then. What do you say?

The Foreign Minister reported the first good news from abroad. Pannouk is finally starting to see their infirmaries empty out. They report, however, that about twenty percent of their population has died and nearly seventy percent was ill but recovered. Those are sobering numbers. However, it has now been with them for a full three years. *I can't imagine doing this for another six months, let alone thirty-two. Somehow we will find a way.*

I have nothing else to report from the Council. Just trying to get the farms in a good place to support us through the next harvest.

- Yuptin

—

Office of the Army Corp of Engineers
Kingdom of Aemis

Dear Yuptin,

Thanks for the update from the Council. There's not much going on in the corp. We now have a plan for fixing the South Aemis Bridge that involves only two engineers on site at any given time. It will take a full two years instead of three months, but it will get done. We'll insist they wear masks and use the army to keep others away. It should work, assuming the Council approves.

I have other news. Agita has developed a cough. It started three days ago, and it has been getting worse. So far, I feel fine, but since I've been living in the same room with her... Well, it seems absurd to suppose that I have not contracted the disease as well. We are looking after one another, and we are making sure that those bringing our food are moving well away from the door before we retrieve it. I have told Forz about this. He should be the only one who knows, besides, I presume, the King. I do not know what to make of it, as we have not left quarantine in these four months, but somehow the plague has found its way to us.

- Terrs

"The real kicker," Yuptin said, as he rode at a slow trot beside Rose, "was that I had broken quarantine. Four times. Two weeks ago I got so sick of my office that I decided to go deliver the day's missives and reports around to the various other council members' rooms myself. I never left the castle and I wore a mask the whole time, so in terms of the severity of the breach, it was pretty mild. I remember it feeling so good to finally be out of that small, dreary office."

"So, when Terrs told you about him and Agita you felt guilty?"

"A bit of that, yes. And anger at the cold, unfair world, infecting two people who had done more than anyone else to keep themselves and others safe. But it was also much more than that. I was stunned by how deeply I was affected. It was not the first time I had known someone who had gotten the plague. Four members of the civil service total had fallen ill by the time I left. And also, there was a letter from a woman I had been engaged to. We had broken it off, but we're still on speaking terms. The letter was about many other things, but she had also mentioned that she had caught the plague. I was not callous to this. In fact, I gave her my best regards and wished her well. My point is that I had handled it. It had been easy. But with Terrs... I still have trouble putting this into words. I find it better if I can back up. Are you familiar with the philosopher Evrys?"

Rose shook her head.

"He had a particular definition of love that is hard for most people to grasp. Most people conceive of love in terms of procreation—the erotic impulse. Evrys imagined something greater for love. Real love, to him, was the desire to see another person thrive, to want them to be well and happy, not merely 'aroused,' but really and truly happy—and oneself deriving a similar happiness from seeing the other person thrive. Such love need not even have a sexual component. One could have such love for a parent, a child, a sibling... or even a friend."

Rose nodded her head slowly.

"Evrys used grand examples to make his point—the king who is able to be a benevolent ruler because he loves his subjects, the soldier who is able to fight harder and better because he loves his comrades in arms. I'd read Evrys as a young person, like most ministers, and so I suppose I had always been thinking of this high and noble love as something that, if I ever found myself feeling it, would be many orders of magnitude more important than my one, insignificant life. There would be a great war or some powerful test of my leadership. True camaraderie with a fellow minister snuck up on me. Rather than one big thing, it invaded my life through a myriad of small things—sword fighting practice, to take just one. Or last year at the Harvest Festival when he and I took the two largest roasts and stuffed ourselves silly."

They had begun descending, the road veering toward the coastline and skirting rocky cliffs. The port drew nearer. They were perhaps only ten minutes away from it now.

"But that still doesn't explain why a man like you runs off chasing tall tales. You admitted yourself in your letters that they'd been embellished many times over."

Yuptin sighed. "A thing about me, Rose, is that I chase solutions. It is why King Aemis has told me he selected me for my role. I love solving problems. The South Aemis Bridge is in disrepair? I engage the Army Corp of Engineering. The farms aren't going to be staffed well enough to grow our food? I will move people around so we all have enough to eat. Terrs and his wife being sick with the plague is the most horrifying problem I have ever encountered. It has no solution. At least, it did not until I remembered our earlier correspondence."

"I saw that. Terrs fed you the story about Reodis. It's a remarkably persistent story."

"Even now, I would tear this entire world apart if it meant that I could guarantee Terrs's and Agita's well-being. I could not sit around and be inactive. I had to do *something*. Even if the medicine doesn't work or doesn't exist, I don't care. I can't just— sit around being one-third as effective at my job while the two of them are going through this! I won't!"

Rose stopped her horse, and Yuptin, realizing she had done so, stopped his as well. She seemed to be glaring at him, though it was hard to tell with the evening sun behind her, casting her in silhouette. Yuptin squinted.

"You told me you had thought through whether or not

your actions were selfish."

"Yes."

"I think you missed something."

"Oh?"

Rose nodded. "So far on your journey, you've interacted with at least six people who could be contagious. You've run yourself ragged, making yourself more prone to illness. Now give Terrs some credit and think about how *he* would feel if *you* were to fall ill. I suppose you could tell me that this Evrys intended the highest love to move in a single direction, but I don't honestly think you believe that. You can't change what will happen to Terrs and Agita. Focus on what you can change. When Terrs gets well, what will be the state of his kingdom's infrastructure? Will his king have all the information he needs to make the best decisions?"

Yuptin shook his head released a heavy sigh. "You're right, of course. I don't suppose you have any idea how maddening it is to be confined to a small, cramped space for months on end?"

Rose remained nonplussed. "We have spaceships. Yes, I'm quite familiar."

Yuptin raised an eyebrow. "None of those here."

Rose grinned wryly. She seemed to be thinking something over just then. Yuptin waited patiently, and finally Rose spoke. "I will tell you this. There are many medications on Reodis. None of them is going to be effective against the plague. They *had* one that was, but they used it all up when merchants brought the disease to their island. They never had much of it."

Yuptin crossed his arms. "Then why work so hard to keep people away?"

"We are worried about visitors finding the stuff that has

nothing to do with the plague. Imagine, if you will, a weapon that can debilitate your enemy's armies by inflicting them with a terrible, contagious disease, while you grant your citizens and soldiers immunity."

"That sounds awful."

"Your societies are not yet ready to handle biological warfare. Most of the societies up there aren't either, despite possessing the weapons." Rose nodded toward the sky. The sun had dipped behind the Western mountains and it was easier to see her now. A halo of orange and red light seemed to be about her head, the last rays of the setting sun.

"How did such things arrive on Reodis?"

Rose shook her head. "A mistake. One of many mistakes over the last fifty years."

"Then the Unholy Night...?"

Rose pursed her lips and nodded. "And more. Those stories would take too long to tell." She turned her horse back up toward the hill. "Are you coming? It would be better for your health if you don't stay at inns. I can keep watch over you and your steed when sleeping outdoors. We want you to be well when you get back to Aemis."

Yuptin looked out once more toward Daicis Port. From his position, he was just elevated enough to see the road reaching out to the south and winding away toward the Kingdom of Fobbyn, from where boats set sail for the island of Reodis.

"Thank you," Yuptin said. "I appreciate the offer."

He turned his steed and they began back up the cliffside road, alongside Rose's white horse and away from the port, at a trot.

Office of Infrastructure and Civil Service

Kingdom of Aemis

Dear Terrs,

I will be going away for some time. By the time you read this message, I will be many miles away. I do not take this action idly or without forethought. I have thought about this decision a great deal. I have another letter out to Dester deputizing him for my post while I am away, and another to the king, explaining my actions. He may feel it fit to communicate them to you, and that is why I must write what I will write next, even though such words have never come easily to me, and I struggle now even under these circumstances.

Your friendship is valuable to me, Terrs. Very much so.

You and Agita will get through this. You are strong and healthy people. You will both fight this plague bravely, and I am sure you will both emerge victorious. I find I must fight as well. Eat well and rest often. Do everything the doctors advise.

I hope to be back very soon. You will hear from me the moment I return.

Your friend,
Yuptin Boeth

Author's Afterword

In 2015, I was attending a Seattle writing group regularly every weekend. On one such occasion, our group arrived, took up our usual tables, and at once started being berated by a man at a nearby table. Normally, I would have spent the first ten minutes of such a writing group thinking about what to write, but that day the man's absurdly anti-social behavior became the basis for a story that came spilling out of me, eventually becoming "We Were Here First." The idea was fairly simple: What if a man such as our verbal assailant found himself the victim of his same behavior, but from perpetrators much more powerful than himself? And so I invented an extrapolation. Who would have power over a straight male knight in a medieval world? Clearly, someone more technologically powerful would have to find their way to him.

I published the story in my second short story collection, *Transmutations of Fire and Void* the next year, and there it remained for four years, an interesting little thing I had put together and no more.

In 2020, the coronavirus pandemic happened, and I suddenly found myself with much more free time to write. I decided to reinstate my practice of writing a short story every weekend. For the first few weekends, each new story was set in its own world, but on June 6, I decided to set that week's story on the planet I'd created for "We Were Here First." As I recall, I wanted to write about how a medieval society had dealt with a novel contagion, and so the medieval world of that original story came readily to mind. That first draft became "One's Own Medicine."

Throughout June and July, I continued to explore the Glissian continent of Ytria. I worked out the physical relationships of the myriad kingdoms by drawing myself a map and decided upon some shared features—where the universities were, where the plague had originated, etc. After July, the writing spree petered out. However, I did end up writing two more stories for the collection. After getting only four hours of sleep one night in early September due to a particularly terrifying nightmare, my friend Aaron Ramos encouraged me to write about that dream, and "All My Dreams" became the result. Just after Christmas, I started thinking about inverting the situation of the plague. What if it was the technological civilization that had a pandemic and the medieval people somehow possessed the cure? "Adaptive Response" is my own personal favorite of all the Ytria stories. I love the way that the inhabitant of the medieval world is ultimately able to demonstrate moral, ethical and even technical superiority in relation to the people who presume themselves to be "more advanced" than he is.

Throughout working on these stories, I benefited from the feedback from Christopher Kulp and Aaron Ramos. As always, my husband Alex is an endless source of inspiration and support, particularly so during 2020, when we found ourselves in lockdown and both going slightly mad with cabin fever. At least we were able to do so together. He is perhaps the only person I can imagine myself being locked up with to good effect rather than ill.

As I write this afterword, the coronavirus pandemic is receding. By the time this book reaches print, the dedication will be out of date. My friend Jon Luke and I have, in fact, been boxing again for about two months now. Those words were written before the results of vaccine clinical trials had been published, during a time when no one knew how long we might have to seal ourselves off from one another. I think the Ytria stories came to me during the pandemic, because the big lesson for me was that, despite all our modern technological prowess, it is how we treat one other that matters. If these chronicles have any unifying theme, it is that at the chaotic intersection of medieval and spacefaring, human beings on both sides of that divide must care about the outcomes of others as well as themselves.

I do not know if there will be any more stories set on Ytria. I certainly won't rule it out. I will, though, borrow a line from Ursula K. Le Guin. If Ytria's people do happen to speak to me again, I promise I'll be there to listen.

Production Dates

We Were Here First	July 26, 2015
One's Own Medicine	June 6, 2020
Ergo Sum	June 27, 2020
A Just War	July 4, 2020
Habitat	July 5, 2020
The Roots and the Spiderweb	July 11, 2020
The Small Things	July 18, 2020
All My Dreams	September 5, 2020
Adaptive Response	December 26, 2020

www.ingramcontent.com/pod-product-compliance
Lightning Source LLC
LaVergne TN
LVHW091120080826
845145LV00008B/1992

* 9 7 8 1 6 2 8 0 2 0 2 9 8 *